I0541116

REMEMBER ME WITH LOVE

Mary Ann Artrip

ISBN 10: 0-9893838-2-2
ISBN 13: 978-0-9893838-2-0
Copyright © Mary Ann Artrip
Second Edition 2015

Without limiting the rights under copyright reserved above, no part of this publication may be reproduced, stored in or introduced into a retrieval system, or transmitted, in any form, or by any means (electronic, mechanical, photocopying, recording, or otherwise) without the prior written permission of the copyright owner. Names, characters, places, and incidents used in this work are fictitious. Any resemblance to actual persons living or dead is purely coincidental.

A Chrysalis Book

Printed in the United States of America

Remembering

Lou Crabtree
The grandest lady of them all
&
Ralph Steve Coleman
The gentlest soul who ever lived

Other books by Mary Ann Artrip

"Moonshadows"
"Surrey Square"
"Rooney Boone"

"Parsnips & Princes"
(A Short Story Collection)

PROLOGUE

When the buzzer sounded from the security gates at the main road, Kate didn't wonder who was calling. She knew. She'd known that this moment was going to happen since the call had come the evening before, just as she got home from the cemetery.

She remained motionless at the window. Jon was dead, nothing else mattered.

She stood with natural grace, shoulders back, chin lifted. Her demeanor suggested a defiance she didn't feel. Touching the shadowed pane of glass, she studied her reflection and frowned. Kate had never liked her looks, even as a child. But now, with the passing years, her face had become too hard—all planes and angles, her jaw-line too sharp, too defined. She studied her eyes—frantic eyes, like the fox searching for a place of safety from the baying hounds, his quickening heart thundering like the exploding hooves of charging horses.

"Poor little fellow," she thought, *"there's no place for either of us to hide."*

An almost invisible frown settled across her forehead and blended with the faint lines of her face, lines that dug deeper, as if searching for a settling place to rest and gather strength. If there was the slightest tremor to Kate's hand as it moved from the window to rest against the drapes, it was indiscernible. *I can deal with this abomination,* she thought: *Jon's death.* All-encompassing to her life though it was, she would, in fact, deal with it. It was the little things that drove her crazy: a car windshield smeared with a smattering of rain, cartons of melting ice cream, a smashed pumpkin which sole purpose was to be a little boy's jack-o'-lantern.

Kate turned her attention to the world beyond the window. The grounds lay dusted with a light skiff of snow that had fallen sometime during the night. Now the low-hanging clouds sweeping through the tops of the tall trees threatened even more. It was not yet ten o'clock, but a heavy mist blocked out the sun and made it seem much earlier. Spring was not arriving with any great fanfare.

The weighted brocade drapes fell back into place as Kate withdrew her hand and turned away. Stepping down two levels into the living room, she walked across the floor and picked up a cup from the coffee table. The cold liquid tasted harsh and bitter upon her tongue, but she paid no mind. There was the faintest china-ping as she replaced the Royal Copenhagen cup back on the matching saucer.

From one corner of the room the massive grandfather clock began counting the hour. Bong. Bong. The chimes sounded hesitant and heavy, begrudgingly giving up the time. Each strike seemed to bear a great burden, a great sadness. Before the count was finished, the security buzzer went off again. It sounded impatient and angry. Kate went to the control panel on the wall and pressed the green button to open the gates. Moments later the doorbell rang. She wiped her damp palms against her dress, took a searing breath, and pulled back the door.

Standing directly in front of her was a face grown familiar over the past weeks, a face seasoned by years of grave consequences.

"Good morning, Mrs. Ames," he said.

Kate met the level gaze and stepped back.

"Lieutenant Simon," she said. "Sergeant Cowan," she acknowledged the second man standing directly behind the first. "Please, come in."

The two men stepped into the room. Sergeant Cowan's cheeks and ears, tinged a pinkish blue from the cold and his white hair brushed up into a sparse pompadour, reminded Kate of a Kewpie doll. He stood with his hands clasped at his back. The cut of his olive green topcoat gaped slightly, revealing the narrow edge of a leather shoulder holster.

Determined to handle the situation with dignity, because it was her nature and the only way she knew, Kate motioned to the sofa. "Have a seat, gentlemen. I have fresh coffee."

"No, thank you, ma'am." Lieutenant Simon shuffled slightly and looked uncomfortable. "Mrs. Ames, we're here to place you under arrest for the murder of your husband, Jonathan Ames." His voice was tinged with a touch of sorrow. "And before you say anything, I must tell you that you have the right to remain silent..."

Kate's mind cut away, the hum of his words buzzing in her brain like a swarm of late-summer hornets. So, the words had finally been spoken. What, then, did she care for rights?

The lieutenant's eyes mirrored a kind of sympathy as he finished the mandatory recital and looked up from the small card in his hand. "Do you understand what I've just said to you, Mrs. Ames?"

Kate nodded. "You've just arrested me for my husband's murder."

"Would you like to call someone? A friend? Legal counsel, perhaps?"

"No. No one."

"Do you want to get a few things together, then?" His voice was kind. "Take your time."

Kate nodded without speaking and left the two men standing near the door. Inside her bedroom, she pulled a small weekender from the top shelf of the closet and opened it on the bed. *What does one pack for incarceration?* she wondered. Easing out a deep drawer of the dresser, she touched whisper-soft lingerie: luxurious silks and satins, creamy chiffons. She leaned a hip against the drawer, shoving it closed. Her practical stuff, from before she married Jon, was in the bottom drawer. She'd often wondered why she kept these things laundered and folded and put away. Did she know all along that the day would come when she would need them again? Probably. She tugged out cotton underwear, flannel gowns, serviceable socks, and packed them in the flowered case. The same case she'd bought for her honeymoon. The happiness that was hers such a short time ago now seemed like a dream from the sleep of a stranger. She continued to pack, with practical consideration, the things she anticipated would be needed.

In the bathroom, she ran a quick comb through her brown hair. The taffy-colored highlights were beginning to fade and would need touching up again before long. She gave a wry smile that such an unimportant thought would cross her mind at a time like this. Pressure was building behind her eyes, then a stinging, as the first tears pushed through and trickled down her face. She swiped them away. What the hell good were tears now? They never helped her in the past. She finished packing, snapped shut the lid on the case and rejoined the men in the other room.

"Mrs. Ames," Lieutenant Simon said, "we'll need the remote control for the front gates. Although we've finished with a thorough investigation of the property, the house and grounds need to be secured in your absence."

"It's in my car," she said. "Over the visor. Do you want me to get it?"

He shook his head. "Sergeant Cowan can do it."

The sergeant made no reply, but turned away to do the chore requested of him.

"And Carl," the lieutenant called after him, "check all the doors and windows and make sure the house is locked up tight."

Sergeant Cowan returned right away and Kate gathered her things. She hesitated a fleeting moment, absorbing every detail of the room. Jon's favorite pipe lay in an ashtray, his hand the last to touch it. Desolation nearly melted her bones. She flipped off the light and the darkened room suddenly seemed colder. The grandfather clock continued its mournful tock-tock-tock. She eased the door shut and heard the lock click. Then she followed the two men to the waiting car.

They drove down the long, curving driveway. Kate sat in the back seat, separated from the two men in front by a rusted metal grill caked with years of dirt and grime. Not knowing if she would ever see her home again, she turned and looked through the rear window. From atop the knoll, *Brandywine* lay shrouded in mist. By the time they reached the main road, the house had disappeared completely.

The car sped onward through the chilled morning. Familiar scenery flashed by, unnoticed. Kate could hear the labored whirring of the heater from beneath the dash, but it did little to thaw the frigid numbness invading her body. Her cold hands cupped together, searching for comfort. Fingers, brittle and easily broken, icicle fingers, clutched her purse and pressed it into her lap. A legion of questions assaulted her mind. Where were the answers? The answers to Jon's life. And death. Leaning her head back to rest against the cracked vinyl upholstery of the seat, she closed her eyes. How had it all happened...

.

ONE

It was early afternoon in mid-September. Kate had cut her workday short and made her autumn pilgrimage to *Heavenly Bounty Farms*. Taking her time, she'd made purchases, visited with the Parkers and then headed home.

Just as she turned off the side lane leading from the farm onto Timberline Road, a looming dark car, out of control, skidded around a curve and headed straight for her. She could see the driver as he fought the steering wheel to gain control of the big Lincoln Navigator. He seemed not to see her until she slammed her hand down on the horn and jammed her foot against the brake. The brakes locked on her Subaru station wagon and the momentum carried her forward and she heard, rather than felt, her head hit the windshield. Her car spun sideways and spewed gravel as the tires dug into the ground, searching for traction. The shopping bag on the seat beside her shot forward and scattered apples and pears across the floorboard, and the perfect pumpkin she had just spent thirty minutes selecting, slammed against the door and smashed.

Over the roaring in her head, Kate could hear screeching of the tires on the other car and smelled the awful odor of burnt rubber. After what seemed an eternity, her little car stopped just short of plunging into a ravine. She barely had time to right herself in the seat before the driver of the other vehicle was at the door of her car.

"I'm sorry," he said. "Are you hurt? I didn't see—"

Kate snatched open the door and stepped out. "How dare you be so careless," she said. "Look what you've done." She pointed inside the car. "That pumpkin was for Jeffy Bailey. I promised we would make a jack-o'-lantern, and now it's ruined."

"I'm sorry—"

"Being sorry isn't going to help much when I have to explain to a little boy why we can't carve a scary face." Kate took a second to catch her breath. "What were you trying to do anyway, kill yourself?" Her head swam and she had to lean against the side of the car for support.

"You're hurt. You'd better sit down before you faint." He took her by the arm and eased her down on the seat. "Will you be okay while I run back and get my phone to call for help?"

"Don't be ridiculous," she snapped. "I'm not going to faint and I don't need your help. I'm fine." Kate jerked her arm out of his grasp. "You still haven't answered my question. What did you mean by driving so fast on such a narrow road? You could've been killed—or worse, I might have been."

Kate was further outraged by the fact that the man was not giving her his full attention. He seemed distracted as he kept glancing over his shoulder and back toward the sharp curve he had just rounded. What *was* he looking for?

"You're right, of course."

He fingered the side of his face. Scratches, thin as threads, trailed parallel across his cheek and down to the corner of his mouth. Blood beaded along the angry lines and was just beginning to scab over. It was evident that the injuries had not occurred during the current speeding incident.

He turned back to Kate. "I should've had my mind on my driving."

"It's a little late for that now." Kate turned on the seat and started to shut the door.

He grabbed it and held it open. "I'm sorry but I can't let you leave. Not until I'm sure you're all right." He tested the door as if he expected it not to work. "How's the car? Is it damaged?"

"The car's not the problem."

"We should at least get each other's names. You may find out later that you're hurt more than you think. You know how insurance people are—cross every tee, and so forth." He took his wallet from an inside pocket and withdrew a business card. "I'm Jonathan Ames. I've lived here in Woodway all my life, over in the western part of the county—farm country." He handed her the card. "Here's my insurance information."

Kate took the card, studied it, and handed it back. "Thank you, Mr. Ames, but I can't imagine actually needing it."

"I suppose you should give me your name."

Kate took a deep breath, her heaving shoulders making it plain that she felt put upon. She clicked her fingernails against the steering wheel.

"My name's Kathleen Spencer," she said and gave her address as 507 Morning Circle #2. Yes, she said, that is here in Woodway. "And I'm insured through Consolidated Investments where I happen to be employed." She started the car and shifted into reverse.

"Good day to you, Mr. Ames," she said as the car eased backward. "In the future try to take pains to drive more carefully." Not waiting for a reply, she left him standing beside the road and she drove away.

Kate's heart was still racing when she pulled into her driveway fifteen minutes later. "*Just help yourself to all of the road, Mr. Big-shot, SUV,*" she fussed as she gathered apples and pears. "*We little cars don't need much room—please take whatever you and your stupid gas-guzzler need.*"

Stretching to retrieve bright orange hunks of the smashed pumpkin from the floorboard, she dropped them into the bag. Grasping the bag by the handles, she dragged it across the seat and shinnied herself out of the car. Next door, at 509 Morning Circle, Mrs. Templeton was busy with her late-summer roses: watering and pruning, keeping them blooming until first frost. Sara Templeton's main reasons for living were her faith, her flowers, and her three-year-old grandson Jeffy. And, as of the day before, Jeffy's new baby sister. Mrs. Templeton waved and Kate smiled and waved back. Glancing around the yard, she was relieved that Jeffy was nowhere in sight. She wasn't looking forward to explaining about the pumpkin.

She crossed the small side porch, balancing the heavy bag on her hip. She fit the key into the lock and shoved open the door with the toe of her shoe. More so than usual, she was glad to be home. After she dumped the bag in the sink and tossed her purse on the counter along with her car keys, she turned and shut the door. Then she felt safe.

Flicking her feet, first one, then the other, her brown leather pumps went flying across the room and clattered to rest in front of the refrigerator. She padded in stockinged feet across the scrubbed linoleum to the living room, picked up the mail from the floor beneath the mail slot, and dropped to the sofa. Smoothing away the frown lines between her eyes, she touched the small knot that had humped itself up on her forehead. Not wearing her seat belt when she drove out to the country was a dumb thing to do. Now she had a headache.

The apartment was quiet. The ticking of a small travel clock on the end table clicked away the minutes. Minutes that had a way of turning, without notice, into years. Kate had neither a high opinion of life in general nor her life in particular, and paid little attention to the passage of time. She tossed the unopened mail on the coffee table, pushed up from the sofa and headed for the bedroom, undressing as she went.

The bedroom strained to accommodate the antique pieces that were the only remaining things Kate possessed which had belonged to her parents. Antique carvings worn smooth in some places and the richness of the wood signified the age and careful tending given to each piece. A full-length cheval mirror stood facing the wall, the brown-papered back turned inward toward the room. Beneath the one window was a lady's writing desk that doubled as a vanity.

Deciding the beige linen dress was wearable at least one more time before being dry-cleaned, Kate fitted a quilted hanger beneath the shoulder pads and brushed at the wrinkles across the back before hanging it in the closet. She stood in front of the dresser, its mirror covered with a pink flowered sheet, and slid the silky pantyhose down the length of her long legs. Her slip dropped to the floor around her ankles and she stepped out. She finished undressing, pulled on a tattered robe, and stuffed her feet into a pair of scuffs.

Back in the kitchen, Kate poured a small glass of wine from a half-empty bottle, sipping occasionally as she prepared a cheese omelet and toasted croissant for her dinner.

She sat in the one chair at the table. The second chair to the dinette set was shoved against the wall and held a wicker basket full of magazines. She thumbed through the mail: phone bill, credit card offers, pre-paid funeral plans. Might've used one of these today, she mused. "Not my time, I guess." She rubbed the goose egg on her forehead and thought again about the man on Timberline Road.

She ate slowly, not particularly savoring the food as much as stretching out the evening. After the meal was over and the kitchen tidied, Kate moved to the undisturbed living room. Twilight was a darkening corridor, a couple of hours to get through until full nightfall, when she'd take a sleeping pill that would shut down her mind for a few hours of nothingness.

She turned on a lamp and glanced around the room. The black eye of the television stared unblinking, as if asking to be turned on. An abandoned book lay on the coffee table. Historical romances had been fun for a while, but buxom wenches and daring firebrands soon lost their appeal in the real world. Suddenly, the natural progression of Kate's evening was interrupted when the phone rang.

She frowned and thought not to answer. It rang again, insistent, and she picked up.

"How's the head?"

Kate recognized the voice. "The head's fine."

"Good. I was worried about you. You got home okay?"

Her hand shook slightly as she drummed her fingers on the receiver. "What can I do for you, Mr. Ames?"

"For one thing, you can call me Jon. Mr. Ames was the man who had the good sense to marry my mother, and then they had the audacity to have me. But both of them have been dead a good number of years now."

"Surely you didn't call to tell me about your birth and the death of your parents."

"Well, no. Interesting as that might be, that's not the reason I called. I truly did want to check and make sure you're all right, but mostly I wanted to ask you to have dinner with me." He chuckled. "To make up for my nearly killing you."

"I appreciate your concern for my welfare and I thank you for it, but I'm afraid dinner is quite out of the question."

"Oh, and why's that?"

"Mr. Ames—Jon, may I be completely honest with you?"

"Please do."

"I don't know you and you certainly don't know me, and frankly I see no reason to change either of those facts. Please don't take this personally because I'm sure you're a prince of a man, but believe me when I tell you that I'm not interested."

He laughed. "Prince? Well, now, I've never been called that. You're presenting me with a royal challenge. I warn you, a prince doesn't give up easily."

"Good night, Mr. Ames." Kate plunked the receiver back on its cradle and sank into the nearest chair.

"God," she muttered. "Who is this person—this Jonathan Ames?" And why had she allowed him to get under her skin? Was it because she couldn't remember the last time a cutting glare from her hard eyes had not wilted a man before he could so much as finish a sentence? But was that not what she wanted? Had she not spent a major portion of the last few years of her life erecting a glacial barrier around her own private world? And to even remotely consider allowing herself to become vulnerable and unprotected was the height of absurdity. To trust again? "I don't think so." She smirked. "At least not in this decade."

TWO

The next morning Kate woke before the alarm went off. Her body resisted when she tried to sit up in bed. The jarring she had taken the day before had settled into stiffness during the night. She faced a black eye when she looked in the small mirror placed high on the bathroom wall. She thought about taking a day off from work, but quickly changed her mind. If she stayed home she would just crawl back into bed and sleep the day away.

Marty's car was the only one in the parking lot when she arrived for work. Alfonse Martin, Kate's boss and the owner of Consolidated Investments, was the only man in Kate's life whom she trusted completely. He and his wife Dixie knew Kate better than anyone, perhaps better than she knew herself, and were the closest thing she had to a family. They were an odd couple: Marty, serious-minded, slight in stature, but he carried himself with an authority that caused people to trust him, which was imperative in the world of finance. Dixie was a jolly ex-saloon singer who loved bright colors, from her hair to her four-inch heels. The couple had moved to the small town of Woodway to open a new business after Marty suffered Wall Street burnout. Kate was looking for a job, and even though she had no experience, Marty made a place for her in his fledgling business. He even encouraged her to go back to college to study financial analysis and investment strategies. She had been married to Evan at the time and thought life was pretty damn terrific.

Kate stepped through the front door of the office building. Located just inside was the reception area containing two desks. The one nearest the door belonged to Rachel Kilgore, receptionist for the small group. A second desk, across the room and off to the left just outside Marty's office, belonged to Sally Harris, Marty's secretary. Kate's office was the first door on the right. The next one down was Kevin Stewart. Kevin was the newest member of the group and turning out to be a financial wizard. Kate liked him a lot and was not at all surprised when young Sally had developed a terrific crush on him.

"Kate," Marty called from his office. "Is that you?"

"It's me. Good morning."

"Come in here for a second, will you? I want you to look at this index and tell me if you recognize a trend."

Kate took the time to drop off her purse and pour a cup of coffee. She carried the cup into his office.

Marty looked up from the report on his desk. "Good Lord! What happened to you?"

Kate touched her eye. "There was a maniac out on Timberline Road yesterday pretending he knew how to drive."

"Are you okay?"

"I'm fine. It looks worse than it is."

There was commotion from the front office as the others arrived for work. Kate repeated the events of the previous evening before everybody settled down. At ten o'clock, she joined Rachel and Sally in the staff lounge for the morning break. The visitor's bell sounded from the front door and Rachel went to tend to it. She came back with a long silver box tucked beneath her arm and cradling a pumpkin in both hands.

"They're for you," she said to Kate.

Kate took the pumpkin and read the note tied to the stem: *For Jeffy Bailey*. She glanced at the box Rachel was still holding.

"Can I open it?" Rachel asked.

Kate frowned and nodded.

Rachel slid off the ribbon and lifted the lid. A dozen long-stemmed pink roses lay wrapped in green tissue paper. She handed the envelope to Kate.

There was no message, only a name. She tapped the card against a thumbnail. "The maniac," she said with a smirk.

Sally smiled. "Well, the maniac picks out beautiful roses."

"The punkin's not bad either," Kevin said from the doorway.

"Would you like me to put the flowers in water?" Rachel asked.

Kate nodded. "And why don't you put them on your desk in the front so everybody can enjoy them."

Kate tried not to think about the flowers for the rest of the day, but each time she passed Rachel's desk she was reminded of the man from Timberline Road.

It was a little after five when Kate pulled into her driveway. Jeffy was rolling through the leaves in the Templeton yard. He came running when he saw the pumpkin.

"You got it." His eyes flew wide and round. "Boy, she's a big one."

Kate laughed. "Are you ready to help me with the carving?"

"Now? Can we do it now?"

She placed the pumpkin on the porch and gave it a pat. "Just as soon as I change my clothes." She opened the door. "You wait right here and I'll be back before you can say *Jack Robinson*."

Jeffy giggled and scooted across the porch and threw his arms around the pumpkin. "I'll keep it safe," he said.

"You do that, Jeffy. We don't want anything to happen to this one."

Kate hurried to change into sweats, gathered up the needed utensils and went back out the door. Jeffy still held the pumpkin.

"Ready?"

He nodded and moved away a few inches to make room for her.

Kate handed him a felt marker. "Here, you hold this while I clean out the inside. I'll need you to help draw the scary-face so I'll know where to cut."

Jeffy held the marker and waited while Kate scooped out the insides and placed them in the plastic bowl. She swiped her hands down the sides of the gray sweatpants and pushed stands of hair back from her forehead with the back of her wrist. She smiled at the little boy waiting so patiently.

"Ready to go to work?"

His blue eyes filled with doubts, but he nodded.

Kate held his tiny hand and helped him guide the marker to make straight, short lines. He watched as she cut where he had drawn, his eyes bright with excitement.

"It's going to be beautiful," he said.

"You know why?"

"Why?"

"Because you helped me. I couldn't have done it without you. Little boys can do just about anything."

"Do you have a little boy?"

Kate didn't answer right away.

"Well, do you?"

"No, Jeffy. I don't."

He looked up at her. "Didn't you want one?"

Kate ruffled his hair. "It would've been my great pleasure," she said.

"Would you like a baby sister?" He lifted the cut-away hat of the jack-o'-lantern and peered inside. "I'll give you mine for this."

Kate laughed. "I don't think your mommy and daddy would appreciate you swapping their new baby girl for a pumpkin," she said. "Besides, the jack-o'-lantern is yours."

"Can I can take it to show Grammy?"

"Do you think you can carry it by yourself?"

He frowned at her. "I'm almost five," he said.

"Almost five. My goodness I didn't realize you were that old. Well then, of course you can carry it by yourself."

Jeffy's look was one of tolerance as he lifted the pumpkin in his arms and started across the yard. "Thank you," he called over his shoulder. "I'll take good care of it and not let my new sister break it."

"You're welcome, Jeffy," Kate said. She stood watching the tiny figure in miniature jeans and tennis shoes wade through the leaves, shoulders bent into his precious burden. She watched until he rounded the corner of the house, then she turned and went inside.

That night Jonathan Ames called again. He barely gave Kate time to say hello.

"It's me again. I'm calling to give you another chance to have dinner with me." He seemed to know what to expect. "Now wait a minute before you hang up. I'm sorry for what happened yesterday, but I can't change it. The only thing I can do is prove to you that I'm not some wild maniac who makes a habit of running defenseless women off the road."

In spite of herself, Kate laughed. "It's funny that you should say that."

"Why?"

"Because that's what I called you today—a maniac."

"Not without good cause, and I don't blame you. But let me make it up to you. Have dinner with me tomorrow night and then maybe I'll go away."

Any idea of accepting a dinner invitation from a man whom she barely knew was as far removed from Kate's mind as to be unimaginable. Still, if it would put an end to the whole affair, perhaps it would be well worth it, but not by much.

"I could fight you on this, you know. I could just hang up and pretend you don't exist."

"You could. But I'd just call back."

"I don't like games, Mr. Ames. And I don't like pressure."

"Then, let's do dinner this one time—*and have done with it*—as Shakespeare would say."

"For this one time?"

"So, it's settled then." He made it sound as if they had just negotiated peace in the Middle East. "I'll make reservations at the Heatherton Inn for seven-thirty, and pick you up around seven."

Kate dropped the receiver back onto its cradle without a reply.

Later, as she twisted and turned beneath the bed covers, Kate replayed the scene on the country road. Why had he been driving like a drunken madman? And the scratches on his face, those ugly, violent scratches. What sort of life did this man lead?

The next day at the office Kate didn't mention her dinner plans for the evening. She felt foolish and a little juvenile about the whole thing. The workday ended before she was ready to face the mysterious Mr. Jonathan Ames again.

Later, her shower over, she sat at the vanity in front of a small mirror and took care with her makeup. She'd already decided what to wear which eliminated any need to ponder her limited wardrobe. Taking her one dressy-dress from its protective covering, she could smell the faint scent of lavender. Heatherton Inn, he'd said. She slipped the chiffon over her head and the pale ivory fell around her hips in fluid gathers. The narrowness of her waist was accentuated when she pulled the zipper up the back. It was almost seven when she slid her feet into the matching pumps. Just as she fastened a short strand of pearls around her neck, the doorbell rang. For a fleeting instant Kate was seized and held fast by an unexplainable second sight, a kind of revelation. *Do I dare let another man—this man—into my life?* she asked herself. *Do I commit such an audacious act as to actually let that happen?* Squaring her shoulders, determined to get the evening over with and behind her as quickly as possible, she headed for the door as the bell sounded a second time.

Jonathan Ames looked friendly enough when Kate opened the door. A smile softened the strong, masculine lines of his face. He was taller than she remembered—six feet or more. His hair was mostly gray and worn rather long and slightly scraggy. He reminded Kate of a college professor, or poet. Keats, perhaps. Beneath the glare of the porch light, his dark eyes were the color of a summer midnight sky. She was surprised at the things she hadn't noticed about him during their first encounter.

"Good evening, Kathleen," he said.

She pulled back the door. "Jon."

The smell of expensive pipe tobacco and imported cologne surrounded him as he came through the doorway. He took up a lot of space in the room, making Kate aware of just how small her apartment was. It seemed large before, as she rattled around the four rooms alone. Now, it just felt small and cramped. Kate motioned toward the sofa.

"The reservations are for seven-thirty," he said. "We probably need to be going."

"I'll get my things." She left him standing in the middle of the room. When she returned, he helped her with her coat, his actions were well-tended and deliberate, as if conducting a business deal that wasn't going particularly well.

In the driveway, Kate stood by the big SUV and waited for Jon to open the door. She glared up at the high seat.

"Even in two-inch pumps, I'm afraid I'm going to need some help," she said.

Jon opened the door and clasped his hands around her waist. "Uppsie, daisy," he said, whisking her off her feet and depositing her on the seat.

Once inside, the warm smell of leather and soft music from the stereo had a calming effect. Kate settled into the seat, fastened the seatbelt, and tried to relax. No exchange of words accompanied his backing out of the driveway.

They drove through the center of town. Kate stole glances at Jon from the corner of her eye. She saw his hand go toward the pipe in the ashtray, then pull back.

"Smoke if you want to," she said.

"I can wait."

"It's okay, really."

He turned to look at her. "You're sure?"

She nodded. "My father smoked a pipe. He had a special blend of apple-cherry tobacco. I loved that smell."

"Your father's dead?"

"Both my parents."

"I'm sorry."

"It was a long time ago," she said. "By the way, thanks for the pumpkin. You made one little boy very happy." She didn't mention the flowers and he didn't ask.

Finally he spoke again. "I hope you're hungry. The food at the Inn is excellent. Have you ever been there?"

"No."

"Well, I think you'll enjoy it, even if you didn't want to come tonight."

"You're right, I didn't want to come. But now that I'm here, let's try to be on our best behavior."

Kate was determined not to mention the previous encounter but had noticed that the scratches on his cheek were beginning to fade.

"Deal," he said. "Let's pretend we've known each other since first grade, and I sat behind you and pulled your pigtails."

Kate smiled in the darkened car. "I never wore pigtails."

"The world's loss," he said, flipping the signal and turning off the road.

The driveway circled around in front of a beautiful eighteenth-century mansion. Jon stopped the car and a parking valet appeared as if by magic and slid beneath the steering wheel as soon as they got out. They started up a shadowed walkway and Jon took Kate's arm as they passed beneath gaslights that wavered and flickered behind frosted globes. They climbed the half-moon steps leading to a veranda that spanned the width of the house. Caned-bottom rocking chairs moved in a slight breeze.

The evening passed in something of a blur. Jon was right about the food being good. Clearly, the Inn catered to the tastes of an older generation, and the band played only the old standards from a gentler time. When he asked her to dance, she accepted.

He held her at medium-nearness and guided her around the floor while the band played *Strangers in the Night*. He was a good dancer. Around ten, he drove Kate home.

He took one hand off the steering wheel and removed the pipe from his mouth. "It's been a good evening," he said. "I hope you didn't find my brand of entertainment a little on the dull side."

Kate remembered the speeding car and the scratched face and had trouble reconciling *that* man with *this* one.

"No," she said.

He pulled into her driveway, left the motor running and walked her to the door. Without speaking, he took the key from her hand, turned the lock, then handed the key back.

"Good night, Kathleen," he said as she stepped through the doorway.

"Good night, Jon."

Kate stood just inside the room and waited for his car to back out of the driveway. Finally she heard the noise level of the engine increase and saw the sweep of headlights as they fanned across the far wall of the living room. Then she was alone again.

THREE

September spilled over into October. The days grew shorter, the nights interminable. As she so often did on Sunday afternoons, Kate left the small town of Woodway and drove deep into the country, her destination certain. She pulled the car onto the shoulder of the road beside a heavy clump of bushes and got out. Hidden in the thicket was a narrow path that led down to a small stream and the secret glen she claimed as her own, a haven she had discovered during her wandering period—those lost years she spent searching for something to believe in. She wasn't sure she ever found it.

Today she took the familiar path through the trees and crossed the rickety old bridge. She shivered and pulled the collar of her coat tighter around her neck. Winter was coming. The woodland was turned out in typical fall fashion: a symphony of color exploding like the crash of cymbals and kettle drums.

Autumn was a humbling experience for Kate and she resented the fact that there could be so much beauty in dying. Death was not a seductive thing to yearn for, to desire and stand in awe of, yet the lure kept calling her back year after year. The chatter of squirrels and the rushing of the brook were the only sounds to break the silence. Pushing her hands deeper into the pockets of her coat, she made her way to the flat rock that was her *pondering* place.

Kate sat down, leaned back against a fallen tree and pulled her knees up to her chin. She sat quietly, not thinking of any particular thing. Suddenly she remembered fifth grade at Woodway Elementary School. Each student was asked to write a poem about autumn and what it meant to them. A poet was the last thing Kate would've considered herself to be but she remembered how easy the lines had flowed onto the paper.

The leaves are falling all around
Upon the houses and the ground
We rake them every windy fall
I love that season most of all

Funny that she should remember the words so clearly after all these years.

The loud caw of a crow stirred her reverie. Clouds were gathering. Kate glanced at her watch, it was almost five o'clock. The sun was setting, drawing out the shadows. She thought about starting back, but made no effort to leave. The wind rose and sent a chorus line of dust-dancers swirling through the trees. The frenzy made her smile. Such was the sum total of her life: *much ado about nothing.*

Her mind wandered to Jonathan Ames. It had been more than a week since that night they went to dinner. She thought he would have called by now, and wondered if his failing to do so annoyed her. *Probably not,* she decided. She thought him pleasant enough, in an odd sort of way. But he seemed a contradiction of terms, the wearer of two faces—a *Pierrot mask*—displaying drama and comedy simultaneously. Certainly he wasn't someone she wanted to get involved with. Still, she couldn't help but be puzzled about him *Why had he bothered to call?* she wondered.

She stretched her legs and leaned back against the tree. She was self-sufficient, self-contained. Such had been required of her for survival. Kate's life had not been easy. She had just started first grade when her father was sent to war and had died in some mysterious place called the 38th Parallel. She never saw her mother smile again after that, and watched as the years of grief and bitterness ate away her life. Kate was a lot like her mother, loving too hard, too desperately. Her divorce from Evan had taught her well.

"Mama," Kate whispered to the wind. "Is this all there is?"

The wind murmured back its reply, but Kate could not discern the answer.

A slight grumbling sounded from gathering clouds that darkened the sky. Then it started to sprinkle. Collecting her purse, Kate dusted dried leaves and twigs from her coat and retraced her steps to the road. By the time she reached the car the wind was whipping the rain sideways, making it nearly impossible to see.

Twenty minutes later she pulled back into her driveway, and as she hurried across the porch she could hear the phone ringing from inside the apartment. She yanked open the door as the phone died in mid-ring. She reached for a dishtowel to wipe her face and mop through her soggy hair.

Later, she carried a cup of hot tea to the sofa, tucked her legs beneath her body and glanced at the phone. She wondered if it would ring again.

She clicked on the television and watched the last half of the local news. Nothing much ever happened in Woodway. The phone rang again just as she started to the kitchen with the empty teacup.

She stared at it through five rings, willing it to stop. She reached out on the sixth.

"Kathleen? It's Jon Ames."

"Hello."

"I tried calling earlier but you must've been out."

"I was."

"How've you been?"

"Fine."

"I would've called sooner but I've been out of town."

"Oh."

"You don't sound the least bit interested."

"No."

"I wanted to tell you how much I enjoyed our dinner the other night."

"I didn't expect you to call again."

"Not even as an act of kindness, to show my appreciation?"

"Not even for that."

"I take it you're not exactly thrilled with my attention." He gave a short laugh. "I'm not a stalker, you know. If you really want me to go away, I will. It's just that you're the least boring person I've met in a long time. And I find so few interesting people coming in and out of my life."

"I'm not interesting, Jon. I'm quite bland actually—vanilla, so to speak."

He laughed. "Well, at least French vanilla."

"If you say so."

"And as long as we're talking about food, how about another night out?"

Kate sucked in a sharp breath and dropped into a chair. "No, Mr. Ames. I'm afraid that's impossible."

"Ah, don't go climbing back up on your high horse."

"I didn't know I was."

"Of course, you did. You know exactly what you're doing."

There was that uneasy feeling again. "Do you charge a fee for psychoanalysis, or is this a free service for friends you've known since first grade?"

He laughed again. "You win. Just remind me not to try to best you in the future."

Kate wondered what made him think they had a future.

"As I said," he continued, interrupting her thoughts, "I'm sorry I took so long about calling, but I was tied up."

"Out of town, you said."

"Washington. The District. Not the state. Don't ever go there and be in a hurry." He grunted. "It's always said that our government only knows how to spend money, and never produce anything. Wrong, wrong, wrong. Those depressing and empty souls have been shut up in that ungodly maze of double dealing and run-soaked lunches until the only thing they know how to create, besides stupidity, is the world's largest supply of red tape."

"I don't know much about that sort of thing."

"Take my word for it. I like to think they're partly responsible for all this gray hair." He paused briefly. "But back to why I called. I know

I promised to go away if you had dinner with me that first time, but I've changed my mind." He laughed. "And that's something I don't do very often—change my mind."

"And you changing your mind is supposed to mean exactly what?"

"That something's important to me, I guess."

What the hell does it matter if a thing is important to you? she thought, and wished she had the nerve to confront him with the question. But she didn't. And what about her—her need to survive? It had taken years to push from memory the earthy pleasures of a warm, loving body next to hers, and she had no intention of ever going down that road again. Not even for this mysterious stranger who seemed to think he could snap his fingers and get instant results. *My dear Mr. Ames,* she thought, *walls don't crumble that easily, even for you.*

"Are you still there?"

"I'm here."

She heard him take a breath. "Thought I'd lost you there for a second." His voice was sounding less sure of himself. "Look, I'm sorry I bothered you and I really do promise this is the last time you'll hear from me, if that's what you want. I'd love to have dinner with you again, but not if it's going to make you uncomfortable."

"Uncomfortable? No, not that."

"So, we'll give it another go?"

Could she see him again and not disturb the established order of things? After all, she had learned her lesson well, had she not? The lesson was that her life could have a *twining* only up to a given point—as God said to the tides: *this far and no farther.* Armed with this knowledge,

Kate felt confident in her ability to control the circumstances surrounding her existence. After all, she'd built her fortress well and chinked it with tears. She would be ever so vigilant against any emotional involvement. In any event, she could always crawl back into the safety of her cocoon.

"All right, Jon." It was as if the earth shifted beneath her feet as she made the decision. Control. She must remain in control. "But this time it's my turn. I may not come up to Heatherton Inn standards but I'm willing to give it my best shot. How about coming here for dinner, Wednesday around seven?"

"You mean a home-cooked meal where you actually put pots and pans on the stove and stir stuff?"

In spite of herself, Kate smiled. "Sounds like it's been a long time since you've had one."

"Too long. But I don't want you going to a lot of trouble just for me."

"No trouble, even though I don't do things on a grand scale. No fine china or silver here. Stoneware dishes and discount store glasses are the most you can hope for."

"Sounds awesome. I'm already looking forward to it. I'll see you Wednesday at seven."

The first of the week flew by. Kate was true to her word and didn't worry about the up-coming dinner. Always having prided herself on her ability to set a decent table, once she decided what she was going to serve, she filed it away in the back of her mind and left it alone.

On Tuesday, Rachel announced to the office she was getting married the week before Christmas.

"Of course you're all invited to the wedding and will be receiving official engraved invitations. It's going to be ever so perfect." With a haughty lift of her chin, she struck a regal pose and marched around the office trailing her pearl-buttoned cardigan behind like a magnificent train. Her eyes sparkled and she seemed about to pop.

"My parents are in a state of shock. Daddy said he would spare no expense. I think they were afraid they'd have me at home forever." She stopped and held up her hands. "No, no, I'm kidding of course. They both like Paul a lot. They think he's quite a catch, which by the way, he is. Sally will be my maid of honor—naturally. I couldn't get through this without her." She laughed. "Not that it's something that has to be *gotten through*. You know what I mean." She paused for a breath. "Oh, I don't know what I'm saying. I'm just so excited."

Kate laughed. "Well, we'd never know it just from looking at you." Then she pulled Sally close to Rachel's side. "You'd better keep an eye on her, she just might explode."

"I'll do my best," Sally said. "But it's going to be hard."

Kevin came out of his office to join the merriment. "Is this going to be what they call *a happening*?"

"Oh, not just *a* happening," Rachel said. "*The* happening."

Marty stood in his doorway and watched the proceedings. "Lord help us all," he said.

Kevin looked at Sally. "If you don't already have an escort, is it too early to offer my services?"

A blush touched Sally's fair complexion. "Your services would be gratefully accepted," she said.

The men returned to their offices, but the excitement lingered for the rest of the day.

FOUR

At six-thirty on Wednesday evening, the meal well on its way, Kate took the time to grab a quick shower and slip into a velour jumpsuit. She had just removed the basket of magazines from the second chair, dusted off the seat and pulled it over to the table, when the doorbell rang. She checked the centerpiece of bronze and magenta mums and decided they were worth the extra ten dollars she'd put out.

Jon came in and offered his coat.

"The evenings are getting colder," he said, rubbing his hands together. He stopped and inhaled deeply. "Something smells heavenly." He pulled a tissue-wrapped package from beneath his arm and handed it to her. The paper was gathered and tied with curly red and green ribbons. "This is for you."

"You didn't have to bring anything."

"I wanted to. Go ahead and open it."

Kate tore away the wrapping paper from a bottle of wine. She looked at the label.

"Since I don't read French, I'm thinking it must be an excellent vintage and that I should be suitably impressed."

He laughed. "I have a feeling you don't impress easily."

Kate's eyes met his straight on and she gave a slight nod.

"Please don't feel that you have to serve it with your meal," he said. "I only brought it along to thank you for tonight."

"There's coffee to go with dinner. But we'll have it later if that's okay."

"Works for me. I think wine makes a great dessert."

"You get five points for agreeing with the hostess," Kate said. "I'm glad we finally found something we can come to terms on."

"Oh, I think maybe we could find lots of things," he said. "It's just a matter of taking the time and the care to uncover them."

She looked at the bottle again. "It must've been terribly expensive."

Jon shook his head. "Can we eat? I'm starved."

Kate showed him to his chair and carried the food to the table. The pot roast bubbled in the baking dish. Miniature carrots and quartered potatoes surrounded the tender beef and still simmered in rich brown gravy. Steam escaped from a small dish as she uncovered snow peas and pearl onions in a creamy cheese sauce. She tossed the crisp garden salad at the table and filled their bowls. Flaky rolls brushed with seasoned butter nestled golden brown beneath the cotton napkin covering the wicker basket.

She knew the meal had been a success when Jon filled his plate for the third time.

He looked up from his food and grinned. "I must apologize for the third helping," he said. "The second was probably acceptable, but the third one will probably cost me my membership in the manner-of-the-month club."

"Who's counting?" Kate said.

"You're not going to take away my points, are you? I don't want to lose my points."

"Your points are safe."

He drained his cup, placed it back on the saucer, and pushed away from the table.

"I can't tell you when I've had such a meal," he said. "This reminds me of the suppers my mother used to cook."

Kate smiled at the compliment, realizing the gravity of its sincerity. She hadn't done all that much, but it was good to know that her efforts were appreciated.

Jon insisted on helping her clear the table and do the dishes. They worked well together. Kate laughed when a plate almost slipped out of his hands.

"I'd hate to break one of these and ruin the whole set," he said.

"Oh, sure." Her voice was slightly mocking. "Then I'd have to make another trip to Target."

He took her wet soapy hands in his. "You should be surrounded by the finest china, Kathleen." He looked at her, his brow slightly furrowed. "Anything less than the best is beneath your dignity."

Kate pulled away. "I don't know that I'd be at ease around things like that. Expensive things have a way of making me nervous, so I guess I'm better off without them."

She took the drying towel from his hands and finished wiping the counter. She could feel his eyes watching her as she concentrated on rinsing the sink and hanging the dishcloths on a rack inside the cabinet door. She turned and smiled.

"But at least I can serve your fantastic wine in genuine crystal stemware," Kate said and handed him the bottle. "You uncork this while I get the glasses. The cork screw is in that drawer over there beneath the cake stand."

Jon looked at the high-domed cover on the cut-glass pedestal and touched the ruby knob. "This is beautiful," he said. "My mother had some cranberry glass. We only used it for company."

Kate nodded. "That piece belonged to my grandmother."

She arranged the bottle and glasses on a tray and Jon carried it to the living room and placed it on the coffee table. Kate slipped a disk into the player and the room softened with music. Jon stretched his long legs beneath the table and rested his back against the pillows.

"All this and Bacharach to round out the evening," he said. "He's one of my favorites."

"Mine too," Kate said. "I'm not sure his musical genius has ever been fully appreciated."

"See, I told you there were other things we could agree on. Do I get five more points?"

"Well, sure, at least five. Music's certainly as important as wine, speaking point-wise, of course."

Jon grinned and shook he head. He pulled a pipe from the pocket of his jacket. "Mind if I smoke?"

"Not at all."

Kate watched as he filled the pipe. It must have been one of his favorites. The wood had mellowed to a golden glow and the bowl fit perfectly into the hollow of his hand. He had good hands, strong and finely lined. The skin, tanned and slightly veined, stretched over smooth knuckles. Pale bronzed hair brushed across the backs and up along the wrists. His motions were distinct and purposeful.

He touched the match. "Talk to me, Kathleen."

"About what?"

"Anything. I like the sound of your voice. Tell me about yourself. Allow me the privilege of knowing who you are; what you are."

Kate studied the glass in her hand and ran her fingers down the stem. She wondered how much of herself she wanted to reveal to this person who was still quite the stranger. Was he really interested? Most likely he was just making polite conversation to fill the awkward gaps in an evening that was beginning to wind down.

"There isn't much to tell," she said.

He settled against the cushions with his pipe and wine and waited for her to continue. His actions were those of a man unhurried and patient.

Kate backed off from anything personal. She talked about her job and told him about Rachel's upcoming wedding.

"I'm looking forward to that," she said. "My life's been pretty much uneventful, but I have been skiing in Vail, and spent New Year's Eve in Times Square—so I guess that counts for something. I've never done anything really dangerous or daring, and don't think I'd like to. Who needs to climb famous mountains or run with the bulls. I love music, semi-classical mostly." She took a sip of wine. "I like to read—mysteries especially: James Patterson, Patricia Cornwell, John Grisham."

He laughed. "Have a need to catch the bad guy, do you?"

She grinned. "I guess I do."

He took her hand. "What else. What else do you like?"

"I love children—"

"Well, I could've told you that when Jeffy Bailey's pumpkin got smashed to smithereens. How did that ever turn out, by the way?"

"Turned out beautifully. The jack-o'-lantern was so perfect that Jeffy wanted to swap his new baby sister for it."

He threw his head back and laughed. "Sounds like a smart kid—or a *very special* jack-o'-lantern." He puffed his pipe. "Well, go on. What else?"

"I'd love cold evenings in front of a fire. But as you can see, I have no fireplace." She looked at him. "That's about it, I'm afraid. Nothing exceptional."

He remained silent for a time.

"Fascinating people always underestimate themselves," he said finally. "You've done much more than you realize." He motioned to the room, pointing with the stem of the pipe. "Look around. You have a lovely home. So it's not the Trump Towers, who needs vulgarity of the spectacular. This space, these wonderful rooms have much more meaning. You might not see its beauty because it's familiar and routine, but to an outsider it's most seductive." He stopped and gave Kate a slight grin. "And I mean that in the purest sense."

Kate nodded.

"Far too often simple beauty and order is not important to people's lives just when the blooming sets in. They let their guard down, plop themselves in front of the television and let it feed their minds. They quit using their bodies and soon the weeds take root, and before long they're trapped inside a bramble patch." He heaved a deep sigh. "Forgive me, when I get on my soapbox I tend to get a little carried away. But it's all true; it should be one of the cardinal sins to waste precious years."

Kate smiled to herself. *Such passion for life,* she thought.

"But look at you." The smile that swept across his face touched his eyes. "You're a classic."

"I've never been called *that* before," Kate said. "I thank you for your compliments and naturally I'm flattered."

"It isn't flattery, Kathleen. I wouldn't do that to you. You'd see straight through it and I'd feel like a fool." He drew on the pipe but it had gone out. "Would I be pushing my luck if I asked you to go with me to the Itzhak Perlman concert in Roanoke next weekend?"

"Sorry," she said, "but unless you can work miracles, no such luck. It's been sold out for weeks."

He grinned. "Let me take a whack at the miracle department." He dropped the pipe into his jacket pocket and stood up. The evening was over.

Kate worked all the next week in anticipation of the weekend. Jon called to say that he was able to get tickets to the much-heralded concert. She was more than a little impressed. They planned to leave on Saturday morning with a *rubber-band* itinerary: flexible and easily stretched. On the way, there was a small antique shop that she had passed many times, always wishing she had the time or adventurous spirit to stop and browse. But she never did. Jon promised they would take the time to check it out. He had also made hotel reservations for the night, engaging two suites he hastened to assure her, to give them a chance to shower and change before the concert, and to stay the night. All the preparations were in order. Kate had even splurged on a new outfit.

On Friday, account ledgers and balance sheets held little interest as Kate watched the clock. Unconsciously, she heard the phone ring. Seconds later her intercom buzzed.

"Kate. Line One."

She pushed down the flashing button.

"Kathleen, it's Jon. Sorry to call you at work."

"That's okay."

"Something's come up. I won't be able to make this weekend. I'm sorry."

"It must be something important."

He didn't confirm the importance of the reason for the cancellation.

"I shouldn't be gone more than a couple of days. I'm sorry, but this is something I just have to deal with. I'll call you when I get back."

"You needn't bother, Jon. It was just a weekend, no big deal for me, and I'm sure it wasn't for you either." She turned her palm over and let the receiver roll out of her hand and clatter down against the cradle. So much for that. She'd been a fool to get involved with him in the first place.

He was gone more than a week. He called to tell her he was back and ask if he could come over. Kate was set to tell him to get lost, when she changed her mind. She wanted to see his face and look him squarely in the eyes when she set him straight about their so-called relationship.

An hour later, when be walked through the doorway, Kate was shocked by his appearance. A look of despair and hopelessness cut deep into the lines of his face, and his eyes sat in dark hollows and took on the color of brackish water. He looked exhausted as he slumped to the sofa. A slight tremor of his hand caught her eye.

"Can I fix you a drink?" she asked.

"Brandy, if you have it."

"Oh, I think there may be some here if I can find it." She fished around in the back of the liquor cabinet. "But it's probably pretty old."

"Old is good," he said.

"Not that kind of old. Old as opposed to *aged*."

She found the bottle and handed him a glass. Sitting down beside him, she waited for him to speak. He leaned back and lit his pipe.

"I didn't take a powder on purpose. You do know that, don't you? If it hadn't been important I wouldn't have bothered."

"I believe you."

"I have no right to expect so much from you. I know you wonder just who the hell I think I am. First I try to run your car off the road, and then have the nerve to plop myself smack down in the middle of your well-ordered life."

Kate grinned. "You pretty well covered it."

"And I have no explanation. Let's just say you came along when I was looking for something—" he made a feeble attempt to smile "—or someone, that made sense."

Kate looked into the pained eyes and felt something stir, something she had long since laid to rest. She cut away from his gaze. "Can I be perfectly honest with you, Jon?"

"Could I stop you?"

She shook her head. "No, because it's important." She had to choose her words carefully; make him understand. "You see, I have no intentions of getting involved in an intimate relationship. For reasons that are none of your business, my life is designed to accommodate one person—me. Now, if you'd like to be friends, I can manage that. But don't ask for more."

"I'm not entitled to more, Kathleen. We all have hallowed ground upon which others are not allowed to tread."

Remembering the scratches on his face the first time they met, Kate touched a fingertip to her cheek then extended her hand. "Friends?"

"Very special friends," he said, accepting her hand. "Come with me Sunday. We'll drive to the country and enjoy God's splendor. He's outdone himself this year. Besides, there's someplace I want to show you."

"I'd like that."

"How about I pick you up around one and we'll make an afternoon of it. Now, I'd better get out of your hair, I've stayed too long already. It's getting late and you have to work tomorrow." He drained his glass and set it back on a coaster.

Kate went with him to the door and retrieved his coat from the closet. He slipped it on, then turned to speak. Instead, he reached out and touched her hair.

"Good night, friend," he said, and was gone.

Kate lingered by the door, her hand still resting on the knob. She could feel doubt and uncertainty closing in around her like a damp winter cloak. She would go with him on his little jaunt, and then she was going to end this involvement with Mr. Jonathan Ames. She was already sorry that it had been allowed to progress this far. She knew better. God, didn't she know better.

FIVE

It was well past ten on Sunday morning when Kate stepped from the shower and padded to the kitchen. She stirred non-dairy creamer into her coffee and carried the cup to the bedroom. When next she emerged, she was wearing faded jeans topped off by an oversized cotton sweater, knee socks and well-worn Reeboks. As a result of repeated washings, the size ten jeans had shrunk considerably and hugged her hips and the curves of her long legs. Suspecting that Jonathan Ames was nothing if not a man of punctuality, she was ready by one o'clock. He arrived on time. Grabbing her old standby, the tweed hacking jacket, Kate met him at the door.

"Hey! Who's this person in faded jeans and old tweed?" Jon looked at the house number over the door. "Right address, all right, and the lady looks slightly familiar, but I'm more used to a perfectly pressed and powdered financial powerhouse."

"Powerhouse?" Kate laughed. "Wait until I tell Marty how important I am. That ought to merit a sizable raise."

"But not today. Today is for us and a special pilgrimage to the country." He pointed to her feet. "Glad you've got on walking shoes."

"So this pilgrimage includes some hiking?"

"It does." He laughed. "And you're perfectly turned out for the activity. Besides, I like looking at you—you look cute."

"Lord, are you living in a different century. Cute is a teenager with spiked purple hair and a cell phone stuck to the side of her head."

"Well, if you say so." He opened the car door. "Scramble on up there," he said. "Might as well learn how, now that you're dressed for mountain climbing."

Kate latched her fingers onto the edge of the seat and hauled herself up.

Jon applauded.

The powerful engine turned over when he touched the key and he backed out of the driveway.

"And where did you say we're going?"

"To a special place."

They drove in silence with only soft cello strings from the stereo to accompany their thoughts. The day was crisp, the sky a startling blue. After a while traffic thinned out, then disappeared altogether as they drove deeper into the country.

"I don't believe I've ever been to this part of Scott County," Kate said, glancing around. "We're getting pretty far out."

"It's the upper tip," Jon said. "Pretty quiet out here. Nothing much ever happens up this way."

"It's beautiful," she said.

Shortly, Jon turned off the main road onto a much smaller one. A sign said: PRIVATE ROAD! KEEP OUT!

Kate felt a little apprehensive. "Is it okay to be here? The owner may take a dim view of Sunday drivers invading his privacy."

"The owner won't mind a bit," Jon said and continued to drive.

The car climbed a slight hill, and there before them was an old farmhouse, nothing that would attract attention, just a simple farmhouse with a couple of outbuildings and a big red barn with a tin roof. When Jon pulled into the yard and shut off the engine, Kate's imagination shifted into high gear: any minute now, a farmer with a twin-barreled shotgun wedged against the hip of his overalls, would shoulder his way thorough the front door and order them off the property.

"Jon." She managed to keep her voice level. "We shouldn't be here. I'm sure the owner didn't put up the 'Keep Out' sign just for kicks."

"The owner does very few things for kicks." He grinned and the lines around his eyes crinkled. "I'm sorry, I should've already told you. Don't worry about invading the owner's privacy. This is where I live."

Kate frowned. She had a problem matching the manner of the man with the common simplicity of the place. She had pictured him in a luxurious condominium complete with pool and tennis courts and an enormous monthly maintenance fee.

Jon laughed. "You can close your mouth now," he said. "And don't look so shocked. Actually, it's very pleasant and I do like privacy." He took her arm. "Let me show you around."

They went up the wide, sturdy steps to the high front porch running the width of the house. The white siding, aged to a misty gray, looked well tended. A row of windows watched out over the porch and showed the hand of recent washings. Off to the left, wicker chairs circled a table where the center had been painted with a bright bouquet of sunflowers. *So*, Kate thought, *he has at least one friend who's an admirer of van Gogh.*

To the right, very near the edge, an old swing creaked back and forth. It looked abandoned and lonely. On beyond, morning glories climbed a trellis that went up and out of sight. The vine, apparently left pretty much to its own devices, had just about taken over that end of the porch.

Over a nameplate beside the door, more flowers. *The artist again*, Kate thought. The door creaked as Jon turned the knob and they entered an interior that was dim and slightly stuffy. A bare bulb dangled from the ceiling at the end of a twisted cord. The room was a clutter of over-stuffed mohair furniture with doily-covered arms and backs. Farm magazines and a large family Bible lay on an octagon-shaped credenza. A corner cabinet was filled with whatnots and assorted bric-a-brac. Kate smiled to herself. There was not a shotgun in sight. Hanging over the front door a blue motto, the letters now only faint shadows with a few stray flecks of silver-sparkle, read: *God Bless This Home*. Everything was clean. Jon spoke for the first time since entering.

"Welcome to my home, Kathleen." He gestured around the room with a sweep of his arm. "It's not my home actually; it belonged to my parents, and my grandparents before them. Papa's family built it back in the early twenties." He smiled. "It's still just about how it's always been. Mama wouldn't allow anything much to be changed."

"They were farmers?"

"Papa was. Mama was a farmer's wife. It was the only life they knew, the only one they ever wanted. But they wanted more for me."

"Parents always do, don't they?"

Jon nodded. "They wanted me to go to college, and even though I didn't think much of the idea, I went. Funny how higher education just about breaks some youngsters, but for me it was easy. I'd always had a knack for electronics, and then along came the computer and anything digitized was like a toy that I just had to figure out. So, after I graduated from Harvard, I was lucky enough to land a position with MIT—they thought I had potential." He scoured his chin and forked back the shock of silver hair. "I was there only a few months when the call came that Papa had suffered a heart attack. It happened so quickly I couldn't get home before he died." He walked to the window and touched the ruffled curtains. "Mama was inconsolable for a while. Then, after she finally accepted his death, I couldn't go away and leave her again. Besides, I never wanted the pressure of working for somebody else. All I ever wanted to do was put things together and see if they'd work—mostly they didn't." He paused and looked at Kate, as if checking to see if she was listening.

"Anyway, after Papa died Mama wouldn't leave, so we continued to live here. I offered to buy her a place in town but she wouldn't hear of it. She said she wanted to be close to Papa and the family." He walked back and straightened a doily on the sofa.

"She died nearly ten years ago, and since I was their only child the place fell to me, and I just stayed on. There's an old cemetery on the hill behind the house. That's where they're buried, along with my grandparents, Papa's parents, that is. I never knew Mama's parents; they died before I was born. I'd like to show it to you." He looked at her. "Then, there's one other place I want you to see." He took her by the arm. "But first, let me show you the rest of the house."

Kate had been a town-raised girl, where milk came from red and white cartons and butter in cute little plastic tubs. And, being a town girl, she was completely intrigued by the country kitchen and its black cast iron cook stove with the warming oven on top and a hot water tank at the side.

Hanging on the wall beside the stove was an implement that looked to be a kind of prier. She lifted it from its holder and turned it over in her hands. Without saying anything, Jon took the lid-lifter and showed her how to place the hook into the eye of the lid and raise the cover from the fire. He handed it back to her and she repeated the procedure. Satisfied, she returned it to its place.

A long table covered with a faded oilcloth almost filled one end of the room. On each side of the table were long wooden benches.

"Jon, if there were only you and your parents, why a table to seat so many people?"

"There were always farm hands helping Papa with the work, and Mama insisted on cooking dinner for them. Out here in the country, we didn't have fancy little things called luncheons. She said they worked hard and, come twelve o'clock, deserved a hot meal; one that would stick to their ribs and hold them over 'til suppertime. And the food she cooked was unbelievable." He took a tobacco pouch from his pocket and began to fill his pipe. "When Papa died and the farming ceased, I think that's what she missed more than anything else. She found it hard to adjust to cooking for the two of us.

"Out here," he said, taking her arm again, "through this back door and off to the left is the bathroom. Papa and I had a devil of a time getting her to agree to indoor plumbing. But the back porch was as close as she would allow it to come. As she said, she wasn't going to have no outhouse inside. 'It ain't healthy,' she'd fuss. She never did completely accept it."

"I would've loved to have known her," Kate said. "She sounds just feisty enough to be interesting."

Guiding her back through the living room, he showed Kate their bedroom. Cabbage roses, once vivid crimson and scarlet, now only shades of pale pink and washed out rouge, covered the walls. The paper had been hung with nails fitted through nickel-sized silver brackets. Pictures lined the dresser behind a brush and comb set. The brush contained strands of hair, much of it gray. Even though the bed was made, the top sheet and double-wedding-ring quilt was folded down, waiting for a tired body to retire for the night. Kate knew the room was just as his mother had left it. Even her nightgown lying across the pillows remained undisturbed.

A picture hung over the bed. The oval wooden frame, carved with delicate curlicues and ivy, circled the glass that had turned milky. The man wore black broadcloth and reminded Kate of Gary Cooper. The young woman smiled up at the tall man while lifting the hem of her white dress away from the grass with one hand and the other one touching a cameo pinned at the center of her lace collar.

"Your parents?"

Jon nodded. "Their wedding day." He closed the door on the room and they turned away.

Kate pointed across the room. "What's behind that door?"

"My bedroom and work area. It's just an assortment of odds and ends and a few projects that I'm currently working on."

"Projects?"

"Gadgets, that sort of thing. I never did tell you what I do for a living, did I? I'm a designer. Inventor. Tinker-person. General goof-off. Any of those terms fit. Some of my designs are quite good, and some perfectly awful."

Kate was intrigued. "Would I be familiar with anything you're responsible for?"

Jon laughed. "I'm afraid not. You couldn't find anything I've done down at the local Home Depot. Mainly my work is in electronics—computer engineering, macro-conductors, that sort of thing. I hold several patents with a few more still pending."

"So that's where you run into the red tape when you were grousing about Washington."

He turned his head away and looked out the window. "Mostly," he said.

Without elaborating on his work or offering to show her his personal quarters, he took her arm and propelled her out of the house.

"Now, if you don't mind, I'd like to show you the cemetery."

They walked through the yard, past a stand of hollyhocks, and up a steep incline behind the house. At the top was a small plateau. A low fence, about waist high, encircled five tombstones. Well-oiled hinges opened smoothly as Jon pulled back the gate. Kate stepped over the tended ground and read inscriptions on the stones. Sandwiched between the two sets of taller stones was a much smaller one. She read the faded words carved into the weather-pitted granite: Jennifer Ann Ames, and beneath the dates were the words: *Gone to play with the baby angels.*

"You had a sister?"

His eyes clouded and he nodded. Kate waited for him to continue. A slight wind caught a puff of smoke from his pipe, swirled it around and carried it away.

"She lived three days—three short days. Just a few meager breaths and then she was gone. There are times I feel so cheated—so utterly and unreversibly cheated—that she was taken from me. From us." He frowned. "We would've been close, and I know she would've made the world a better place. Maybe if she were born today modern medicine could save her. It was a long time ago and back then babies died very often with no one knowing the reason. I guess, like everything else, medicine has come a long way." He brushed his fingers along the top of the stone.

"I was only seven when it happened, but I remember it as if it were this morning." He seemed to be reliving the pain. "It was one of the hottest days of the year. Mama was still in bed from the long hard labor. Mostly I remember the tears. Mothers are expected to cry, I suppose. But men, well, they're tough—taught early on not to show their feelings." He stuck his hands into his pockets and looked off into the distance.

"One day I went into the barn looking for Papa. I found him in one of the stalls; he hadn't heard me come in. There, alone in his grief, he was crying and beating his fists against the wall. Such weeping, Kathleen, I hope never to hear again. I was quiet as a mouse when I backed out of the barn. Somehow, even though I was only seven, I knew I couldn't intrude on his sorrow. Later, when he came into the house he seemed fine, only I knew he wasn't." He pointed. "Over there's his grave. He was a fine man, an honest and dependable man. When he gave you his hand on something, you knew he would never go back on his word."

"You were named for him."

"Mama said there was no more honorable name than that of Jonathan Ames. It's been a big responsibility to carry, and there've been times I haven't given it the respect it deserves."

Kate was doubtful that this man could ever be disrespectful.

Beside that grave lay a final one. Kate knew it had to be Jon's mother. She touched her hand to the cold marble and read the inscription: Rebekka Ann Ames, Beloved Wife and Mother. Kate felt awkward as tears gathered in her eyes and she tried to wipe them away before he could see. *Why has he brought me here and forced upon himself so much pain?* she wondered. Turning, she reached for his hand. It was a slight gesture, but it seemed right.

"Now," he said, breaking the grief-laden silence, "remember I said we were going to do some walking? It's about a mile beyond that ridge." He pointed toward the east. "Can you make it?"

"I can make it," Kate said. "You're the one who said I was dressed for mountain climbing."

"So I did," he said, and they headed down the backside of the hill, the walk slow and leisurely. Their attention was drawn overhead to the loud honking of a flight of Canada geese. The long, stretched-out line of bodies formed the V-shaped formation and looked like a crack drill team. They seemed to fly with effortless motion.

"Did you ever wonder if the lead goose knows he's the head honcho?" Jon asked.

"Does he?"

"Probably."

Kate could find no reason to doubt his opinion. "I like the way they all stay together."

"Canada's are very devoted. If one becomes ill or can't fly and has to land, another goes with him—" he grinned "—or her. And they stay together until the afflicted one recovers or dies."

"Is that true?"

"Absolutely."

They walked on. Jon pointed out things he wanted her to see: rabbits playing hide-and-seek in the golden sagebrush, a mother doe and her yearling, the spotted pair only visible when they moved, a hawk gliding smooth circles against a canvas of autumn sky. Kate's laughter came easy and often. The sun had already started to go down and she gave a vague and fleeting thought to the time. But it didn't seem important. At last, they crested the rise of a small hill and there before them, across a wide expanse of meadow, was a glorious knoll. Mighty oaks and poplars and maples crowned the curve of the ridge and extended down the grass-covered slopes. Kate stood gazing, her hands on her hips.

"How lovely," she said. "Can we climb to the top?"

"This is what I wanted to show you. Do you like it?"

"*Like?* Now, that's a puny word. I don't merely like it, Jon. It's breathtaking. It's majestic." She picked up speed, eager to get to the summit. Jon hurried to catch up with her.

"Whoa, wait, slow down a minute," he said, catching her by the arm. "There's no hurry."

By the time they reached the top, both were out of breath. Kate plopped to the ground and stretched out beneath the spreading arms of a giant poplar. The fluted pods on the high limbs were empty now of the tulip-shaped flowers they had held only a few weeks earlier.

Jon dropped down beside her. "You do like it, don't you?"

"It's beautiful. I could stay here forever." She sat up and looked around. "Do you own it?"

"It's all part of the farm: from where we turned off onto the private road, past here and over another quarter mile or so. I guess there's about five hundred acres in all. A developer's been trying to buy it for a year now. I think I'm almost persuaded."

"You're not serious? You wouldn't consider selling this knoll, would you? Look at that sunset. Just look at it. How could you possibly entertain the idea of parting with it?" She looked at him. "Is it the money?"

"No, Kathleen, it's not the money." He plucked a blade of grass. "But the county needs room to grow, to expand and improve. Selling would mean more jobs, more desperately needed revenue." He shredded the grass. "If I do agree to sell, it'll only be that parcel over near the main road." He pointed. "Back here, down into the meadow there and across to the cemetery, I'd never part with. I figure there's about fifty acres I'll keep and sell off the rest."

"The farmhouse. Will you sell that?"

He seemed to have made up his mind. "It only holds memories, and memories sometimes need to be put to rest. Start to build new ones, so to speak."

"Where will you live? Will you move to town?"

He laughed as he got to his feet and dusted twigs from the seat of his pants. "For only the shortest time possible. I'm a country boy, I'd never live in town for long. I thought maybe I'd build here, up on this knoll." He took her hand and pulled her up. "What do you think?"

"I couldn't imagine a more perfect spot."

As if reluctant to leave, they stood for a moment longer. "Nature has never been more at her finest than she is today," Jon said.

Kate nodded and knew this day would be hard to forget.

The walk back to the farmhouse was more hurried. By the time they reached the car, only lingering shadows remained from the sun that had gone down past the horizon.

"I didn't realize it was so late," Kate said.

"It really isn't. It only seems so out here in the country with all the trees and hills around."

He helped her up onto the seat and closed the door. They were both silent on the drive back.

"Tired?" he asked as they neared her duplex.

"I guess I am, a little." She leaned her head back. "Running around in the woods like a young colt takes a lot of energy." She glanced over at him and smiled. "And at our age."

"Oh, I don't know," he said, pulling into the driveway. "We're doing okay."

"Would you like to come in?"

"No, but thanks. I think what we both need right now is a nice hot shower and a good night's sleep."

"I believe you're right." She smiled at him. "Good night, Jon. Thank you for a lovely day."

"Thank you for sharing it with me. It meant a lot." He reached for the door handle beside him.

"Please, don't bother to see me in. I'll be fine."

"It's no bother." He tucked a stray lock back from her brow. "I brought you from your door—I'll always see that you get safely back."

He took her arm, walked her across the sidewalk and opened the door.

The jacket and cotton sweater felt heavy and damp as Kate stepped into the warm room. She began stripping in the hallway and by the time she reached the shower she was naked. Not until the hot water hit her back did she realize how bone-tired she actually was. As the water ran over her shoulders and cascaded down her body, Kate's mind clicked off automatically. With a detachment she'd long become accustomed to, she soaped and lathered and rinsed, never once giving thought to what lay beneath her hands.

Feeling refreshed from the shower, a rumbling in her stomach reminded her that she'd eaten nothing since breakfast. She heated a quick can of soup, decided that was all she needed and, although the hour was still early, she went to bed.

Kate's slumber was fitful and restless as bizarre images invaded her dreams. She found herself standing on a hill. The wind was howling as it whipped about, uprooting sunflowers that were dripping globs of scarlet paint. A drop landed on Kate's hand and when she touched it, it wasn't paint at all, but blood. Mingled with the noise of the wind, she could hear a desolate wailing, not unlike the sound of weeping. Someone was in pain, but she couldn't get close enough to offer comfort. Something was keeping her enclosed within a tight space, as if being held prisoner. There was a dark cloud overhead, but it wasn't a cloud at all, rather something shadowed and sinister, blotting out the sun. She felt threatened. The wind increased and suddenly there was a loud crash. Kate woke, gasping for breath. The bed covers were tangled around her and damp with perspiration. Across the room, the curtains flapped wildly from wind and rain coming through the half-opened window. A flower vase on her makeup vanity had blown over and lay shattered. Grateful for having been retrieved from the nightmare, she closed the window and returned to bed. The dream caused her to shudder. Kate was too much of a realist to believe in omens, yet she felt weighted down by a sense of foreboding. The remainder of the night passed under the canopy of an uneasy sleep.

Autumn continued to push the days forward. Kate thought of Jon often. He had not called, but she thought he would. She was not overly pleased with the knowledge that it mattered. Almost two weeks passed before his phone call came.

"Kathleen, it's Jon."

She laughed. "By this time I do recognize your voice."

"I've missed you," he confided. "I've thought of you every day."

"Have you been out of town again?"

"No. I've been here on the farm since I last saw you. In fact, you're the first person I've spoken to since I took you home that Sunday night. I've had lots of things to think about, a lot on my mind."

"You haven't been off that farm in almost two weeks—that doesn't sound like you. Are you okay?"

His sigh sounded heavy and tired. "I'm fine. Actually, the phone did ring a couple of times but I didn't bother with it."

Kate had a feeling that most calls this man received would carry some degree of importance—but apparently not for the past couple of weeks.

"I just called," he interrupted her thoughts, "because I wanted you to know that I'm going away for a while, until after the first of the year most likely. I would've liked to have had our first holiday celebration together—but it didn't work out that way. There's something I have to take care of. Something which mustn't be postponed any longer. I'll call when I get back." He paused for the span of a heartbeat. "But I'll be thinking of you while I'm gone."

Kate refused to let herself be saddened. While it was true that she had been looking forward to spending time with him through the Christmas season and having him beside her on New Year's Eve, she knew she was getting far too involved and that this was probably for the best. She told herself she was glad he was going away.

"I've got to go now. Good-bye, Kathleen." He hung up abruptly.

Slowly she replaced the receiver back into its cradle and pushed away the lump growing in her chest. Sure there was disappointment, but she had been disappointed in the past and dealt with it. She would do so again.

"So, that's that," she muttered to herself as she considered this man who had so recently invaded her life: this mystery man.

What was the matter that had to be *taken care of*? Was it another woman? Someone he knew in Washington? He went there often enough, he had surely made any number of friends. Some had to be female and serious. But serious enough to warrant *taking care of*? He made it sound as if it were something he had to finish, to put an end to.

Her head swam as she tried to sort out the pieces. Like a jigsaw puzzle that had to be put together with great patience, the pieces would take a long time to fit, and even then would not go together easily.

SIX

The approaching holiday season loomed empty and without promise. Kate found herself actually dreading her favorite time of year. The one redeeming factor was Rachel's wedding, and from all indications it was growing into quite a production.

An anticipation factor had raised the overall atmosphere of the office to a new high, as Rachel's happiness became contagious and the entire staff got into the spirit of her wedding. One whole week was spent in the selection of a wedding gown as she and Sally plowed through stacks of magazines. At first they would agree on the perfect dress, only to change their minds an hour later. Kevin kidded them at every turn.

"Poor Paul," he lamented. "The old fellow never had a chance." He looked at the two heads huddled together at Rachel's desk and feigned concern. "Don't you two know that we bachelors are becoming an endangered species? Are we less important than the spotted owl or the snail darter? Soon I'll be left to carry on alone."

"Oh, pooh," Rachel said. "Just you wait, your day's coming." She looked at Kate standing in the doorway of her office. "Tell him, Kate. Tell him that sooner or later he'll be a willing—no, eager—victim."

"Sooner, I'd say," Kate said.

Kevin threw his hands up in mock surrender. "Prime your weapons, ladies. I'll be back for the firing squad in about an hour. Even the condemned has to eat." He looked at Sally and winked as he went out the door.

Sally blushed and she and Rachel looked at each other and laughed.

"Kate, come see this dress and tell me what you think," Rachel said. "Sally and I both like it, but would you look at it, please? You have such good taste and, well, I just don't know."

Kate closed the folder she held in her hands and tucked it beneath her arm. She stepped over to the desk and looked at the picture. The gown was a beauty. The scalloped sweetheart neckline would be a perfect frame for Rachel's oval face, and the ivory color would set off her olive skin and long, dark hair.

"I think it's the right dress," Kate said.

"See. I told you," Sally said. "And it's available in a size four so there'll be almost no alteration problems."

"Okay, it's settled." Rachel closed the book and gave it a final pat. "This is the first dress I try on."

Kate turned from the girls, wandered to the door of Marty's office and looked in. He sat at his desk, an open file spread out before him.

He looked up and smiled. "Hi."

"Busy?"

"Not really. Just looking over the Deaver's file. Come in." He motioned to the chair in front of his desk. "Sit."

"I don't want to interrupt."

"Nonsense, you could never do that. By the way, thank you."

"For what?"

"Helping to clear up the dress business."

"Oh, that. I hope you're not getting put out by all of this wedding stuff."

"It's okay. It can't last much longer so let them have their girl time. Now, how about you? Are you all right?"

"I'm fine."

"Well, you look a little peaked to me. Kate, are you getting enough rest?"

"Sure, Marty." Kate wanted to change the subject. "How's Dixie?"

"She's well. As a matter of fact she was just asking about you the other day. She wondered when you're coming out to the house."

"I'll get out there one day soon. I miss her."

"How about Thanksgiving?"

"I can't, Marty. I've been invited next door to Sara Templeton's. Her family's coming and I'm anxious to see Jeffy and the new baby."

"Dix will be disappointed."

"Tell her I'll call soon."

Marty looked at Kate and smiled. "Anytime you're ready. You know you're always welcome." He turned his attention back to the file.

Kate flipped open the folder on her lap, studied it for a moment, and closed it again. She sat for another minute before getting up and wandering into the outer office.

The days crawled by. Rachel's last day of work came with a final hurrah; work virtually came to a standstill. The pace had slackened naturally because of the holidays, which was a blessing because Kate doubted seriously there could be much concentrated attention given to such mundane matters as securities, investments, or tax shelters. Marty brought champagne to toast the bride and presented

Rachel with a check for five-hundred dollars as a wedding gift. Kevin, undaunted in his stand for bachelorhood, relented and gave her a dozen yellow roses. A tiny teakwood music box, inlaid with jade and coral, was Sally's gift. Rachel lifted the lid and the group listened to a few bars of *We've Only Just Begun*.

Kate's gift was the last to be opened. After weeks of searching, she'd finally found the right present. Rachel folded back the tissue paper to reveal a beautiful gown of white batiste. The long sleeves were gathered at the wrists with delicate tea roses embroidered in the palest shades of ivory and pink. Tiny green leaves formed a garland that joined the roses in bands encircling the wrists, and the deeply gathered front and back yokes were trimmed with identical roses. Kate could hear the groan of her checking account from the price of the gown, but had no regrets for having bought it.

Tears gathered in Rachel's smoky eyes as she accepted the gifts. "Thank you all. You're so dear to me."

"Now, how about a toast," Marty said, filling the glasses. "Who wants to make it?

They all looked at each other and laughed. "I think it should be the maid of honor," Kate said.

A faint blush crept over Sally's flawless complexion and her blue eyes misted. Her chin trembled as she started to speak.

"To the kindest, dearest friend a girl could ever have. Even though we wish you weren't moving away and will miss you dreadfully, we wish for you and your future with Paul, the very best the world has to offer." She raised her glass in Rachel's direction, and the others did likewise. "To Rachel" Sally toasted: "*May you have sun-filled days and star-filled nights, and dreams to wrap around you. But more than this, much more than this, may love always go with you.*"

Kate was not surprised to find that Sally had the soul of a poet. She had always displayed a tenderness seldom seen in one so young.

"That was beautiful," Kate said and noticed that Kevin looked at Sally with a new kind of fascinated appreciation.

Sally seemed embarrassed by all the attention and tried to wave it away.

They drank and laughed through the embraces and made promises to keep in touch. And they would, at least in their memories.

Rachel's wedding day dawned crisp and cold with only a wisp of winter clouds. Throughout the morning and while she was dressing, Kate thought of Jon. She wondered where he was, what he was doing. He lingered just at the fringes of her mind all the way to the church and while the haunting voices from the choir loft sang *Ave Maria*.

A hush fell over the crowd, and the people turned in their seats as the wedding march sounded and the procession began its slow trek down the aisle. Sally was the last of the attendants to enter before the bride. Her rich burgundy dress reflected a blush of pink against her face giving her alabaster complexion a rosy glow and made her eyes sparkle. Then the crescendo of the music increased and the bride appeared. Escorted by her parents, Rachel entered the sanctuary and the guests stood. The long train of her dress, the dress chosen so carefully and so dearly, brushed rose petals from the white bridal path as she passed. Paul stood waiting at the altar, handsome and elegant in his formal cutaway. When Rachel reached his side, they looked at each other and smiled; a smile that held the secret of the ages. Then they joined hands and pledged to each other the love that would unite their lives. Kate touched her cheek, surprised to find it wet.

Good cheer and celebration reigned supreme at the reception. Toasts of love and best wishes rained down on the beaming couple. From a corner of the room, a three-piece orchestra played Mozart. Dixie's heavily ringed fingers caught Kate's eye, motioning her over. Kate accepted a glass of champagne from a passing waiter, threaded her way through the crowd, and plopped down beside Dixie at the lace-covered table. The dear friend looked festive in her emerald green dress that billowed out from her substantial figure. Pearls adorned her throat and her ears. Her red hair was a series of little corkscrews that covered her head. With a smile that was a bright slash of red, she reminded Kate of Aunt Pittypat from Atlanta.

"Well, hello stranger," she said.

"It *has* been a while," Kate admitted.

"Come out to the house for Christmas, Kate. While Marty watches football we'll catch up on all the latest gossip."

"I'll have to let you know, Dixie. Something might come up and I won't be able to make it."

"What *might* come up? Kate, do you have a new beau?" Dixie fancied herself as having keen perception. "Marty said you'd been looking peaked lately but you don't look sick to me. If I had to guess, I'd say you're a woman in love."

Kate laughed at the absurdity of the idea. "Dixie, you're incorrigible."

"Of course I am, and proud of it. What else do you expect from the best damn torch singer who always showed more cleavage than was deemed decent." She leaned forward. "Ah, could I tell you stories: which roulette wheel was rigged, where the good booze was kept, who was banging who—"

"Dixie!"

"Well, I could, and you still haven't answered my question."

Kate shook her head. "Now there," she said, pointing to Sally dancing with Kevin, "is a girl in love."

Marty arrived at their table and asked his wife to dance. Kate watched them walk away and was shocked to feel an unexplained anger toward Dixie. The anger left her shaken and quite frightened. She set the glass on the table, collected her coat and left the reception.

SEVEN

Christmas day crept in and vanished without any encouragement from Kate. She didn't visit the Martins. She wasn't ready to deal with Dixie's inquisition. Gifts and cards had been delivered to her apartment and were appreciated, but still she felt empty.

Returning to work restored some semblance of order to her life the following week. There lingered about the office the leftover flavor of the wedding and Christmas, but a meager amount of work did manage to get done. Kate left Consolidated Investments early on New Year's Eve and drove by the liquor store. With a modest bottle of chardonnay tucked securely under her arm, she headed home.

Much later, with the music of Bacharach as her only companion, Kate sat on the sofa and drained her glass. Her lips felt thick and her tongue too burdensome for her mouth. She clamped her hands to the sides of her head to keep it from lifting off her shoulders. A couple of times she felt the sofa move. Pouring another glass, she was surprised to discover the bottle was nearly empty. She couldn't remember drinking all the wine by herself, but she must have, she reasoned, since she was all alone. The ticking of the travel clock on the end table punctuated the stillness of the room. As Kate listened, the ticking grew louder and louder, faster and faster. She wanted to scream at it to stop. She was not yet ready to surrender the present so quickly. Through blurred vision, she squinted at the numbers on the dial. As best she could to make out, the time was quarter to midnight. Wallowing in her self-pity and feeling quite the drunken martyr, Kate wondered if, like the Bacharach song said, the new year would bring one less bell to answer. *What the hell*, she thought, *it probably will*. That decided, she went to bed and was promptly whistling a soft snore.

A faint, repetitive noise sounding far away, pushed through Kate's sleep and reached her fuzzy brain. She struggled against the intrusion and burrowed deeper under the covers. Suddenly she was wide-awake and clear-headed. She switched on the bedside lamp and reached for the phone. A steady hum of the dial tone was all that was on the line. She looked at the digital clock on the nightstand; it was a minute past twelve. It could only have been one person calling. From somewhere, out there at the beginning of the new year, Jon had taken the time to call. Now she knew he had not forgotten. Lying back on the pillows, she closed her eyes and drifted back to sleep, a trace of a smile upon her lips.

Deep into January, winter had the small town of Woodway in a firm grip. Snowdrifts wedged against the houses and frosted over the windowpanes. White peaks stood high on the roofs and scalloped canopies hung precariously from the eaves like finely tatted lace. There was an occasional scattered ray of sunshine, only to be darkened by snow clouds and cold mist.

Kate was filled with a restless anticipation that gnawed at her insides. Jon said he would return sometime after the first of the year, and now it was the middle of January. Would he be back? Of course, he would. There was the farm to see to, the house to build. Had something happened during his long absence to make him change his mind? Kate had no answers. She waited.

It was the middle of February. The sun made a rare appearance and brought a welcome respite to an otherwise dreary month. Cabin fever forced Kate from the confines of her small apartment, and she felt a need to visit her *pondering* place. The roads were clear but snow still covered the ground and curled in the fields like waves of ocean foam. The woods lay silent beneath its winter blanket. The old bridge was a slab of white and Kate broke the snow with her fresh boot prints. She waded to the edge of the swollen brook and stood watching as it swept along, carrying little snow-covered islands of leaves and frozen twigs. The water seemed to mock her in its glorious freedom as it tumbled over moss-covered stones, then gurgle and disappear beneath opaque circles of ice patches where the water was shallow. Dainty layers of rime crystals danced along the edges of the rushing stream and clung to the banks.

Snow had partially melted from her rock. Kate sat down and turned her face to the sun. And she thought about Jon. *Something out of the ordinary was keeping him away*, she reasoned. Were there bonds in another part of his life—separate and apart from her—that he couldn't break? Causes, and people, to which he was committed? It was possible. Even probable. Unlike Kate, the boundaries of Woodway did not mark the limits of his life. Part of him belonged to the world beyond; a world of which Kate knew very little. And she couldn't believe that Jon would give up a cause easily. She believed his sincerity when he said he would be back, but unpredictable circumstances had a way of altering best-laid plans. Considering this, she was able to leave her wooded sanctuary believing that he had not deliberately lied to her.

Back in the apartment Kate danced on one foot as she tugged at the slippery rubber boot. One more good pull and her foot would be free. Just as she braced herself against the cabinet, the phone rang. She hobbled from the kitchen, trailing water across the living room carpet.

"'lo."

"You're out of breath," the familiar voice said.

Her hand fisted around the receiver. She made no reply.

"Kathleen, are you there?"

"I just came through the—my boot was stuck and I couldn't—" Damn it, she was babbling. She took a breath. "When did you get back?"

"Last night, late. I tried calling earlier today but there was no answer."

No answer? She bit back the sarcastic words. *Of course there was no answer. I was out in the woods thinking about you.* "How was your trip?"

"Difficult," he said.

He had been gone nearly three months and the most he could manage about the trip was that it had been *difficult.*

"How soon can I see you?" he asked, breaking her concentration. "Kathleen, are you there?"

"I'm here."

"Are you sure you're okay?"

"Would you care to come over tonight? I'll whip up some supper."

"I don't want you doing anything other than what you've already planned."

"Just soup and a sandwich."

"Sounds good. Sure you don't mind?"

She rubbed her brow. "No, Jon, I don't mind."

"I'll see you in an hour then."

"Hell, yes, I mind," Kate muttered as she hung up the receiver. "Why couldn't I be honest enough to tell him that?" Who was this man, *this master of intrigue,* who had crept into her life? The thought of seeing him again left her feeling slightly unstable.

He looked spectacular when Kate opened the door a short time later. He came in and gave her a quick hug.

"You look more lovely than I remember," he said.

Conversation during the meal consisted of small talk, with Kate contributing answers to a long list of questions about the events that had taken place in his absence. They cleared the table and carried coffee cups to the living room. Comfortably stretched out on the sofa, he pulled the pipe from his pocket and tamped in the tobacco.

"Thanks for not asking questions," he said.

Kate knew, without explanation, that he was talking about his extended absence.

"An important chapter has closed in my life," he went on to confess. "And right now I cannot—*will not*—talk about it. Maybe someday I'll be able to tell you. But only when I think you're ready and that you'll understand."

Kate nodded. "We all have things we can't talk about. Believe me, I know."

"But for now," he said, reaching into his pocket, "I brought you a belated Christmas present. I hope you like it." He handed her a small box wrapped in gold foil.

"I didn't get you anything."

"Never mind about that. Go ahead, open it."

Carefully Kate peeled back the tape. Beneath the expensive wrapping paper lay a purple velvet box. She gasped as she opened the lid to reveal a pear-shaped diamond suspended on a delicate gold chain.

"Oh, Jon, to say you shouldn't have is entirely inadequate. But really, you shouldn't have."

Laughing, he lifted the jewel from its velvet bed. "Try it on."

"In a minute. I want to look at it first." She touched the stone with a hesitant finger. "You were terribly extravagant. It must be worth a fortune."

Again he laughed. "I can see by your reaction that you genuinely like it."

"It's the most beautiful thing I've ever been given. I suppose the proper thing to do would be to refuse to accept it. But please don't expect me to do that."

"I expect no such thing."

"I'll treasure it always."

"It pleases me far more than you realize to give you something that is so obviously appreciated. Wear it often. The two of you compliment each other. You were made to wear beautiful things, Kathleen, and I hope this is just the first of many."

"Thank you, Jon. You're a good and generous man and I count myself privileged to have you for a friend."

"Don't heap praises upon my shoulders, my dear. I neither deserve, nor want them."

"But—"

A slight frown creased his brow as he pressed a finger lightly against her lips. Properly chastised by the mild rebuke, Kate lowered her eyes and fell silent. The rest of the evening she felt like she was walking the rim of a volcano; a volcano that seemed peaceful on the surface but held violent rumblings within its depths.

EIGHT

Together they saw March in like a lion, and then out like a lamb. April was pure enchantment. There was a new springiness to Kate's step. Gone was the malaise of the past, the days she was barely able to get through. Together they attended lectures and auctions, browsed old bookstores, and once had driven more than a hundred miles to attend a piano concert. Kate was constantly amazed at the similarities in their likes and dislikes. She respected Jon's judgment and frequently asked his opinion. He, in turn, accorded her the respect to which he seemed to think she was entitled.

At first Kate expected Jon to make demands of her, demands that could never be fulfilled. She dreaded the time she would have to deal with it, knowing it would put an end to a relationship that was becoming more important to her all the time. However the demands never came. She had always considered him aloof and slightly reserved, but finally managed to let her guard down completely after coming to the inevitable conclusion that he wanted no more from her than she was prepared to give.

Jon finalized the sale of the outlying acres to the development firm. Holding true to his word, he retained the fifty acres to the east, which included the family cemetery and his beloved knoll where he intended to build the new house. Together they looked at floor plans, discarding one after the other.

"Well, I see right now," he said, closing the last blueprint book, "the plans for the house will have to be original. Of everything we've looked at, nothing even comes close."

Kate poured fresh coffee. "This house is important to you, isn't it?"

"Too important to settle for anything less that what we really want."

The spoon fell from fingers that had gone numb as the '*we*' was not lost on her.

The following weekend they went out to the farmhouse one last time to collect the remainder of Jon's personal belongings. He had already moved most of the things into a rented house in town. There remained only a small number of items to be gathered. Quietly he moved from room to room, as if reliving the past. Kate left him alone with his memories and wandered into the kitchen she had grown to love. In her mind, she could see Jon's mother at the old cook stove preparing one of her huge meals. She imagined Jon, as a little boy, and the sound the screen door would make as it slammed shut behind him when he dashed into the kitchen. She could see his face streaked with dirt and sweat and hear his mother tell him to wash up for supper.

She wandered back into the living room. Jon was nowhere in sight. Peering out the front door, she saw his retreating back as he made his way up the hill toward the cemetery. Taking a step to follow, she changed her mind. He needed the time for himself.

Turning back to the room, Kate noticed the door to his bedroom was open. Cautiously, she went over and looked in. Except for a box in the corner, the room was empty. She ventured in slowly. Off to the far end of the room was a second door. It too was open. On the other side of the door was a smaller space with a long, narrow table that looked as if it had seen many hours of use. She walked its length, running her hand across the top. The wood was smooth as satin except towards either end where gouge marks, perhaps from heavy-duty pushpins, might've been used to hold down diagrams or drawings. Overhead hung a large light bulb nestled beneath a metal reflector. On the back wall was a network of power strips, switches and mysterious-looking black boxes with dials.

As she turned back to the larger room, her eyes darted to the box. It looked to contain books, *textbooks probably*, she thought, and lots of note pads. Sticking out from between the stacks was the corner of what appeared to be a picture. Feeling guilty, Kate glanced out the window. Jon was just coming through the gate on his way back down the hill. Cautiously, she slid the picture out. From the surroundings and the glossy paper, it was obvious that the black and white photograph had been taken at a fancy dinner club.

Kate looked at the exquisite face smiling up at Jon and knew that this was an important figure in his life. The platinum hair, long and silky, was caught up and held by a diamond-studded band. Tendrils fell casually down to shoulders that looked creamy and luminous. Large, misty eyes, framed by meticulously mascaraed lashes in the small doll-like face, mirrored unabashed adoration as they gazed at Jon. The Grecian gown, draped high across the front and gathered at the shoulders by diamond clips, gave a hint of innocent allure. A wide gold band wrapped twice around the smooth upper arm, and manicured fingers cradled a crystal goblet. The other hand rested just at the point of the pixie chin. On the third finger of the left hand was an enormous emerald-cut diamond ring. *An engagement ring*, Kate thought. She turned the photograph over and on the back was an inscription: *To Jonnie—Owner of my soul. Keeper of my destiny. Julie.* The handwriting was intricate and flowing, and Kate thought it was somehow related to the artwork on the porch.

For the first time since knowing Jon, Kate felt the power of jealousy and wanted to hate all that the photo represented. Hurriedly she placed it back where she found it and left the room. She would've liked to have had more time with the picture, to study it. She had barely looked at Jon's face, but was left with the distinct impression that he was extremely happy.

Kate was standing in the front door as he entered the yard. "Ready to go?"

He nodded. "Just let me get the last box of materials from the bedroom. It's just some textbooks and research materials that I want to keep."

He came back with the box tucked under his arm and carried it to the car. Kate noticed that the edge of the picture was no longer showing between the stacks. He shoved the box onto the back seat and they drove from the farmhouse for the last time.

Sleep was a long time coming that night. Kate twisted and turned until she pulled the top sheet away from the bottom of the bed. Each time she closed her eyes she was haunted by the beautiful face in the picture. *Why had they broken up?* she wondered. Was Julie the object of Jon's last trip, the important chapter he had closed in his life? The thing he had to put and end to? But she's gorgeous. Kate winced. *Next to her, I'm a church mouse.* How could two such perfectly matched creatures come to a parting of the ways? And who had made the decision? *Surely not Julie.* The radiance of the face in the picture could have only been inspired by a love of epic proportions. Kate wondered when the picture had been taken. *Was it after we started seeing each other? Could it have been on his last trip? Was night-clubbing with a beautiful woman the reason he was gone for such a long time?* Remembering the pain that flickered across Jon's face after his return, Kate knew she could never ask him about his past. But she could not turn the picture, nor the questions, from her mind.

NINE

Jon called two days later to tell Kate that he had found the right architect to do the house plans.

"I've already given him a general idea of what we want," he said. "We have to come up with a list of the basics and he'll draw from that." There was that 'we' again. "You will help me, won't you, Kathleen?"

"I'd love to. When do we start?"

"Tonight, if that's okay. The sooner the better."

"Great. Come over and we'll see what two brilliant minds can come up with."

Later, Kate whipped up a quick omelet and they ate standing by the sink holding their plates. Then Jon carried what was left of the pot of coffee to the living room, and they settled on the couch with paper and freshly sharpened pencils. Jon began by drawing rough designs from which Kate took notes and made suggestions. It was almost midnight before they looked up from their work. The house was beginning to come together and take on its own special personality. Being an engineer, Jon was concerned with construction details, pitches and elevations. Kate, on the other hand, added a more aesthetic quality, giving harmony and comfort and continuity to the eye. Some ideas were discussed and promptly discarded. Where Kate was conservative, Jon tended toward the more extravagant. The only thing on which they totally disagreed was the indoor swimming pool. Kate thought it was a luxury and terribly pretentious, but Jon was adamant in his insistence that it be included.

"But Jon, swimming pools are ego-boosters and very little else. It's like: *See my pool. Ha-ha, you don't have one.*"

"*You?* And which *you* would that be? Who's even going to know it's there?"

"Company. Visitors."

"I don't plan on having visitors who need to be impressed. Do you?"

Kate thought how bizarre the conversation was beginning to sound.

"Well, you might just as well install tennis courts and a helicopter pad."

Jon grinned. "Hey, that might not be a bad idea—the tennis courts, I mean. The helicopter pad we could add later."

"Jon."

"I was kidding. Such seriousness."

Kate looked at him and raised an eyebrow. "I do tend to carry on, don't I?"

"It wouldn't hurt to lighten up," he admitted. "But back to the pool. Think about it. Doctors tell us that swimming is one of the best forms of exercise; something about the pressure of the water balancing against the strain on the body. Outside, I agree, it wouldn't make a whole lot of sense. But an indoor pool can be used the year around." He gave a determined nod. "I get the final vote."

"Oh."

"I have more points than you, and you gave them to me. So I say it stays. I may concede to you on something else, say, the tennis court. But the pool definitely stays." He tapped his pipe against the side of the ashtray and dropped it into his pocket. The matter was settled.

He stood and arched his back, Jon stretched his arms over his head. "Look at the time. I didn't mean to take such advantage of you on a work night." He smiled. "Thanks for the help. I couldn't have done it without you. You had some very good ideas."

Kate beamed at the compliment. "Why, thank you, sir. I'm glad to know that I was appreciated."

He opened the door and stood with his hand on the knob. "You are more than just appreciated," he said and dropped a kiss on her forehead. "You were indispensable."

Kate closed the door behind him and brushed her fingertips across the burning skin where his lips had touched. She pressed her brow as if trying to seal the kiss into place. Her hand froze. A horrifying paralysis moved down her arm and spread across her shoulders, before engulfing her body and weighing her down. Fear, far greater than any she had ever known, coursed through her veins. Deadly fear. She leaned against the door. *"It's true,"* she hissed. *"You were so sure of yourself; so confident that you'd keep things under control. You fool. You poor, stupid fool."*

As if to heap indignation upon revelation, the platinum blonde in the picture flashed across Kate's mind. Such beauty. Such perfection. She clinched her fists and pressed them against her chest. A tear slipped from between her tightly closed eyes and rolled down her cheek. "Damn," she whispered. *"Damn, damn, damn."*

The next day from her office, Kate called Dixie.

"Hi, sweetie," Dixie said. "I wondered when you were going to call. I thought about buzzing you, but I never know when I'll interrupt something important. I know how it is when you hold down a demanding job."

"Not too demanding, Dixie. Your husband's a teddy bear to work for."

"How've you been? You sound sad."

Kate gave a feeble laugh. "You know me too well."

"Tell you what. Why don't we go out tonight, just you and me. Somewhere fancy. My treat."

"You know I need to talk."

"Meet me at seven at the Golden Lion. Now, let me get back to my show. Monique's about to come out of her coma and boy is she going to be pissed when she finds out—"

"Love you, Dixie."

"Same here, darling. See you tonight."

At seven-thirty the maitre d' led Kate and Dixie through the main part of the restaurant to a quiet corner of the room. Kate knew Dixie had requested the specific table for its privacy. After they were seated and cocktails ordered, Dixie pulled a pack of Virginia Slims from her purse and picked up a book of matches from the ashtray. Kate waited until she lit the cigarette and inhaled the first puff before she spoke.

"I've done a foolish thing, Dixie."

"I don't believe it. You don't have it in you."

Kate leaned forward, her fists on the edge of the table. "Dixie," she said in a kind of painful growl, "I'm in love."

"I knew it," Dixie cried triumphantly. "I told Marty, but he said I'd been watching too many soaps." She reached over and laid her hands on top of Kate's knotted fists. "I think it's stupendous."

"Stupid is more like it."

"I take it you haven't told the lucky man."

"Told him? I've barely told myself. Dixie, I'm scared."

"Does he know about—"

"Of course not. And I don't want to talk about it."

"Kate, you have to talk about it. It was a long time ago and you have to give it a rest, and get on with your life. There are good men in this world. Good, decent men."

"You mean like Evan?"

"Evan was a detestable slug that somebody should've poured salt on. He deserted you when you needed him most. Oh, don't think I didn't notice what was going on. I could see him starting to pull away even while you were still flat of your back in the hospital."

"He said I made him uncomfortable; that he was afraid he'd hurt me." Kate sneered. "I tried to make him love me—*to make love to me.* Hell, Dixie, I even begged him. Do you know how demeaning it is to beg your husband to touch you?" She shook her head. "No. You wouldn't. You and Marty are too close."

"Kate—"

"Well, never again, my friend. I can promise you that. There is no need great enough for me to lower myself to that depth. Never again will I spill my guts to a man who can't stand to put his hands on me. I'll not fight to save another marriage the way I did with Evan."

"Sweetie, that marriage wasn't worth saving. Maybe it was all part of a larger plan. Sometimes we don't know what God has in store for us."

"Don't talk to me about that charlatan."

Dixie waved her off before she blasphemed again. She'd heard it all before. She smiled and hoped The Almighty was in a good mood and feeling especially tolerable. "Lord, Kate, are you still blaming God for not having a baby while you were married to Evan?"

"He could've, you know. I would've been a good mother. What was one baby to the all-powerful Creator of the universe? I prayed, Dixie. Just one tiny baby was all I ever asked for." She lowered her voice. "You know what I used to do after Evan and I had sex? I'd press my legs together so the baby couldn't drain out. Other women just hop right out of bed and go to the bathroom. Not me. Oh, no. I'd lay there like an idiot—not moving a muscle. A baby meant that much. Evan and the marriage I could live without, but a baby would love me for me, *just for me*, Dixie, no matter what." She paused and took a deep breath. "Whoever said prayers get answered, just plain lied. It's a crock."

"It is true, Kate. It's just that sometimes the answer is *no*."

"Especially to those of us who are not one of the *beautiful people*."

"Kate—"

"Oh, it's okay, Dixie. I've always known I'm on the rather plain side." She laughed. "Accepted it actually."

"So you're not a classic beauty like Grace Kelly or a modern day Scarlett Johansson." She frowned. "Have you ever noticed how many of those girls look alike. I think they all go to the same plastic surgeon and he only has one pattern." Dixie stubbed out her cigarette. "You, my dearest Kate, are an original. As a matter of fact, I think you're probably the most beautiful woman I've ever known."

Kate winched. "Why, because I have a *good personality*?"

Dixie hooted. "Your personality is in the crapper." She lit another cigarette. "You know who you remind me of? Ingrid Bergman. You even look a little like her, and she by the way, thought she was plain too."

"She was exquisite."

Dixie tucked the cigarette into the corner of her mouth and cuffed Kate on the chin. "Here's looking at you, kid."

Their laughter was interrupted when the waiter came to take their order. Kate shook her head as if to clear away her thoughts. It was good to talk it out with the only person who truly understood.

TEN

A week later Jon invited Kate to join him on a holiday. Her love for him made her reckless enough to accept an invitation to fly to New York to attend opening night of *La Boheme*.

Assuming in the past that Jon was relatively well off, she found herself wondering if he was a little more than just comfortable. He certainly commanded the attention of someone rich, and while not famous, at least widely known and recognized. Upon their arrival in New York, Kate had the idea they were not among strangers.

They had just stepped into the lobby of their hotel when a brightly garnished woman, hurrying and breathless, rushed toward them.

"Precious Jonathan." Her gloved-hands fluttered against his arm like colorful butterflies. "How wonderful to see you. You must come out to the house after the opera; you are here to for the opening? We're having a little *thing*—" she flicked her fingers "—for the Maestro. He'll be simply crushed if he knows you're in town and don't come." She pulled in a hurried breath. "You know this is the first time he's conducted in New York and I think the poor dear's a little nervous. Seeing you will cheer him up. So don't disappoint me, sweetkins. See you back at the house. Ta, ta," she trilled and hurried away before Jon could reply.

Kate stood with her mouth open. "Who was that?"

"That, my dear Kathleen, is one of a rare breed. Courtney Sinclair Westfield, is a career party-giver and professional hobnobber."

"Are we going?"

His look turned serious. "But, my dear, we simply must."

"Else Maestro will be crushed?"

"Absolutely." They laughed as he took her arm and guided her into an elevator.

In the sitting room of Kate's suite, a fruit basket wrapped in gold transparent paper covered the top of the table on which it sat. Champagne, cloistered in white linen, rested on its side in a silver bucket. In the bedroom, long-stemmed roses arranged in a crystal vase along with forget-me-nots, stood on the nightstand. A small square box lay on the pillow in the center of the king-sized bed. The card carried no message only Jon's bold signature. Kate opened the box to find a bottle of *Bellodgia* perfume. She took off the top and smelled the floral scent. It reminded her of springtime.

Later, she sank into the enormous tub and leaned her head back against the tiled wall and tried to catch her breath. She had come so far, so fast, could she take it all in?

"Kate, old girl," she spoke aloud, her words bouncing around the ceramic room, "get a grip on reality. This world isn't real. You may have it for one week then it's back to the business of shoring up the barriers of your life. You were stupid to become so weak, and now the cracks in the wall have to be reinforced. In the meantime don't forget who you are, what you are. The instant you forget, all is lost." *But for this one week*, she promised herself silently, *I'm going to be someone special, someone Jon will be proud of.*

For the opening, Kate dressed as if there would be no other nights. "Formal," he told her, in answer to her question of what one wears to opening night of a grand opera. As extra insurance, Kate bought two gowns. She shuddered to think of the shambles she had made of her savings account. Choosing for this night her most extravagant purchase, she pushed from mind the six hundred dollars for the dress and cape. Feeling the silk caress her skin, she knew her decision about the dress had been right. The long sleeves clung closely to her arms, ending in a wisp of a ruffle at the wrists. She raised her hand and whiffed the pulse spot where she had applied the gift perfume. Jon's taste for excellence seemed to be boundless. Her only piece of jewelry was the beloved pendant. Fascinated, she watched in the mirror as the diamond caught the light and sparkled against the black silk of the dress. A knock sounded at the door just as she reached for the cape. Squaring her shoulders, Kate lifted her chin, determined to meet the cream of New York society head-on.

Upon their arrival at Lincoln Center, it was obvious from the beginning that tonight was to be the event of the season. Kate saw several well-known personalities from the world of entertainment and was introduced to at least one senator. Affecting a rather stiff composure, she was determined not to appear light-years above her social station. Jon held her arm possessively as he guided her through the crowd.

The lights dimmed and rode upward. The audience settled back into their seats as the orchestra began the overture. A chill of excitement tingled up Kate's spine as the curtain lifted.

She laughed at the plight of the poor impoverished Bohemians and at the end, heartbroken, she wept as poor Mimi hacked and coughed herself to a complete and utter demise. Even with the intermission, the performance was over much too quickly, and the players made repeated curtain calls. Kate continued to applaud long after her palms burned and turned red.

During their exit from the building, John was stopped time and time again for a handshake, a hearty pat on the back, or a whispered private joke. Kate was introduced to dozens of strangers, and she stood by his side and listened to his easy banter and levity. She marveled at his ability to maintain an air of approachability while still keeping people at arm's length. Finally, they were able to make it to their waiting car.

Courtney Sinclair Westfield's stately mansion was ablaze with light when Kate and Jon stepped from the stretch-limousine around midnight. He took her arm as they approached the entrance.

"Good evening, Mr. Ames," the doorman said.

"Henry," Jon said and swept Kate through the double arches.

The ballroom was crowded with beautiful people displaying the brightest plumage the best couturiers had to offer. They seemed to know they were a special lot, a chosen few. The ring of laughter, the call of greetings from across the room, the clink of crystal and silver, made Kate's head spin. Waiters, dressed in spotless linen, covered the huge room with champagne-laden trays. Jon collected a glass for each of them.

"Here," he said with a smile, "you must surely need this by now."

"I really do, but could you hold it for a minute? I just spotted the powder room. Will you excuse me?"

"You go right ahead. I'll wait for you there." He gestured to a small divan tucked away in a corner.

The powder room turned out to be several tiny alcoves separated and closed off by folding doors. Selecting the first one that was unoccupied, Kate sat down on a rattan bench. *Just a minute to catch my breath before I go back out there*, she thought.

A giggle came from nearby, penetrating the thin walls. "Haley, I can't believe this man you've fixed me up with." The voice sounded very young. "Is he old enough to be my grandfather, or what?"

"But Buffy dear, he has money. Lots and lots of gorgeous money. And if I know you, and I think I do, you'll end up with a good chunk of it before long."

Uncomfortable at overhearing such a private conversation, Kate collected her things to leave.

"So, speaking of money, did you happen to see Jonathan Ames?"

Kate halted in midair and dropped back down.

"Now there's a catch for you. He's one gorgeous hunk of man. He wouldn't be hard to take even without money."

"In your dreams. Wonder who the Mother Teresa is."

"Buffy, that's a terrible thing to say. She might not be the prettiest little thing in the room, but God, is she's loaded with class."

"But she's *old*."

"You think everybody over twenty-five is ancient. Although I'll admit, she does look older than Julie. Wonder what ever happened to the two of them?"

"Julie's a bitch."

There was a slight laugh. "Julie isn't a bitch. You didn't like her because she was beautiful and mysterious."

"Mysterious, my ass. An expensive and over-rated whore is more like it."

"But she did have a certain style."

"With his money she could buy all the style she wanted."

"I haven't seen her in ages. Have you?"

"Norman and I ran into them at some charity benefit a couple years back. I bumped into her in the powder room. The poor thing said she was having her period and asked if I had a Midol. Then she flashed me her new lumineer smile, that must have cost King Jonathan a fortune, told me to give Norman her love, and sailed away."

"Did you?"

"Did I what?"

"Give Norman her love"

"He didn't need it. He had mine."

"Yeah, you loved him all right. Loved him to death."

"Don't be tacky, Haley. It was *not* my fault Norman died. You know he had a bad heart."

"I know he did. I'm sorry."

"I don't want to talk about Norman, and I don't want to talk about Julie. Okay?"

"Okay, baby." A fastener on a purse clicked. "Let's get you back to grandpa moneybags before he finds somebody else to spend all that moola on."

Kate heard them leave. Feeling heat rise to her face, she turned on the tap and splashed cold water on her face. Then she took a few extra minutes to redo her makeup and tidy up. When she returned to the room, Jon was standing in the corner surrounded by a small crowd. He moved from their midst to meet her.

"Was I gone terribly long?" Kate asked. Listening to the conversation it seemed as if time had stood still.

"No, not long," he said and handed her the champagne which she eagerly accepted. "Are you okay?" he asked with concern. "You're pale and your hands are like ice."

"It's just all the excitement. Did you see the Maestro yet?"

Jonathan laughed. "I did. I think he's hitting the bourbon pretty hard right about now." He pointed to a woman headed in their direction. "Ah, here's somebody I want you to meet."

"Jonathan," she said. "How good to see you again."

"Gabriella," he said and took her hand. "I'd like you to meet Kathleen Spencer." He smiled at

Kate. "Gaby was the head in the box for tonight's performance."

"Head in the box?"

Gabriella boomed out laughter that shook the room. "Well, the rest of me was in there, too."

"The head in the box," Jon continued, "is the prompter. She's keeps the actors on track during the performance."

"And she's in a box?"

Jon nodded. "At the edge of the stage. Most people never know she's there."

Gabriella shook her finger. "Oh, but the cast knows," she said. "Oh, do they ever—testy bunch that they are."

Across the room, somebody called her name and she gave a big smile and turned away.

Kate was suddenly aware of two women, their heads together and glancing in her direction, and had a feeling she was being sized-up by Buffy and Haley. She forced her lips into a fixed smile that hurt her face.

ELEVEN

By the end of their stay in New York, Kate was glad to be on the plane headed for Woodway.

Upon their arrival back home the architect had completed the blueprints for the house. Jon brought them over and unrolled them on top of the cleared kitchen table.

"Well, what do you think?" he asked expectantly.

Kate stood with her hands on her hips gazing down at the curling sheets of paper. "It's hard to tell," she said, biting her lip. "It's like looking at a piece of material and trying to visualize the finished dress."

"Here, let me show you. This is the way it will lay out, if you're facing the front of the house," he said, holding down the sheet. "Over here to the right is the area where you come into the kitchen and dining area from the terrace and parking spaces." He pulled the sheets apart. "Here is the master suite tucked in between the kitchen and the front of the house. This next page takes us from the dining room to the living room and further on is my work studio." Kate reached to help him hold down the curing sheets. "And this hallway leading from the living room branches off to the great room—see, here on the outside wall is where the stone fireplace will be, and over there the two guest rooms sort of tucked in at the back of the house, toward the woods. And this final sheet is the pool, that's across from the dining area, and will be on the right when you come in from the terrace."

"Oh, the pool. How could I have forgotten that," she said and smiled.

"Well, what do you think?"

"I think it'll be beautiful. How soon do they expect to begin construction?"

"As soon as they can cut a road into the building site. The architect said he would talk to the grading people tomorrow."

"Then you've already committed and given them the go-ahead to proceed?"

"Indeed, I have."

They sat together on the sofa. "You're really excited about the house aren't you?"

"I guess I am," he said, and puffed his pipe. "I like putting things together. This is almost like an invention, but not quite. You and I came up with the basic idea but someone else will actually put it down on paper and do the construction. And now that we've come this far I can't wait to get started. How about coming out to the knoll this weekend to look around. We need to figure out how the house is to be situated."

We.

"Besides, there is something else I want to talk to you about and the knoll seems the most appropriate place."

"I'd love to," she said and wondered why he sounded so mysterious.

It was late afternoon on Sunday when Jon picked Kate up for their trip to the knoll. It was a most magnificent evening for a ride in the country; summer was nearly gone. Here and there patches of leaves were already changing colors. Kate looked from the car window and imagined the beauty of the countryside when it would be dressed in its full autumn finery. Jon had been amazingly quiet on the drive out. She glanced at him from the corner of her eye, the ever-present pipe clinched in his teeth. *He has something on his mind*, she thought. *Something important.*

The private road sign that once led to the farm had been torn away from the post. Even the fence was gone. All traces of the narrow road lay crushed beneath the wheels of giant earthmoving equipment. In the distance Kate could make out the beginnings of the shopping mall near where the old farmhouse once stood.

"The place has certainly changed," she said.

Jon barely glanced in the direction of the development. "The new house will be about two miles on past here," he said.

A few moments later, Jon pulled the car well off the road and parked. Stakes, fastened with little red flags, had been placed in the exact location where the road was to be graded.

"We have to walk from here," he said.

The air was sharp and clean and pure. Kate breathed deeply and felt renewed. Overhead, birds fussed at having been interrupted by outsiders. The lay of the land rose gently before them and continued an upward rise until it met the knoll. It looked deceptively near.

"There's a good quarter-mile walk ahead of us," Jon said, "so we might as well take our time."

Kate nodded and automatically slowed her pace. He pointed to a squirrel as it scampered down the trunk of a tree. Kate laughed as the fur ball stopped, clacked at them, then scurried off. Jon took her hand to help her across a fallen tree, and once on the other side continued to hold it securely in his own.

"You know the one thing I like most about you?" he asked.

"What?"

"There's nothing phony about you. You are what you are. No hidden agenda, no games, no barrage of questions. I never feel pressure from you, Kathleen. And you make silence acceptable. With you, empty spaces don't have to be filled with idle chatter. I've never known another woman with that quality. Believe me, it's rare."

Kate's mind rushed back over all the times she had forced herself to remain silent and not question him. She doubted that she was as rare as he thought.

"Well, here we are again," he said as they reached the knoll. He spread his arms and casually dropped one about her shoulders. "Is it as pretty as you remembered?"

"Prettier," she said honestly. "It's truly the most tranquil spot in all the world."

"Maybe not the entire world, but it does come awfully close. Now, take a good long look and tell me how you think our house should be situated."

Our house.

"Let's walk around a bit, look at it from all sides," she suggested, slightly shaken. After carefully examining the hill from all directions, she squinted into the sunset. "This way, I think," she said, showing him with her hands.

"I hoped that's what you'd say, because I've always seen it that way, too. Perhaps you should have been a designer."

"I'm just a financial broker." She laughed. "An overworked, underpaid financial broker."

"How about changing careers, Kathleen," he said and reached into his pocket. "Would you consider, at this stage in your life, giving up your current occupation and taking on the terribly burdensome job of being my wife?"

He raised the lid of a jewelry box and picked up an acorn-sized diamond from its bed of satin. It shot sparks from his fingers when he held the ring out to her.

"I'm a complex person, Kathleen. I'll never be the perfect husband, but I will try to make you happy. I can provide more than adequately for you, and in return, the only thing I ask is for you to have patience with me."

Kate was unable to speak. At all cost, she knew she couldn't let the protective wall around her start to crumble, or she would be trapped with no way out. She loved this man who stood before her. In spite of all the nuance and mystery surrounding him, she loved him with a fierceness that left her fragile and weak weakness. Tears, bright as the diamond Jon held in his fingers, glistened in her eyes and spilled over.

She pushed his hand away. "I can't marry you," she said. "Please take me home."

"I didn't mean to make you cry."

"It's not your fault, you've got to believe that." She turned and stumbled. "Can we just go away from here? Now."

"Of course," he said, dropping the ring into his pocket and hurrying to catch up to her.

Kate lurched back along the path they had just come. Her feet and legs had no feeling, causing her hard steps to rattle her body like broken bones. The roaring inside her temples threatened to explode her head. There was a great pressure against her chest and she labored to breathe. *I'm not strong enough to get through this,* she kept thinking. *I just have to give the pain to a higher power and let death take me off this knoll.* She refused to look in Jon's direction. *Damn him to the pits of hell, he has no right to do this to me.*

If Jon wondered what was going on, he gave no sign. He didn't try to get her to talk, and for that Kate was grateful. They traveled their own distances, back through the woods, each carrying secrets that would not be left on the wooded hillside.

TWELVE

Kate tumbled off the seat almost before the car came to a full stop and lurched up the sidewalk. As the apartment door slammed behind her, pain knotted like a pounding fist inside her stomach, doubling her over, and she crumpled to the floor. Great sobs ripped her body as the dam holding back a torrent of tears threatened to break. Clasping her arms around her body, she feared for her sanity and tried to pray to an uncertain god. Finally the spillway opened and scalding tears flooded her face, draining the vessel that housed the very core of her spirit. She welcomed the pain.

Her body spent, she dragged herself to the bathroom and ripped away her clothes. Turning on the shower, she stepped in, and stood there while the hot water beat against her head and plastered down her hair. She stood still and let the water cascade over her body, her ugly and grievous—her most grievous body—and she wept.

The old tattered robe hung from the hook on the back of the door and was limp with dampness when she reached for it a short time later. Kate pulled it around her wet naked body and went in search of a drink. She would need something more than wine this night; something to bring on forgetfulness and blessed oblivion.

There was a light tap on the door just as she was coming down the darkened hallway. She flipped on a lamp and the knock sounded again.

She pressed her ear against the door. "Who is it?"

"Kathleen, it's me."

"Go away. I'm very tired."

"I'm not going. Not until we talk."

Kate turned the knob and opened the door a crack. She brushed the wet hair from her eyes and pulled the robe tighter about her body. "There's nothing to talk about."

"I think there is," he said, pushing the door open and stepping into the room. "Kathleen, this is hard for me—forcing myself into a place where I'm not wanted, I mean. Don't make it any harder."

She stood with her hand on the door. "Jon, I can't deal with this tonight. Please don't make me."

"Just tell me what's wrong and I'll go. I won't leave until you do."

"It's none of your damn business and you have no right to do this to me."

"I do have a right. I just asked you to marry me, that gives me the right. Now tell me Kathleen, what's wrong?"

Kate slammed the door and faced him. Her red eyes blazed in anger. At that moment she hated him above all men.

"Wrong?" Frayed nerves crackled and snapped, heartbreak and bitterness boiled over. "Do you really want to know what's wrong, Jon? Why I can't marry you?" The words tore from her throat as she snatched back the robe and stood naked before him.

"Take a hard look, Jon. I'm a shell, that's all I am. Do you really want to be married to a *shell*?" She felt herself losing her grip on reality. She lifted her chin and glared at him. "Go ahead, Jon, it's okay to look. I never do, but you can. See the handiwork the surgeons were so proud of. They said I beat the odds—beat the big 'C.' It was generally believed among the team of doctors that breasts were not so awfully important anyway, so they just scooped them up like so much hamburger and hacked them away."

"Oh, God," Jon said and closed the robe over her scarred body. He gathered her to him and wrapped her in his arms. "I know it must have been—"

"No." She clinched her hands against his chest. "No, you don't know how it must have been, or what it cost me. You can't know what it's like to have the one you love look at you with disgust and loathing. As if you've done something on purpose, something so despicable that you're no longer worthy of love. *Unclean* is the word that comes to mind."

Kate pushed him away and dropped her head. "I'm sorry, Jon. I had no right to do that to you. You deserve better."

"Damn it, Kathleen, don't apologize for what you are. Don't ever do that. There are no perfect people, so don't even try." He put his hands on her shoulders and gave her a shake. "I didn't propose marriage to a shell, or whatever else you want to call it. You know me better than that."

Kate tried to twist away. She felt the pressure of his hands tighten. "Why did you come back?" she whispered. "You didn't have to, you know."

"Yes, I did."

"Why?

"Because I made a commitment to you out there on the knoll—our knoll. Because I want the rest of my life to have some redeeming value. Because you are the finest, gentlest, most honest person I know and I'd like to spend the rest of my life with you." He reached for her hand. "I ask you again: will you marry me?"

"You'll end up hating me, and I'll hate you for it."

"I won't. I could never hate you."

"You say that now."

"Marry me, Kathleen. Let me prove it to you."

"Tell me, Jon. How can I?"

"You can because you need to trust again. We both have shadows from the past hovering over our shoulders but they can't be allowed to shape and control the future. I won't let them. I won't. We can make it together. It'll take time but eventually it'll come, you'll see." He paused and took a heavy breath. "I'd like your answer now, and I'll go."

Kate felt her body go slack, the knots that were her fists relaxed and her fingers dropped. She nodded her head.

"Say it," Jon said. "Say it out loud."

"I'll marry you, Jon." Her throat was raw, making her voice raspy and weak.

He pulled the ring from his pocket where he'd dropped it earlier, and slipped it on her finger.

"I've imposed enough on you for one day, but when you're feeling stronger think about setting a date. I don't want to rush you, but I'd like it to be soon."

After he'd gone Kate went to the kitchen and made a cup of tea. She stirred in honey and lemon and carried the cup to the sofa and sat down. Through a mist of tears she looked at the ring on her finger. Dare she do this thing—marry this man? Images of another ring flashed through her mind. *Where is Julie now?* she wondered. Was she the shadow that he was so determined would not control his future? Of all the reasons he had given her for coming here tonight, love had not been one of them. Somehow, Kate continued to believe, Jon's love had been spent on another; perhaps exhausted to the extent that there was none left over. *What a fierce love it must have been*, she thought.

"I don't know what the future holds," she spoke with soft conviction. "But I'll marry Jonathan Ames and the devil can have the sins of the past."

The next morning the ring and Kate's engagement caused quite a stir at the office. Sally and Lynn, the girl who replaced Rachel, huddled around her and gazed in wonder at such a gem. Even Marty was impressed when she told him about Jon.

"So, Dix was right," he said. "She said there was a man in your life; said you had that look. Have you set a date yet?"

"Not yet."

"Well, I wish you the best, and that's probably what you're getting. I don't know much about Jonathan Ames—not many people around here do. His family was farmers and well thought of. But after he went off to school, and especially after he lost both his parents, he just sort of drifted out of circulation." He smiled. "Gone a lot, I understand, but even when he's here he keeps pretty much to himself." He smiled again. "I'm not telling you anything you don't already know. You're a lucky girl, Kate. Be happy."

"Oh, Kate," Sally said, her blue eyes sparkling, "I can see it all now, an autumn wedding. You'll be spectacular."

Kate laughed. "I've never been spectacular in my life, Sally," she said. "But I do like the idea of a fall wedding."

At home that night Kate settled on the sofa, propped her feet on the coffee table and held a calendar against her legs. She was determined to set a date. The more she thought about Sally's suggestion the more she liked it. October. It must be October. Satisfied with the month, she only had to pick a specific day. If she planned for the middle of the month, that would give her six weeks. She looked at the calendar. Six weeks would be about right.

Jon seemed pleased the next night when he stopped by and she told him.

"Here," be said, "I want you to have this." He dropped the cameo pin into her hand—the one from the wedding photograph of his parents. "It belonged to the first woman I ever loved. And now it's only right that it go to the second woman in my life."

Kate thumbed the profile carved into the rose-hued pearl. "Thank you, Jon. I'm honored."

"Your next step, in my opinion, is to give up your job. No, wait," he said, holding up his hands, staying her objections. "I know that smacks of being a kept woman, but I don't mean that at all. I'm as committed to you now as if we were already married, so why wait." He led her to the sofa and they sat down. "Humor me on this one point, Kathleen. Turn in your two-week notice tomorrow and leave the rest to me, please. I want to be the one you depend on." He smiled. "Besides, you'll need all your time for shopping, and for me."

"I'm just not sure I can take money from you. I'm not made that way." She shook her head and ran a hand across her brow. "I'm afraid I'm saying this rather badly, but independence runs too deep in my veins and old habits die hard. Jon, don't put me in a position to have to ask you for anything."

"You don't have to ask." He handed her a small leather case. "These are for you. No questions asked, no balances kept."

Turning the case over in her hands, Kate looked inside and found credit cards printed with her name.

"You've gone to a lot of trouble for me, haven't you? You really want to do this."

He took her hands and looked at her. "I want to take care of you now."

"I'll be careful with expenses, Jon. I'm not an extravagant person."

"You don't have to be careful. Be as extravagant as you wish."

"Can I ask you something about that, Jon?"

"About money? Anything."

She hesitated. "Are you rich? I mean, very rich?"

He laughed. "My accountants tell me I am, even though I don't spend much time thinking about it. Now don't feel embarrassed. How else do you get answers, if you don't ask? Besides, you have every right to know. I should've already told you."

His eyes leveled with hers. "The money's come honestly, Kathleen, through a lot of hard work and a little luck. Some of my designs were vital breakthroughs in the complicated world of digital technology. A couple were successful enough to have been utilized by the space program. Others were bought by private concerns that pay very generous royalties. A lot of this is legal jargon that I don't understand and I won't bore you with it, but as of the day you accepted my proposal my attorneys have been in the process of rewriting the dispensation of my estate."

"You didn't have to do that."

"Of course, I did. I want you to know this, Kathleen. You need to know for your own protection. If anything should happen to me, you'll become a very wealthy lady." He reached into his pocket and pulled out his wallet. "In the event anything should ever happen, that you would need help, you're to contact my advisors in New York. Whether it's financial, legal, or otherwise, you're to call them. Do you understand?" He handed her a business card. "Now, promise me."

She accepted the card with hesitation. A sudden chill caused her to shudder. "I promise."

He seemed to sense her air of foreboding and turned her to face him. "We must be realistic, so don't be frightened. I've just asked you to give up your job, your sole means of livelihood. I now have a responsibility to you. This is the way I want it. So keep the card and hopefully I'll be around for a long time and you'll never have to use it."

"Thank you, Jon." She leaned over and gave him a light kiss.

"You're quite welcome," he said and smiled. "By the way, the construction crew has almost finished the new road. They hope to start on the house by the middle of the month. The architect promised to have it completed by the first of the year, if the weather cooperates. Hopefully by the time we get back from our honeymoon we can start with the furnishing and get moved in."

"The honeymoon. My goodness, I hadn't thought about that."

"Not your department," he said. "Travel is my considerable expertise and frankly I'm good at it. The first thing we have to do is get you a passport. There are lots of places I want to show you and it's going to take a couple of months. Your job is to take care of yourself and see that you have everything you need."

"I've never done much traveling."

"Well I have, so that automatically puts me in charge." He grinned. "Besides, I still have my points."

"Lord, I've created a monster with a measly ten points."

He stood up and pulled her to her feet. At the door, he bent his head and kissed her parted lips. "Good night, Kathleen. Sweet dreams."

The following morning Kate gave Marty her notice. "I'll be glad to work extra hours to train my replacement."

"Thanks Kate, but Kevin will have to double up on his work load to include yours. As of right now I'm not planning to replace you. Business has been off lately and the forecast doesn't look promising."

"I'm sorry to hear that."

"Not to worry, my dear. You have enough to think about without filling your head with business. It's just a little slow right now." He patted her arm. "Anyway, things will turn around, you'll see."

Nonetheless, on the drive home, Kate found herself worrying about Marty and his beloved business. There were too few like him, men of total honesty and integrity, to spare even one. The thought of the failure of Consolidated Investments left her deeply depressed and she wished there was some magical solution to make everything good again.

From out of a perfectly cloudless sky, raindrops plopped against the windshield and mixed with the fine layer of dust covering the glass. If she turned on the wipers, it would just smear the dirt and make a mess. Should she leave it alone or try cleaning it off? The immediate indecision of what to do seemed monumental. *Why does everything have to be so complicated*, she wondered.

THIRTEEN

The two weeks passed. Kate explained, and apologized, about the wedding. Jon had expressly requested a private ceremony to be presided over by a judge who was a personal friend of his. The wedding was to take place in chambers with only two of his aides as witnesses. They all seemed to understand, with the exception of Dixie, who huffed and puffed and said she was entitled. But she relented slightly after Kate agreed to a dinner for just the two of them. They dined at Mario's.

"You look wonderful," Dixie said.

"Do I?"

"Love agrees with you. You must be getting lots of good sex."

"Dixie!"

"God, you're a prude." She picked up the small box lying beside her plate. "Here," she said. "This is for you."

Kate took the lid off and lifted out a line-bracelet of red-enameled ladybugs held together by a gold braid. "It's beautiful," she said.

"Ladybugs are supposed to be lucky."

"You know damn well I don't believe in luck. Anybody who'd trust their life to a roll of the dice or a four-leaf clover should be locked away. But thanks for the gift." Kate smiled. "I really do love it."

Dixie waved the bracelet away. "Now then, when am I going to get to meet this man who's made you look so terrific?"

Kate frowned. "I don't know, Dixie. He's awfully private."

"Why? What's he got to hide?"

Kate shifted on her seat and straightened the napkin on her lap. When Dixie saw them together, would she know that Jon didn't love her? *She would know*, Kate decided.

"Nothing," she said. "He's just a very reserved and private person, that's all."

Dixie pulled her bow-shaped mouth into a pucker as she raised her hand to signal for a waiter. But her eyes narrowed and squinted slightly and looked suspicious.

A feeling of disjointedness followed Kate home from work the last day. Lethargically she parked the car, unlocked the door of the apartment and headed straight for bed. Turning off the world, she pulled the covers over her head and slept.

Rebounding the next morning, Kate felt revived and full of energy. There was barely four weeks before the wedding and she would need every day of those weeks. She decided to begin shopping for her trousseau in Shasta Bay, which was larger than Woodway and offered a great shopping experience. Plus it was only a couple of hours away. The phone rang just as she poured her second cup of coffee. It was Jon.

"I called you last night," he said.

"Did you? I'm sorry. The phone didn't wake me. Yesterday wasn't an easy day to get through. I came home mentally exhausted and collapsed into bed."

"How are you now? You sound fine."

"Today, I'm great. As a matter of fact I was thinking about shopping."

"Shop away," he encouraged. "Would you like me to go with you?"

"Maybe next time."

"Well, be careful driving. I'll call you tonight." He rang off.

Kate hung up the phone. She was anxious to be on her way and attending to the affairs of her wedding. On the drive to Shasta, she listened to an oldies-but-goodies radio station, singing along with Streisand and Diamond: *You don't bring me flowers anymore.* When she couldn't keep up with the words, she switched the dial to a talk show. The topic under discussion was "The recession and what to do about it." The subject mattered to her, but not today. She flipped off the radio and turned her attention to the road ahead.

In Kate's opinion, Shasta Bay had it all. She very rarely visited the tony shopping mecca, she plainly couldn't afford it, but mostly it wasn't a place she cared to spend much time by herself. Its quaint shops, boutiques, and milliners catered to the long-legged blondes—golden girls with rich inheritances, or couples. Especially couples in love.

But today the world was different. At her leisure, she strolled the fashionable squares, stopping occasionally to peer into windows. Selecting a most exclusive-looking shop, she entered with a purposeful stride. Draped around rattan busts were imported silk scarves pinned with hundred dollar gold clips. Andy Warhol T-shirts and Liz Taylor fragrances in crystal bottles were displayed on mirrored glass shelves. Toward the back and to the right, separated by a pair of wicker mannequins in evening clothes, was the tailoring room with bolts of woolens and cashmeres. Kate hadn't given any thought to the fact that there was a segment of society who knew nothing but custom-made clothes. She suddenly had a feeling she would be exposed right away as an impostor and encouraged to leave. As she turned back toward the door, an impeccably tailored lady approached to offer assistance.

"Don't go," the clerk said. "We have that effect on lots of people." Her eyes held kindness. "May I help you with something?"

Four hours later Kate laughed over a glass of sherry. She had been measured, taped and sized until her head whirled. The entire shop had come to her rescue and put themselves entirely at her disposal. They made suggestions and offered advice, which she gratefully accepted. She was encouraged to take her time and select just the right fabrics and patterns.

"Four weeks doesn't give us much time," the clerk said. "But don't you worry, we'll manage. Can you come back in a week for your first fitting?"

"I'll be here," Kate said with confidence.

She was famished when she left the shop around three and walked the few steps to a nearby restaurant. The place was casually subdued and mid-afternoon quiet. In the dim elegance only a few patrons were dining.

After eating, Kate lingered over a comforting cup of herbal tea and felt satisfied with how her day was going. She enjoyed the shopping more than she expected, and although she could have spent far more than she did, her conservative nature had kicked in and monitored her ability to be reckless. Glancing down at the ring on her finger, she felt good just looking at it. True, it was of enormous value, it frightened her to think about how much it must have cost, but that wasn't its real significance. No, it was more than that. To Kate it represented an extension of herself, someone on the other end—a giver. That was the important thing, the only thing really, which mattered. She signaled for the check. She was anxious to be home. To be in her own surroundings where familiarity had filled the empty space in her existence and soothed her spirit. A place where she felt safe. And to be with Jon.

Two hours later she kicked her shoes into a corner of the kitchen just as the phone rang.

"Hello."

"Hi, there. How did your day go?"

"Great. As a matter of fact I just got home."

"Well, take the time to rest for awhile and don't worry about supper. How does the Heatherton Inn sound?"

"Right now it sounds terrific."

"I'll pick you up around eight. And Kathleen, I'm glad you're home," he said and hung up the phone.

Why is he glad? she wondered. He had never said he loved her. Not once. She knew he cared for her, he had proven that many times over. *But love?* Kate thought not. For some reason she couldn't shake the feeling that she could've been almost anybody. Simply, Jon had made the decision to get married and she just happened to be the one selected. They blended well together. She, in her own fashion, actually complemented him. He, in turn, fit well into any situation. He was the only man Kate had ever known who fit the description: *a man for all seasons*. Scolding herself for having such an analytical mind, she released the telephone receiver.

"Don't analyze this thing to death," she fussed at herself. "Be happy with things the way they are and don't look for a hidden agenda. You might just find it."

Later at the Inn, they dined on steaming platters of fresh seafood, danced a couple of times, and talked in hushed tones over after-dinner drinks.

"I talked to Judge Hampton today," Jon said, looking up from his brandy. "He's delighted about the wedding. He informed me flatly that he would've considered it a personal affront had he not been asked to do the honors." He reached for her hand. "He wants to meet with us on Friday evening for prenuptial counseling. I told him I thought we were a little old for that sort of thing, but he insisted. Do you mind?"

"Of course I don't mind. I've never known a judge before. Is he terribly stuffy and rigid?"

"Only on the bench," Jon said and smiled. "Actually he's a very personable fellow. A little old-fashioned for my taste but I think you'll like him. And we'll need to set aside a couple of hours sometime soon to run to the clerk's office for the licenses."

Kate nodded. "I'm looking forward to meeting him." She raised her wine glass and could see the reflection of the sparkle of her eyes in the pale gold liquid. "To the judge."

"And to you," Jon said.

FOURTEEN

On Friday evening, Kate felt a little nervous as she and Jon waited in an outer office.

The secretary was busy clearing her desk. "His Honor will be with you in just a minute," she said. "He had an unexpected telephone call."

"Why don't you run along," Jon said. "We'll be fine."

"I think I will, if you don't mind." She glanced at the closed door. "I'm sure he'll be right out." She gathered her coat and purse. "Well, good night."

Jon looked at Kate. "Do you feel like a kid waiting to see the principal?"

Kate nodded, but before she could reply, the door opened and a boulder of a man with a heavy mantle of steel-colored hair entered the room.

"Jonathan," he said and held out his hand, "sorry to keep you waiting."

Jon took Kate's arm and together they stood. "Walt, it's good to see you," Jon said, clasping the out-stretched hand. "It's been too long."

"This must be the lady you were telling me about. Kathleen, isn't it? Well my dear, I certainly am glad to meet you. Please, come in and have a seat." He ushered them into his chambers.

The room was small. Books lined the walls to the ceiling on three sides. A picture of Ronald W. Reagan hung over a bricked fireplace. The drapes were open and the windows already darkened with nightfall. A soft light from a lamp on the large cluttered desk lit the room. The judge gestured to the two chairs.

"Here, make yourselves comfortable. Nancy made fresh coffee before she left."

"Coffee would be lovely," Kate said. "Would you like me to pour?"

"I'm impressed," the judge said to Jon. "A lady who actually offers to serve others." He looked at Kate and smiled. "If you don't mind."

After the coffee was poured the judge sat behind his desk and faced them.

"Now then, you two are getting married. Splendid. Splendid. I couldn't be happier." He cleared his throat. "The speech I generally give is directed at a much younger couple, so I'll dispense with the usual and talk to you as mature adults. After marriage, a relationship is never the same. It can either strengthen your friendship or wreck it. Marriage is not as easy as a stroll through a rose garden, nor is it as hard as digging ditches. But it is work—dedicated and diligent work."

Jon gave the judge a smile of tolerance. "Walt, what happened to the dispensation?"

"Sorry," the judge said. "We're all a little over the hill here, but let's be realistic. There will be problems, both major and minor. As you well know Jonathan, things are not always as they seem. There are extenuating circumstances, augmentations if you will, to the wedding of any two independent individuals. That goes doubly so for people who have fashioned their lives to suit themselves, lives that are in fact more reclusive than inclusive. This brings other forces into the marriage, and how you deal with these outside entities says a lot for your maturity and wisdom."

He leaned back in the chair and gazed at the ceiling. "Supreme Court Justice Oliver Wendell Holmes said of his court, but it fits aptly in describing marriage: *'We are very quiet here, but it is the quiet of a storm center.'* And, as you know," the judge went on, "storms are unpredictable. They can blow themselves out and nobody gets hurt. On the other hand, they can churn around getting stronger and stronger until they have to vent their energies. You must be vigilant and not let the storm get out of control. Be honest with each other in all things. I repeat—in all things, Jonathan."

"Now, Walt. Don't start."

Kate studied the cup in her hand. She sensed an electrically charged current between the two men, something unseen but very real.

Jon continued. "You fret too much, Walt. We'll be fine. Kathleen's a terrific person."

"I concur completely," the judge said. "I think you're lucky to have her."

Jon nodded. "Very lucky."

"Nonetheless," the judge continued, "honesty, that's the important thing." He brought his hands together and pressed his forefingers against his lips. His brow bunched beneath the heavy hair. "Don't keep secrets, Jonathan. They're damning. They have a way of bringing unexpected tragedy, and all too often upon the innocent." Tension crackled in the room as the two men seemed to face off against each other.

"My goodness, you two have a way of sobering one's thoughts," Kate said. "Are you sure you really like each other?"

"Very much so." The judge waved a hand in Jon's direction. "I've known this man all his life. Knew his parents when I was a lad; fine people, they were. I worked on their farm to help put myself through law school. I remember when Jon here was born and how proud they were. And the sadness over the loss of baby Jennifer. Jon has always been like a son to me, a son I never had. There's not a whole lot in this world I wouldn't do for him. I would've been mighty upset had I not been asked to unite the two of you in marriage; looking forward to it."

"We appreciate you taking the time," Jon said.

"Time is precious, Jonathan. Once it's gone, you can't get it back. Then all you have are memories." He shook his head as if to clear away old embers. "Forgive an old man his mental meanderings. I've kept you long enough." He pushed back from his desk and stood. "Congratulations Jon. And to you, Kathleen, my very best wishes. I hope you'll be happy."

They stood up, the meeting over. Kate extended her hand. "It's been a pleasure to meet you, sir. Thank you for your valuable time and words of counsel. We'll try to live by them."

"I hope so, my dear. I hope so." He glanced at Jon. "If I don't see you again before the twelfth, I'll expect you here at seven o'clock sharp."

"Thanks, Walt. We'll be here."

The judge opened the door for the pair and patted Jon on the back as they left. Neither spoke until they were inside the car.

"Well, what did you think of the imminent Judge Hampton?" Jon asked.

"He seems to be a man of conviction. No head in the clouds for him, very down to earth and straight forward."

"He's that, all right. I've always considered him a conservative's conservative," he said, turning the key to start the car.

"Is he married?"

Jon turned the key loose and placed his hands on the steering wheel. "He was. To his beautiful Victoria."

"What happened?"

"Polio. It was back in the early sixtes. He never quite got over the loss. When she died it was as if a light went out in his soul." He shook his head and touched the key again. The car sprang to life.

"I'm sorry," Kate said as she settled back in the seat and watched as he turned on the heater and adjusted the volume on the stereo. She liked watching him.

The first few days of unemployment went smoother than Kate expected. For the first time there was a shortage of hours in her days. A thing as simple as a luncheon with Dixie had to be scheduled in advance. Time dwindled down and was whittled away almost before she realized it.

It was a week before the wedding. They sat close together, listening to Gershwin's *Rhapsody in Blue* and snacking on cheese and fruit from a tray in front of them.

"Kathleen, you look tired. You're not doing too much, are you? You must take care of yourself."

"I'm fine. You have no idea what's involved in getting ready for a wedding."

A shadowed passed over his face. "I guess I don't."

"I don't mind, really I don't. I could've gotten Dixie to help. She offered. But for some reason this was something I wanted to do myself." She smiled. "I guess I'm being selfish by not wanting to share the experience with anybody else."

"Selfish? You. I hardly think so, my dear."

"Whatever it is, it's almost over. Tomorrow's my final fitting."

"What time are you leaving?"

"Early, I guess. It's a couple of hour's drive, so I should leave by ten. Why?"

"I just wondered. I may be over before you leave, if that's okay."

"Well, sure, it's okay. Are you coming for any special reason? I mean, you don't usually visit in the mornings, but sure, it's okay." She touched his arm. "It's nice to see you anytime." Suddenly she pulled her hand away and laughed. "You're up to something, aren't you? Why do I always get this feeling when you're about to surprise me?"

"I'm sure I have no idea what you're talking about." He winked at her as he got up from the sofa, gave her a hug and went out the door.

The next morning the alarm sounded at seven and Kate pushed herself out of the warm bed. It took a second cup of coffee to clear the lingering sleep from her brain. She flipped on the radio hoping for a good weather report. The day looked a little overcast and she hated driving in the rain.

Brightened by a cooperative meteorologist, she turned toward the bedroom. A car horn blasted from the driveway. She knew it was Jon. The doorbell rang as she tightened the belt to her robe.

"He certainly sounds impatient," she murmured, smoothing down her hair as best she could and opening the door.

"Good morning, my dear. Don't you look lovely."

"Thank you. It's just an old thing I threw on."

He reached for her hand. "Come outside, I have something to show you." He pulled her through the doorway.

"You bought a new car," she said, seeing the silver Lexus in the driveway. "It's beautiful."

"Glad you like it. Here are the keys."

"But Jon, I have a car." She looked at the aged station wagon parked in front of the shiny new car. "Well okay, I *almost* have a car."

He pointed a finger. "That, we'll donate to Goodwill. Go on, get in. Let's see if it's a proper fit."

Kate slid through the door onto the soft leather.

"Perfect," she said. "I'm afraid I'm becoming a bit spoiled."

"I could never spoil you enough," he said. "Now, how about driving me back to my place. You have important things to do today."

"I'm not even dressed," she protested.

"You look fine. Drive."

Kate marveled at the way the car responded to her slightest touch. Pulling into the parking lot at his temporary dwelling, she leaned over and gave him a quick kiss.

"You're too good to me, you know. I feel most undeserving."

He touched her cheek. "There is no one more deserving. Have a good day and drive carefully. The car's a hunk of machinery and can be replaced. You can't."

FIFTEEN

On Saturday, Kate and Jon drove to the country to see how the house was coming along. A new private road sprouting off the main one led to what would eventually be the entrance of the driveway. But today they were able to roll across the rutted road and right up to the front door. The one-level house sprawled over a good portion of the knoll.

"It looks nearly finished." Kate said

"I'm afraid they're just beginning. The outside part goes up right away but once they start the between-the-walls stuff—wiring and plumbing, boring stuff like that—work can go on for days and you can barely tell anything's been done."

Jon took Kate's hand and helped her around a pile of material near the door and they crossed the threshold. The inside of the house was like a hulking skeleton. Their steps echoed.

"It's really big," Kate said as she looked around.

"When the walls go up and everything gets sectioned off you can get a better perspective," Jon explained. "Right now it's just a maze of two-by-fours and crossbeams. Here, let me show you where they're excavating for the pool." He took her arm and led her off to the right. A large backhoe, stilled for the day, sat beside a gaping hole in the ground.

"You know," Kate said, "the more I think about the pool the more I'm inclined to agree that it was a good idea."

Jon smiled as if he knew she would come around to his way of thinking. They walked back through the house and stood in the breakfast room looking out over the side terrace.

"I only hope I can manage such a place." Kate's voice held a definite doubt. "It's going to take a lot of work."

"We'll get you some help. Not full time, I know you wouldn't stand for that, but maybe someone to come in a few times a week and for any special occasions we might have." He pointed to a small building set back in the trees. "Gardener's shed," he said. "For the grounds keeper. I wouldn't dream of trying to do it all by myself."

The idea of having a housekeeper would take some getting used to. Kate was just coming to realize how drastically her life was changing.

She gazed down the dirt road and visualized a long, winding driveway.

"Jon, this is more than an ordinary house, isn't it? I get the feeling that it's becoming, well, more along the lines of a country estate; a secluded manor house."

"I guess that's a good way to describe it. There'll be a high fence surrounding the grounds with a security gate at the entrance." He glanced at her. "Does the idea bother you?"

"I guess not. I just never imagined myself living on an estate. It's a little unsettling."

"Well, don't let it intimidate you. It's just a house with a roof and some walls—so what if the walls are a little more fancy than we're used to."

He gave her the smile she had come to love so dearly. "We'll get used to it, I promise."

Kate felt the threatening of tears when he referred to them as *we,* and wondered if ever a man had been more adored than Jonathan Ames. She shook her head to clear her muddled thoughts.

"What about a name?" she asked. "Estates have to be titled, you know. Something like *Dragonwyck* and *Ravensmoon?*"

Jon laughed. "My dear, you've been reading too many Gothic novels," he said. "Nothing that ominous for us. I've decided on *Brandywine.* Brandy for me, wine for you—if you approve, of course."

Kate smiled. "Sounds like a winner to me."

The sun was just going down as they left the knoll.

"I'm glad they were able to save most of the trees," she said. "Look how the sun filters patterns of light on the ground. It's truly an enchanting place."

"We *are* going to be happy here."

A note of desperation sounded in his voice, as if he were willing the declaration to be true.

Days tumbled by in a hurry; fall days, glorious and busy. The twelfth of October dawned under a brilliant autumn sky. Kate had slept little the night before. Jon had not come over, but she talked to him briefly on the phone. Now, in a panic, she turned in the middle of the floor. She knew there had to be something left undone. Bags were packed and sat waiting. The apartment was spotless. Forcing herself to eat a light breakfast, Kate kept one eye on the clock.

Sidney, her hairdresser, had agreed to take her as his last customer of the day, but that wasn't until four o'clock. "Slow down Kate," she cautioned herself. "You'll make yourself sick." The phone rang.

She snatched it. "Jon?"

"You sound as if you've worked yourself into a full scale panic," he said.

Kate laughed. "I guess I have. I'm so glad you called. Is everything okay? What's wrong?"

"Nothing's wrong, so stop worrying. I only called to say good morning and that I'll see you about six-thirty."

"Will that give us enough time? We can't be late for the judge."

"We'll have plenty of time," he assured her. "It's only a ten minute drive to his office. Now I have a couple of things to do, so I'll see you later."

The day passed. Kate did little things to help hurry the time: she talked on the phone, twice to Dixie who offered to come over and keep her company, but Kate declined. She polished her fingernails and toenails: *pearl mist*, plucked at flawless eyebrows, and gave herself a facial.

Later, Kate looked in the mirror and was satisfied with the way Sidney had done her hair. The blonde highlights feathered across her forehead and brushed toward her face, forming a wispy frame. A rumbling in her stomach reminded her that she had eaten nothing since breakfast. She toasted a piece of whole wheat bread and spread it with orange marmalade. Draining an almost empty milk carton, she forced herself to sit at the table and eat slowly.

Outside twilight was beginning to gather and soon streetlights would flicker on.

After a cool shower, Kate fastened the hated bra into place and positioned the gel-filled packets. Then she stepped into the silk unders. Removing the tissue paper from between the folds of her wedding dress, she lifted it from the box. The mauve, hand-woven linen felt luxurious beneath her touch. Antique lace, heavy in its richness edged the hem and trimmed the tuxedo bib. An obi belt cinched the waist and gathered in the fullness of the tea-length skirt. She fastened the cameo pin just over the point where she could feel the beating of her heart. She hoped Jon's mother would be pleased. She sat down on the bed to wait.

As she waited, doubts nipped around the edges of her mind. Was she doing the right thing? She clasped her hands beneath her chin.

"Mama," she whispered. *"Is it okay that he doesn't love me? Can I love enough for the both of us?"* The doorbell interrupted her thoughts and she hurried to answer.

Jon was wearing a new chesterfield topcoat and Kate thought he looked remarkably handsome with the white silk scarf casually thrown around his neck. He was carrying two packages. The first was a bottle of wine.

"Do we have time?" Kate asked.

"We'll take time," he said. "By the way you look lovely. New dress?"

"Just wait until you get the bill," she warned.

"Which reminds me," he said, placing the packages on the end table. "As of right now I'm confiscating your credit cards. Come on, hand them over."

Kate picked up her purse, took the cards out of her wallet and reached them to him. "Is anything wrong?"

"Here's your replacements," he said and handed her a small leather folder embossed with her new name.

She looked at the bright shiny cards tucked behind clear plastic. "Kathleen Spencer Ames," she said. "I like the sound of that."

"So do I," he said. "Now, how about the wine? I want to propose a toast."

She pointed to the box on the table. "What's that?"

"Never mind what that is, Bright Eyes. First, we drink the champagne."

Kate poured the wine into her best crystal. They faced each other with raised glasses.

"To you," Jon said. "Thank you for being so patient and trusting and for accepting my proposal. I pray to God that I never give you cause to regret it."

"And to you, Jon. Thank you for being so good to me and making me feel so special."

"You are special," he said. "I wait for the day you believe that as much as I do." He picked up the box. "This is for you."

Kate hefted it in her hand. "It's heavy."

"Go ahead, open it."

She took the lid off and lifted a corner of the jeweler's cloth. She gasped. "Jon, do you know what this is?"

He threw his head back and laughed. "No, what?"

"It's a *Faberge* Easter egg." Her brows tucked and wrinkled her forehead. "I've read about them, and seen pictures, but I never thought I'd actually see one in person. I thought they were only found in museums and Russian castles. Are you sure it's okay to have this?"

He brushed a stray tuft of hair from her cheek. "No, it's against the law," he said. "We're going to keep it hidden away in some dark corner at *Brandywine.*"

"Jon!"

"I'm kidding, Kathleen. Of course it's all right."

Kate lifted the egg from the box and held it in her hand. The golden shell was crowned with diamonds and encircled by fiery rubies and sapphires. Emeralds cascaded down the sides like willowing branches, and flickered an icy green. The gems blended together and scattered a prism of color against her hand. She lifted the hinged lid to a hummingbird suspended in flight. Its wings were spun platinum tracery and looked deceptively fragile.

"It's hard to understand the Russian history behind a thing of such beauty," she said. "And to think that some of these remarkable works of art were purposefully destroyed." Her hand trembled as she placed it back into the box and handed it to him. "Keep it for me, will you Jon?"

"Yes, my dear, whatever you say." He glanced at his watch. "We'd better be going now."

The only light in the old courthouse glowed from the back of the building. Jon led Kate inside through a side entrance.

"Right on time," Judge Hampton said. "Nancy and my bailiff stayed over to act as witnesses."

"Then can we get started, Walt? We have a plane waiting."

The judge looked up as the others entered the room. "Fine. Fine," he said. "Jon, you stand here. Kate, you're here on his left. Now we can commence."

Kate listened to the vows of devotion she and Jon were pledging. Could they hold true to their promises of putting the other first in their lives? She had heard the words when she married Evan and thought they meant something then. They hadn't. *Would they this time?*

Finally the judge proclaimed: "By the power vested in me by the state, I now pronounce you husband and wife. Jon, you may kiss your bride." Kate felt the light brush of Jon's lips against hers.

"Well now, a short toast and off with the two of you," the judge ordered.

More wine was poured and toasts were made amid hugs and handshakes. Jon and Kate left the courthouse to the sounds of best wishes ringing behind them.

At the Woodway municipal airport a small charter plane sat idling, waiting to take the newly weds to their connecting international flight. Kate's mind was reeling from the effects of the wine and she barely heard the increased whine of the engines as the plane taxied down the runway and lifted off. Kate was on her way for her first trip to Europe.

SIXTEEN

It was after midnight the next night when they arrived at their hotel in Paris. The lobby was a sunburst of scarlet plushes, gold brocades, rouged railings. Kate tried to take it all in as Jon signed the register and pointed out their bags to the captain. In the elevator Kate rested her head against the wall and stifled a yawn. Jon's smile was one of understanding and he took her arm when the door opened.

They entered their suite and Jon dismissed the bellhop by folding some bills and pressing them into his hand. Then he removed his coat and draped it across the back of a chair.

"Hungry?" he asked. "We could have a midnight tiffin."

"Tiffin?"

Jon smiled. "A meal."

"Could we have this *tiffin* thing tomorrow? I'd much rather have a bath."

"A bath it is," he said and slipped Kate's coat from her shoulders and laid it beside his on the chair.

Kate picked up the flowered overnight case and headed toward the bedroom. Jon followed behind and flipped on the light.

"Your bath's over there." He pointed to the left.

Without replying, Kate kicked off her shoes, padded across the white carpet to the blue and white ceramic bathroom and closed the door behind her. She stood still for a moment.

Everything seemed so stilted and unnatural, like a badly directed play. *What am I doing in Paris with this stranger?* she wondered, and thought perhaps Jon was having the same thoughts.

She took time with the bath and preparing for her bridal bed. The long pink gown was laced at the scalloped neckline with velvet ribbons, and the satin shimmered as it slid down her body and hugged her hips. She was wearing nothing underneath. At last she was ready. She reached for the knob, her hand lingering. Then she opened the door. The room was dim, lit only by a small lamp on the nightstand. Kate heard the clink of crystal from the sitting room and knew Jon was making drinks. She turned off the lamp and slipped between soft sheets that covered the acre of bed. A moment later he appeared in the doorway wearing a dressing gown and holding a pitcher and two goblets.

"I made martinis," he said.

The light coming from behind him was the only illumination of the bedroom. Kate watched as he set the pitcher on a side table and filled the glasses. She fluffed the pillows and propped herself up against the headboard as Jon carried the drinks to the bed. He settled in beside her, leaned over and kissed her cheek, then proposed a toast.

"To you, Mrs. Ames," he said.

Kate smiled. "Mrs. Ames. I like the sound of that."

"Welcome to Paris, and you're doubly welcome to my name," he said.

Kate laughed. "I hope to have your name a lot longer than I have Paris."

"You will." He drained his glass and rattled the ice cubes. "Another?"

Kate shook her head.

Jon placed the glasses back on the table and turned on his side to face her. "You must be tired."

"Not really. The bath was a wonderful restorer."

He touched her arm. "Must be the French water."

Kate moved closer and laid her head on his shoulder. She turned and kissed him on the neck and put her hand inside the dressing gown. Then she reached down, untied the sash and slid her arms around his waist. She could feel the buttons on his pajamas and started to undo them when she felt his arms press into the small of her back, pulling her closer. Then his hands moved up to her neck and cupped her face. He kissed her. Kate opened her mouth to get the full taste of him. Her breathing had become harsh and dry and she was not aware for the span of a heartbeat that he was pulling away. Her passion faded, leaving traces of shame and humiliation.

"I'm sorry," Jon said.

"It's not your fault." Kate turned away, moving to her side of the bed and tightening the velvet ribbons at the neckline of her gown.

Of course it wasn't his fault. Why did she not know that before she made an absolute fool of herself. She felt the touch of his hand against her back. It lingered for a moment then fell away. The bed seemed a place of desolation, a barren stretch of desert to bleach the bones and dry up the spirit.

Only when exhaustion finally overcame her, did she drop off. When she woke the following morning, he was already up and dressed. The previous night wasn't mentioned.

Paris in autumn wove her spell as enchantress. Kate felt herself being pulled into the mystique of the city and wallowed wantonly in its splendor. Eager to learn and experience as much as humanly possible in the short time they had, she felt sorry for Jon as she darted about and bombarded him with questions. Like a sponge, she soaked up the French atmosphere and begged for more. Her stack of tourist brochures grew as they strolled the *Champs-Elysees* and explored quaint shops. Awestruck, she stood with Jon before the majestic Notre Dame Cathedral. She studied the rule of Napoleon, first Emperor of France, and of his military genius. France was brimming over with history and her hundreds of years of kings and emperors, some literally quite mad. Of all the characters from the past she was getting to know intimately, the one whom she felt would have been a kindred spirit was the young nobleman, Lafayette. How daring he must have been to disregard royal objections and sail to America to help the rag-tag bunch of colonists fight for independence.

"Can't we stay a few more days?" she pleaded. "There's so much more to learn, so much I don't know."

"I wish we could Kathleen, but there isn't enough time. There are other places to see. We'll come back again, I promise."

Jon had been the perfect traveling companion. Taking the time to explain things, he was never bored or impatient with her inquisitive mind. *He's seen it all before,* Kate thought. No matter where they went there were people who knew him.

Jon was especially attentive during the day. It was as if he was trying to make up for failing to fulfill his role in the marital bed. Kate knew it would take time—a lot of time. Maybe it would never happen. But she could wait. The time would not come when she would beg him to make love to her.

Their days were glorious. Their nights continued in a set pattern. So seemed the natural order of things.

They toured most of Europe, seeing all the places Kate had imagined; places she often wondered about. They danced in Spain, bought Black-Watch and Stewart plaids in Scotland, and watched the changing of the Guard in London. In Switzerland, Kate fell in love with a massive grandfather clock the moment she laid eyes on it. Beneath the leaded crystal door, the face of the clock was marked with ebony numerals and the hands gold filigree. The chimes, struck and tuned by a master-craftsman, were mellow to the point of bringing the listener to tears. The fact that the clock cost twenty-five thousand dollars had not the slightest impact on Jon and he insisted on having it shipped home.

Italy. The final stop of their itinerary. Rome airport was a bee-hive of activity. Security guards with weapons slung across their shoulders, went about their jobs with utmost seriousness, and kept a wary eye on the crowds. Jon guided Kate to a waiting limousine while others stood in line for taxis. The driver maneuvered the big car in and out of the erratic traffic. Horns tooted feverishly as little cars scurried about. The whole city seemed in a hurry.

Their hotel was located just off Saint Peter's Square and within easy walking distance of the Basilica. After checking in, Kate slipped into a jogging suit and Reeboks and dragged Jon out the door.

Upon entering the Cathedral, Kate felt the very walls themselves shrouded in mystery. The looming marble altars and the works of Michelangelo and Bernini made her feel like a tiny speck of insignificance. With an appreciation that made the passage of time go unnoticed, they lingered until suppertime drove them outside in search of a restaurant.

Jon retained a car and driver for the length of their stay. They visited each of the Seven Hills, and at one abbey, Kate placed her hand inside The *Mouth of Truth* and halfway expected the stone circle to close down on her wrist. The chauffeur explained Rome's history, both mythological and factual. His stories of Remus and Romulus and the she-wolf held Kate enraptured as she strained to catch every word.

Of all that Rome had to offer, the Coliseum left the strongest impact upon Kate's mind and seared her soul—permanently, she feared. Grand arches formed the doors to stairways that were the stages for the sweeping entrances of Emperors and their courts. The stones, laid with such precision, had been trod into uneven ledges by millions of footsteps. Kate was convinced that if she stood perfectly still, and was very quiet, she could hear the roar of the masses and the clash of armor of the gladiators as they fought to the death. Not willing to tempt the pagan gods, she hurried on.

Leaving the car and driver behind, Kate and Jon took the train to Naples. They sat in a private compartment and dined on hard rolls filled with white ham and cheese, and drank cold beer. The Italian landscape whizzed by as the wheels clicked off the miles and the train was sucked into tunnels of blackness that cut through the mountains. They spent two nights in Naples before taking a ferry to the Isle of Capri. At the dock, a driver waited and drove them up the narrow winding street to the top of the island. Hotel personnel, forearms draped with white linen, stood in a receiving line as Kate and Jon entered the Caesar Augustus Hotel.

They settled into their rooms before being escorted to a terrace overlooking the Bay of Naples, where they dined on pasta and seafood. After dinner, a large glass bowl of fruit covered with water was brought to their table. Grapes, large as golf balls, were crisp and lingered sweet upon Kate's tongue.

They toured around Capri in a powerful speedboat that skimmed across the choppy waters. Multicolored coral formations decorated the shoreline and overhead battlement stations looked out across the bay. At the entrance to the Blue Grotto, an oarsman stood at one end of a small wooden boat, waiting for them. He was holding a long slender pole. The boat rocked gently beneath her feet when Jon helped Kate from the larger vessel into the smaller one. The pilot poled in the direction of a small gap in the side of the bluff. Without speaking, he motioned for them to bend low on their seats and pulled the boat through the hole with a heavy chain looped across the top of the mouth of the cave. Blackness engulfed them on the other side. Jon took Kate's hand as the oarsman stood and pushed away from the darkened entrance.

When they had gone a little way into the other side of the cave, the boat turned in a semi-circle bringing into view the opening they had just entered. Kate held up a hand to guard her eyes against the brilliant color. Light filtering through the opening garnished the water, turning it a clear and resplendent azure blue. The place had certainly been well named. Kate remained silent as the oarsman poled around the interior of the cave and sang an aria from some unfamiliar opera. His vibrant tenor voice reverberated off stonewalls and echoed up secret chambers that branched off from the larger room.

"This was a favorite playground for the Roman gentry," Jon said. "One can easily understand why."

Kate leaned over the edge of the boat and trailed her fingers in the blue water. "If only these walls could talk," she said, looking around.

Jon laughed. "It's probably best that they can't."

They remained inside the grotto only a couple minutes more before leaving the blue calm of the cave and returning to the world outside.

After Capri, they stayed in an obscure little village tucked away on a hillside. Enjoying the winding down of the day, they sat side by side in the warm twilight. Kate casually tilted her head and let it come to rest on Jon's shoulder. The view from the terrazzo was peaceful and calm as a slight breeze drifted across the balcony. In the distance, bells pealed from a mountain monastery calling the faithful to evening prayer. Religion had never been an important part of Kate's life, but the somber tolling brought tears to her eyes, calling up ideas of eternity, of this life and what lay beyond. *We have such a little speck of time together,* she thought. *So little time to do what we will to justify our passage through history.* Had she done enough? Did anyone ever?

Jon stirred beside her.

"Do you believe in God, Jon?"

He nodded.

"I suppose I do. One would have to be a fool to look at the order and precision in sunrises and sunsets, the ebb and flow of tides and the phases of the moon—not to mention the perfect placement of the planets—and put it all down to coincidence." He grinned and patted her arm. "And I, my dear, am no fool."

Kate laughed. "No. You're surely not that."

"And now we only have one more week before we go home," he said. "Have you enjoyed Europe?"

"It's been a dream come true."

"I know in some ways this trip has been a disappointment to you." She could hear the pain in his voice.

"Sssh," she whispered. "You don't have to explain." In the semi-darkness Kate thought she saw a flicker of relief cross his face. "You've been so good to me. You've given me things I only dreamed about in the past. Jon, you owe me nothing."

"I owe you everything, Kathleen." He shifted his body against hers. "Contrary to what most people think, money is way near the bottom of the list for making a happy life. Comfortable? Okay, I'll give you that. But happy? Not even close." He took her hand. "A man has to feel from the core of his being what he's all about. Lose that and your whole life threatens to fall apart. And for years I felt myself unraveling."

Kate frowned up at him.

Jon gave a faint smile and nodded. "Yeah, I don't understand it either. It was like I had been knitted together and the stitches were dropping and I was coming apart a little at a time. There was a time I was sure that sooner or later there'd be nothing left but a little nest of ragged yarn." He squeezed her hand. "But now the unwinding—the *unraveling*—has slowed and nearly stopped." He kissed her cheek. "Thank you for that, my dear."

Kate smiled in the darkness. She felt safe and protected. And in a strange way even loved.

The last of their time was spent back in Rome. The day came to leave and Jon helped the driver load their luggage into the back of the limousine.

"Don't forget the one final stop we have to make," he reminded the driver.

"No sir. I surely won't."

"What final stop, Jon? I thought we were on the way to the airport."

"We are. But there's one place we've failed to visit."

The car wound through the streets. Kate watched the city through smoke-tinted windows. As anxious as she was to return home, she hated to leave this place with its warm and wonderful people. The car slowed, then stopped. Jon reached across her and pushed a button to lower the window.

"Look at that fountain," Kate said. Then she covered her mouth with her hand and her eyes widened. "The *Trevi?*"

Jon nodded.

"My goodness. How could I have forgotten it?"

"You can't leave Rome without making a wish." He reached into his pocket and handed her a coin. "Here. One coin. One wish. Make it a good one."

Kate scrambled from the car and felt the spray of the water as she descended the steps.

"One wish," she whispered. "Only one." Closing her eyes she wished with all her might, kissed the coin warmed by her hand, and tossed it into the sparkling water.

The water bubbled gently as the coin fell and settled among the many others lying on the bottom. Kate watched until the water stilled around it before she turned away. Now she was free to return home

.

SEVENTEEN

Europe seemed far away as the plane touched down in Woodway. It was good to be home and the sound of English being spoken all around her was music to Kate's ears. Jon's Lincoln Navigator appeared as if by magic and they drove home. The tiny apartment looked inviting when Jon opened the door a short time later. They had agreed to stay there until the house was completed.

"Let's get a few things unpacked and drive out to see the house," he suggested. "I'm anxious to see how much they've gotten done since we've been away."

As they drove through the country, a blanket of snow covered the hills and clung to the trees and the bushes that lined the road. A brightly lit sign announcing the development of the new Woodway Mall stood in close proximity to where the private road once ran. Ten minutes later, they were at the private road that led to the entrance of their new home. Stone columns stood on either side of the driveway spanned by an arch that wove the name *Brandywine* into the intricate ironwork. The newly paved drive curved its way toward the house, using the tall trees as a natural border along each side. Male voices and hearty shouts punctuated the late-evening sounds as the men loaded equipment into the back of a truck. The whirring of a saw fell silent.

"They seem to be getting ready to leave for the day," Jon said. He stopped the car in the middle of the driveway that circled around in front of the house.

"Looks pretty good from here, don't you think?"

"It's quite a house," Kate said. "Can we go inside?"

"Sure. Let's drive around to the parking area." He executed a U-turn in the driveway and continued toward the right side of the house. The entire wall facing the terrace and parking area consisted of sliding glass doors. They got out of the car and started up the flagstone steps.

A mackinaw clad 'Paul Bunyon' rounded the corner of the house, a roll of blueprints tucked under his arm.

"Mr. Ames, welcome back, sir."

"Sam, it's good to see you." Jon held out his hand. "May I introduce Mrs. Ames. We were anxious to get home. How's it going?"

"Nice to meet you, ma'am," Sam said and nodded at Kate. He looked at Jon. "It's going just fine. We've been lucky with the weather holding. This is the first snow of any size that we've had so far. If you have the time I'd like to go over a couple of things with you."

"You go ahead, Jon," Kate said. "I'll go inside and look around, if it's okay."

"Help yourself, ma'am," Sam said. "But be careful, there's tools lying around with loose cords. It's easy to trip."

"Thank you, Sam." She watched as the two men walked away, their heads bent over the unrolled sheets of paper.

From the terrace, Kate entered the breakfast room and wandered around peeking into closets and cabinets and opening drawers. The house was beautifully proportioned, from the massive master bedroom to the completely equipped kitchen. Facing the front of the house, she stepped down into the living room and tried to picture how it would look once the carpet and wall coverings were in place and the furniture arranged. Further on past the living room was a closed door. It opened to a room lined with shelves and wide files built into the walls. *Jon's studio*, she thought. She knew that each shelf and file had been meticulously designed for a specific purpose.

The rest of the house was equally impressive. A stone fireplace spanned the width of the den, and from the window-seats there was a view of the back woods. The two guest suites—for visitors they'd probably never have—were well situated for privacy and opened onto a secluded back terrace. Back down the hallway toward the way she'd come, a closed door beckoned. Kate pushed it open and was delighted to see the finished pool room. The pool was filled and lights blinked beneath the surface of the still water. Overhead, retractable skylights took up most of the ceiling. The pool itself nearly filled the floor except for a walkway that circled the room.

"I see you've found my favorite room," Jon said, coming up behind her and touching her shoulders.

"I'm surprised it's already filled."

"To see if there are any leaks and to check the heating and filter system," he explained. "You've seen the rest of the house?"

Kate nodded. "I'm impressed. It really turned out beautifully. You should be proud."

"*We* should be proud, Kathleen. You had as much to do with making this a reality as I did. Sam tells me another two weeks will finish it up. After a couple days of rest you can get started on the decorating."

"But you'll help me, won't you?"

"Of course, I will. I only meant that you have complete control. Whatever you want to do is fine with me. I trust your taste completely."

The following two weeks were a myriad of decisions. Every minute of their time was occupied with choices: furniture, fabrics, patterns and color selections. The days had been so fast-paced that Kate was rather surprised when she woke one Friday morning to discover a free, uncommitted day. Jon left a note that he had gone to the house and wouldn't return until evening. Kate glanced at the sofa where he spent his nights. The bedclothes were put away and the cushions straightened.

It seemed like old times when Kate stepped through the front door at Consolidated Investments a couple of hours later. Everything was as if she had never been away.

"We've really missed you," Sally said, giving her a big hug. "You look awesome."

"*Awesome*?" Kate smiled. "Well, maybe I am." She glanced around the room. "I wanted to come by sooner, but I just couldn't find the time."

Marty came out of his office, a wide grin on his face. "Kate, it's so good to see you. How's that husband of yours?"

"Fine, Marty. We both are. How are things here?"

"Steady," he said. "But tell us about your trip, and how about that house you two are building? It's causing quite a stir, let me tell you."

For the next hour, the group talked over top each other, with so much to say, so much to catch up on.

Leaving the office later, Kate had the distinct feeling that the business at CI was steadily declining. She felt a sickening ache in the pit of her stomach for the man who had been like a father to her. What had once been a thriving small-town business was now being over-shadowed by giant conglomerates: corporations staffed with microchip personnel who stored clients as factored ratios and statistics, rather than individual people with diverse personalities and needs. Kate wished there was something she could do, but was left with a feeling of helplessness.

For a week vans rumbled up the driveway at *Brandywine,* unloaded their contents, and drove away again. Moving day came at last. Kate and Jon had taken the last of their things from the apartment and Jon went on ahead. With a final look around the empty rooms, Kate turned her back on the small apartment, and the hollow life it had housed and protected for so many years, and walked out the door.

The big gates at *Brandywine* swung open at a touch of the remote control, and closed again behind her. Jon was already at the house. Kate parked her car beside his and joined him inside. Always the one for toasts on special occasions, he had the drinks poured and waiting.

"To you, lovely lady, and to the beautiful home you helped me create," he said, holding forth a snifter of his favorite brandy.

Kate dropped down beside him on the Tuscany sofa. "And to you for making all this possible and asking me to be part of it."

The indirect lighting painted the room with muted brush strokes and for the first time since she could remember, Kate felt safe from the outside world. Safe and protected, and maybe someday even loved.

He swirled the snifter, took a sip, and set it on the coffee table. "How about a swim?"

Kate smiled. "I'm beat. It's a hot shower and an early turn in for me, if you don't mind."

"Of course not. You go on. I think I'll stay up and read for a while. There's some new material I want to catch up on."

Later, Kate woke with the strangeness of a new place. Her footfalls hushed in the deep carpet as she made her way through the dimly lit house. A soft light glowed from a single lamp left burning in the living room. The grandfather clock struck three. The door of the studio stood open. Quietly she looked inside. Jon had fallen asleep on the dark brown leather couch, an opened book across his chest. It rose and fell with his even breathing. Kate eased the door shut and turned away.

EIGHTEEN

The world beyond the walls of *Brandywine* went by unnoticed as Kate and Jon took up their new lives. Hand-in-hand they walked about the couple of acres enclosed within the security fence. They had braved the cold to look over the area to decide how best to proceed with the landscaping. Soggy patches of moss from newly melted snow squished beneath their feet and cushioned their steps. Winter sun penetrated the tall trees, but the wind remained bitter as it swept through the stark limbs and rustled the few remaining parchment leaves.

"It's going to be a big job," Jon said, looking around the woodland and back toward the house, now a good distance behind them.

"Why don't we leave it just as it is, in its natural state," Kate said. "Especially this far out. It's in excellent condition and anything we try to do couldn't make it any lovelier than it already is. The moss and wild flowers and the new saplings are all it needs." As she turned her head to look around, the hood of her coat slid from her hair. She tried to pull it back into place, but her mitten-covered hands did not want to cooperate.

"You're probably right," Jon said. "If it hasn't become overrun with briars and thick underbrush by now, I guess it never will. We can groom the ground over near the house and keep that tended, but this far out we can't improve on what nature has already given us."

Kate smiled and continued to tug at the stubborn hood.

"Here." Jon turned her toward him. "Let me do that."

Child-like and trusting, Kate stood before him as he unknotted the strings and pulled the hood into place. Cinching the fabric close to her face, he tucked her hair in around the edges and tightened the cord beneath her chin.

"Too tight?"

Kate shook her head

Jon tied a bow and pulled the zipper all the way to the top. "Better?"

Kate grinned. "Much," she said as a staggering gust of wind howled across the knoll.

"You ready to start back?"

"In a few minutes." Kate shaded her eyes and squinted into the evening sun. "Jon, where's the cemetery from here?"

"Over there." He pointed off toward the left. "Across the meadow and just beyond that far ridge. If you come straight down from where the sun is now, you'd just about be on the hill."

"And the new mall?"

"Much further over and to the right. More toward the main road."

"I'm glad we can't see it from here."

"Well, we're pretty far away. Maybe not as the crow flies, but it's a good eight to ten minute drive." He took her arm and steered her in the direction of the house.

"I'm getting you back inside," he said. "The wind's kicking up pretty good and I don't want you catching cold."

They walked back to the house, passing the caretaker's building on the way. "I've been thinking about the gardener," he said. "I think I'll start looking around for somebody."

"But we just got moved in."

"I know, but there's a lot to be done now. No use putting everything off to the last minute and expect one person to handle it. We don't want to overwhelm him before he even gets started."

Kate nodded. Being overwhelmed was something she had come to understand.

The next afternoon Kate sat in the breakfast room looking out over the terrace. Jon came around the corner of the house and up the steps. Following close on his heels was a man she had never seen before. A cumbersome limp twisted his hip to one side as he walked, making him seem slight and frail. The hat on his bowed head was mottled with sweat circles, and the ragged braided band dangled loose cords in several places. Jon slid back the glass door.

"Kathleen, this is our new gardener, Silas Hawkins."

The man came to a stop directly behind Jon and dragged the hat from his head.

"Hello, Silas," Kate said. "I'm pleased to meet you."

Silas Hawkins barely glanced up as he stood rolling the brim of the hat between fingers tanned and cracked as old leather. His jagged fingernails and torn cuticles were caked with dirt that had a look of permanence.

"Ma'am," he said.

"Silas tells me that his wife would be interested in helping in the house," Jon said. "He assures me she's an excellent housekeeper and cook."

Silas nodded and glanced up. A pale light glinted in his watery blue eyes as a smile turned up the corners of his chapped lips. He had a missing front tooth, but the remaining ones were surprisingly white and looked strong and healthy. He was younger than Kate first thought. Suddenly he was no longer just an obscure little figure who worked with the soil and got his clothes dirty.

He's stronger than he looks, Kate thought, and decided that here was a man who was honest above all else. She liked him.

"What's your wife's name, Silas?"

"Emily."

"Do you and Emily have children? Perhaps you could bring them over."

"No ma'am, we don't. Emily lost a baby, but she don't like to talk about it."

Kate had to look away from the sadness in his eyes. She fastened her gaze on the surrounding woodland. "Why don't you bring Emily over so we can get acquainted?"

"I'll bring her tomorrow, if that's not too soon?"

"Tomorrow's fine," Kate said.

"Thank you, ma'am. Now if you'll excuse me, I'll get back to work." He squashed the hat back on his head and made for the old pick-up truck parked by the caretaker's building.

Jon watched him for a second. "I think he's what some people would call an *employment risk*."

"Why?"

"Because he *looks* unstable. But did you see his eyes? I've got a feeling that Silas Hawkins is one hell of a dependable soul."

Kate smiled. "I think you're right."

"They must be having a pretty rough time. I ran into him at Wilson's Nursery and when I offered him this job, he jumped at it. If you can possibly use his wife in the house, I'm sure it will be a big help."

"I'll use her," Kate said without question.

Emily came the next morning when Silas arrived for work. Kate liked her from the start. She was a runty little thing, not especially pretty, more standoffish, and unsure of herself. Even though Silas continued to call Jon, Mr. Ames, Kate insisted from the very beginning that Emily call her by her first name. Before many days had passed, it was as if they had always known each other.

Judge Hampton was the recipient of the first official invitation to *Brandywine* and lost no time in accepting. Kate wanted the evening to be perfect and spent a lot of time on the menu. An hour before he was to arrive, she and Emily were busy in the kitchen.

"Check the roast, will you, Emily," Kate said. "It may need basting."

Emily stood at the sink, idly running water over her hands.

Kate frowned. "Emily?"

She turned. "I'm sorry. What did you say?"

"See about basting the roast."

She turned off the water and dried her hands on her apron. She walked to the stove and stood with her hand on the handle of the oven.

"Are you okay?" Kate asked.

Emily shook her head, lowered the door and slid out the roasting pan. She picked up the brush and turned to Kate.

"I'm pregnant."

"You're what?" Kate's heart quickened. "Oh my, Emily, that's fantastic news."

Tears gathered in Emily's eyes. "What if I lose this one, too?'

"You won't," Kate said. "We'll see that you have the best care available, that you eat right and don't overdo." She walked over and laid her arm around Emily's shoulders. "This time you're going to have a healthy baby and I'm going to get to keep it a lot."

Emily laughed and cried and hugged Kate. "What would I do without you?"

"Me? You're the one having a baby."

Dinner preparation took on a whole new mood. They both smiled a lot and laughed at the slightest thing. Together they laid the formal dining room with imported china and crystal, then stood back to admire their efforts.

The judge arrived. He and Jon seemed genuinely glad to see each other. Throughout the evening, Kate sensed a penetrating curiosity on the judge's part. Over after-dinner coffee in the living room, he seemed to be filled with a kind of restlessness. Kate took her cue from Jon, and was silent as the older man set his cup on the end table and pushed himself up from the chair. He paced the room, his breathing heavy and sounding like it took great effort. He lifted the Faberge egg from its pedestal and turned it slowly in his hands. Placing it back on the table, he turned to study an original watercolor hanging beneath tract lighting. He turned and spoke.

"Jonathan, may I speak to you in private?"

"Walt—"

"Now, Jonathan." His voice was firm. He turned to Kate. "Will you excuse us, my dear? This will only take a minute." He walked toward the studio without looking back. Jon followed him into the room and closed the door.

While she waited, Kate poured fresh coffee into their cups. She could hear slightly raised voices coming from the other room.

"You cannot continue in this fashion," she heard the judge say. "My God, boy..." his voice trailed away. Jon murmured a muffled reply that she couldn't make out

Moments later the door flung open and the men emerged. Red-faced and visibly shaken, the judge snatched his coat from the back of a chair and huffed from the room. He slammed the door behind him.

"Is everything all right?" Kate asked. "Judge Hampton seemed awfully upset."

"He'll be fine once he cools down," Jon said. "His Honor is righting the axis of the planet. Its current position doesn't quite suit him."

"Well, I hope this doesn't hurt your friendship. I know how important he is to you."

Jon smiled. "Oh, I think not, my dear. Walt's sensibilities are not that easily bruised." He seemed to dismiss the entire incident as trivial.

Kate cleared the dishes from the living room as Jon turned away and reentered his study. She didn't see him again until the next day.

Swimming had become an important part of Kate and Jon's routine. On nights when the moon was full, or nearly full and stars crowded the sky, Jon would turn off the lights in the room, roll back the retractable skylights, and they'd float on their backs and watch the moon ride across the opening, leaving only shadows and the flickering lights beneath the water.

John wore his swimming trunks like a model. He had a good body, strong and solid with elongated muscles that ran the length of his long legs. The lines of his shoulders were wide and set square out from a smooth chest that tapered to a narrow waist and flat belly. He was an excellent swimmer and very patient in teaching Kate the finer points of breathing and stroking. After a while, her flailing and splashing was replaced with a degree of precision and control. He praised her for her accomplishments, and his praise was all that mattered.

It had taken Kate some time to find swimsuits that accommodated her special needs, but she finally did. They were cut high across the front with a padded built-in bra, little cap sleeves, and a crisscrossed back that made sure everything stayed in place. *Okay, so they're not microscopic bits of material held together with strings,* she reasoned. That wouldn't've been her style even if her body was perfect. And she loved swimming. Something about the water, the seduction of the moist caressing, stirred a primal need within her. But the need to mate went unfulfilled.

Ensconced within the walls of the luxurious home, the bonding between them continued. Jon still spent nights in his studio, but occasionally Kate caught glimpses of him at the door of the master bedroom. The first time it happened she almost called out to him, but quickly stopped herself, knowing instinctively that he would retreat. Her patience was inexhaustible. She waited.

A mid-winter storm was raging. They sat on the sofa in the den drinking mulled wine, the Scrabble board on the cushion between them. Over the snapping and crackling of the logs in the fireplace, sleet pelted the windows like mortar rounds. Thunder rolled in the distance and the lights flickered.

Kate sat cross-legged across from Jon and watched as a frown settled between his eyes and he studied his letters. He cast an obviously surreptitious glance in Kate's direction. The tiles clicked as be arranged them on the board.

"*Zyzzyva?* That's not a word and you know it," she said.

"Is too." A smile played around the corners of his serious mouth.

"Okay then, what is it?"

"It's a kind of bug."

"A bug!"

"Well, not a bug exactly."

The board and tiles tumbled to the floor as Kate fell against him, laughing.

"You just this minute made that up, I know you did. I'm never going to play with you again."

He dropped a kiss on her hair. "That's what you said the last time when I got you with *ixylyl.*"

Suddenly a sharp crack of thunder rent the air as a keen flash of lightning split the blackness on the other side of the windows. The lights flickered and went out. The room plunged into darkness except for the light from the fire. Kate started to pull away from where she had fallen, but Jon put his arm around her and held her against his chest. The flames in the fireplace licked around a large log and traced shadows against the walls. There was a sizzling sound as an errant drop of rain found its way down the chimney and caused the fire to sputter.

Kate continued to lean against his chest, his arms around her. *What's he thinking,* she wondered. *Is he measuring his present life against some past one? Comparing me to others he has known? Julie, perhaps. Or is he instead remembering the ugliness lying just beneath this beautiful yellow cashmere sweater covering my body?* The thought made her pull away.

"Looks like the power's going to be off for a while," he said. "I'd better check and make sure the emergency lighting is working. Why don't you curl up here on the sofa and I'll keep the fire going. The power may be off for some time."

Kate kicked back against the pillows. "I think I will," she said.

Jon pulled the chenille throw from the sofa back and tucked it in around her body before he went to check the lighting.

Sometime during the night, Kate roused in her sleep and was vaguely aware of Jon sitting in front of the fire, his back resting against the sofa cushion. Her stirring caught his attention and he tucked her hand beneath the cover before turning his gaze back to the fire.

A heavy snowfall covered the grounds in late January. Jon succeeded in enticing Kate to join him for a walk around the grounds. She pulled on heavy snow boots and dressed in layers of clothes.

"Are you sure you can walk in all of that?" he chided.

Kate's bright eyes peeked out at him from beneath the chinchilla-lined hood. She smoothed the fur away from her mouth and stuck her tongue out at him.

Jon rolled his eyes toward the heavens as if petitioning for patience. He helped her down the terrace steps and kept an arm around her waist as they waded through the deep snow.

Kate planted her feet and waved her arms wide. "Isn't it beautiful?"

"You're beautiful," Jon said.

She held her breath, waiting for him to continue. But he seemed almost embarrassed and bent and scooped up a hand full of snow. Slowly, he began forming it into a ball.

Kate pointed a gloved finger.

"Jonathan Ames, don't you dare throw that. If you throw that snowball you'll be extremely sorry."

The ball whizzed past her head and she was left with no recourse but to retaliate. The battle was underway. Kate lost her footing and tumbled into a deep snow bank. Graciously, Jon offered his hand, which she grasped firmly and proceeded to pull him down beside her. A cloud of white powder filled the air as snow was kicked up and flew in all directions, while the grunt-filled wrestling match continued.

Finally, an exhausted Kate begged for time-out and Jon rolled her onto her back and helped her to her feet. With his arms around her bundled-body, his eyes met hers and held fast. She watched as he lowered his head and covered her cold mouth with his. The taste of him was like nectar to a starving body that would have continued to survive on bread and water. Unspoken words hung between them as they started back to the house, but Kate had seen something in his eyes she had never seen before. She felt the faint ripplings of hope as she thought she recognized the fragile beginnings of love.

NINETEEN

There was an unexpected break in the winter weather. Kate and Jon sat at the breakfast table as the early February sun streamed through the windows and warmed the room.

"Do you think winter is starting to wind down?"

"I doubt it," he said and continued to read the paper.

"Well, I hope so." The phone rang. "Sit still and finish your paper," she said. "I'll get it."

Stepping across the room, she reached over the counter and lifted the receiver.

"Hello." Kate could hear a hint of breathing on the line. "Hello," she repeated. Suddenly the line went dead. "Well, that was strange," she said, returning to the table.

He put the paper down. "Who was it?"

"I don't know. Someone was there, I'm sure of it. But then, they just hung up."

"Probably a wrong number," he reasoned as a frown, ever so slightly, creased his forehead.

"I guess so," she said. "Still, I had the feeling the call was intentional. They didn't hang up right away."

"Don't worry about it. I'm sure it was nothing."

The break in the weather failed to hold. A blast of icy winds whipped down from Canada and paralyzed the Northeast in a firm grip. Kate pushed a button by the terrace doors to close the heavy drapes against the onslaught. The room darkened and just as she reached to flip on the light switch, the phone rang. She heard Jon answer in his studio. A few moments later he stepped into the living room.

"Any coffee?" His manner seemed uneasy.

"Just brewed a fresh pot. How about some hot apple pie to keep it company?"

"Ah, lady, how well you know me," he said and rubbed his stomach. "Come join me and let's talk."

Kate gathered cups and saucers from the cabinet and took silverware from the drawer. Jon poured steaming coffee into their cups and cut huge slabs of pie. An aroma of apples and cinnamon filled the kitchen. They sat on stools at a small side bar.

"What do you want to talk about? Is anything wrong?"

He twirled his fork on the flaky piecrust and shook his head. "I guess it's just the weather. It can quit any time it wants to. I've had enough."

Kate nodded. "But we'll have to be patient and let this spell run its course."

"We don't have to put up with it, you know. We could go away for a while."

"Where would we go?"

"To beautiful beaches and the bluest sky in the world. Have you ever been to Nags Head?"

She shook her head. "But I always wondered what a place with such a name would look like."

"Well, let's go and I'll show you. I just flipped on the weather channel hoping this mess is about to go away—which, by the way it isn't. But I did see something interesting. Seems like there's a freak trough of warm air working its way up from the Gulf and meandering along the lower east coast. If we leave right now, we'll hit North Carolina about the time it does. Walt has a summerhouse at the Outer Banks and said we could use it any time we wanted." He looked around the darkened room. "I think the time has come."

"It sounds too good. How soon could we go?"

He glanced at his wristwatch. "How 'bout in thirty minutes?"

"Thirty minutes? You're serious."

"Only if we want to catch the sunshine and warm breezes."

"Do you want me to check the airline schedule?"

"Pshaw on the airlines. The main roads are being cleared, so throw a few clothes in a tote bag and I'll warm up the car. The emergency compartment is fully stocked."

"I'd better give Emily a call."

"Never mind. I'll leave Silas a note."

Less than thirty minutes later, they were heading out the door.

The roads had been scraped and graveled, but the first hundred miles was slow going. Even though the car was cozy and comfortable, Kate was aware of how carefully Jon was driving. He kept both hands firmly on the steering wheel and the big Lincoln Navigator maintained an even speed. Gradually the gray skies began to lighten.

"Well, now just look at that," Jon said peering through the windshield toward the sky. "There really is a sun up there. If it won't come to us we'll just have to go to it."

"This was a wonderful idea, Jon. Just think of all the awful stuff we left behind."

"And that's where it belongs. *All* of it. Where we're heading is warm sunshine and miles of gloriously deserted beaches. I promise, you're going to love it." He patted her hand and reached for his pipe.

Kate rested her head against the back of the seat and watched the sky turn to a brilliant blue as the car rolled away the miles. Soon the mountains fell away and the landscape flattened to the distant horizon.

Like Judge Hampton, his beach house had a certain grace. The rooms were spacious and airy and urged those present to comfort themselves. Jon showed Kate where to put her bag.

"You take this room and I'll bunk in Walt's bedroom. I never could sleep in a strange place and I'll probably be up half the night. No use keeping you awake."

Later, Kate sat in a pink and blue canvas-covered patio chair and watched Jon put steaks on the grill. Off to the right of the patio, situated beneath the cooling shade of pine trees, was a lattice-wrapped gazebo. It looked inviting and Kate made a mental note to check it out before they left. Only a few yards beyond, the Atlantic continued its relentless ebb and flow.

"Nice of Walt to keep such a well-stocked larder," Jon said as he turned the steaks and they sizzled. "He should get down here more often. It'd do wonders for his health."

"He's not well?"

"Heart trouble. He's had it for years. I can't imagine not having him around, but he's going to die if he doesn't slow down and give some of the work to younger people. The doctors have warned him and I stay on his back all the time, but it's like arguing with a fence post."

"I'm sorry he's sick. I wish there was something we could do."

"Well, we can't. He's as good a man as you'd ever hope to meet and I love him, but he's a hardheaded old warhorse and there's not much chance he'll ever be anything else."

A slight breeze fanned across the patio. Kate leaned against the padded back of the chair and closed her eyes. "I could get used to this."

"Why don't we get a place down here?"

"Jon, could we?"

"As soon as we get everything squared away at home we'll come down and take our time looking around. Maybe next winter we won't have to sponge off Walt." He buttered thick slices of bread and turned them onto the grill. "It's almost ready. Hungry?"

Kate jumped to her feet. "Starved. I'll pour the iced tea and toss the salad; olive oil okay?"

"Sure."

Kate unfolded a red-checkered tablecloth and fanned it out, then picked a handful of azaleas that bordered the walkway and stuffed them into a plastic tumbler. Jon plucked a single flower from the bouquet and tucked it into her hair. She placed her hand over his and held it there. Overhead a flock of seagulls congregated and their screeching intruded upon the intimacy. The magical moment was over.

The days at the ocean flew by. Time seemed to be of little value as they squandered it without a second thought. They took a short cruise up the coastline, passing beneath creaking and straining drawbridges. One full day was spent at Kill Devil Hills, the birthplace of aviation. Kate loved it when they visited the two-room shack with its overhanging sleeping-loft that the famous brothers referred to as their *two-story house.*

"You would've had a lot in common with those two characters," she told Jon. "I'm sure you three would have found a lot to talk about."

Jon smiled at the thought. "Can you imagine Orville and Wilbur watching a launching of the space shuttle?"

Of all North Carolina had to offer, a special stretch of deserted beach was Kate's favorite thing. To get there they had to get permission to cross a private game preserve. The beach was empty and ran on for miles. Waves rolled in and broke over their bare feet, splashing water on the cuffs of Jon's rolled-up pants and wetting the ruffle of Kate's long peasant skirt. The sky was filled with the cries of seabirds as they seemed determined to drown out the roaring of the surf with their screeching.

Kate stooped to inspect the bounty the sea had left upon the sand. She loaded Jon down with starfish and sand dollars until his hands could hold no more and he begged for mercy. Finally, she relented and chose only two shells for keeping and dropped them into her skirt pockets. The rest she allowed him to leave on the beach.

Walking back to the car, Jon showed Kate the hunting lodge that had been a private residence at one time. In its heyday it was a mansion among mansions. "It was called *The House of Seven Chimneys.*"

"Why?"

He pointed toward the roof. "Because it has seven chimneys."

"Is that unusual?"

"It is when it only has six fireplaces."

Kate slapped him on the shoulder where the wet shirt clung to his skin. "There you go, making things up again."

He held up his hands. "Trust me, it's the truth. The lady who built the house wanted more chimneys than any other house around. Somebody nearby had a house with six chimneys so she insisted on seven."

"But what does the seventh one go to?"

"Nothing."

"That's silly."

"Maybe. But at least she had more chimneys than anybody else," he said. "I guess that counts for something."

"I guess," Kate agreed.

On the stroll back to the car, Kate stopped, bent over and placed her hands on her knees.

"I'll race you back to the car. Readysetgo."

She took off up the beach, her bare feet kicking sand out behind her. Midway through the race, Jon easily overtook her and was lounging against the car fender, legs crossed and looking bored, when she arrived.

"What kept you?"

Kate was gasping as she leaned over to catch her breath. Jon swooped her up and held her against him. She wound her arms around his neck and buried her face into his chest. His shirt tasted of sweat and salt.

They put off leaving North Carolina. Every day there was a different reason for staying. Even a weenie roast became an important event.

"We'll build a fire down by the water and burn our hotdogs to a crisp. So what if we get sand in our lemonade." He closed the lid on the picnic basket. "Doesn't that sound like fun?"

"I can hardly wait," Kate said. She gathered up a blanket and a small portable radio as they went out the door.

They only had to walk a few yards to the water's edge. Jon went in search of driftwood for the fire and Kate spread out the blanket. Then she stood with her hands on her hips gazing out at the far horizon. The blood-red sun was just beginning to slide down into the restless black water. For some reason it reminded Kate of Emily and the fullness of her body. She felt Jon's hands on her shoulder.

"Beautiful, isn't it?"

Kate turned and smiled. "Better get the fire going. It'll be dark soon."

Later, they stretched out on the blanket and looked into the navy-blue heavens. The night was crystal clear and each star seemed to stand in its own glory. Kate shivered as a cool breeze whipped in off the water. Jon pulled her next to him and wrapped his arms around her body.

"There's the Big Dipper," he said, pointing skyward. "And over there is his little brother. They're in the constellation Ursa Minor, or *Little Bear*."

Kate turned to look at him. "Is there anything you don't know?"

"Oh, my dear, I don't know the really important things: how to make the world a better place, how to prevent ignorance, how to erase hunger and poverty."

He flipped over onto his stomach and switched on the radio. Undecipherable babble blasted forth in all its ear-splitting pandemonium. "Or, that," he said. "For the life of me I can't figure out the appeal that kind of coarseness and vulgarity has to anybody with a lick of sense." He twirled the dial until he found real music, music that could be tolerated without the gnashing of teeth. He turned to pull Kate back into his arms. They lay quietly, listening to Mantovani and the waves. And their world was at peace. Or was it? she wondered.

The next afternoon Kate brought up the subject of leaving.

"Jon, if we're going to stay much longer I'm going to have to go shopping for something to wear." She held up a side of her skirt and touched a sleeve of her cotton sweater. "This is the last outfit I have and if I wash it one more time it's going to fall apart."

"Tomorrow. You can go shopping tomorrow. Right now let's go for a walk on the beach."

"But it looks like there's a storm coming up."

"We won't go far."

They walked a short way, keeping in sight of the house. The waves were beginning to heave and toss. A distant rumble echoed across threatening skies just before a thin streak of lightning shot down and touched the water. All at once the skies opened up and drenched the land. Ducking his head against the savage wind, Jon grabbed Kate by the hand and dragged her back toward shelter. The gazebo was the nearest thing to offer any measure of protection. Jon pulled her inside. Breathlessly, Kate wiped her face with the hem of her skirt and twisted water from her hair.

"Whew, that came up fast," Jon said.

Kate laughed and looked around the inside of the small structure. "I'd been wanting to visit this place anyway."

Except for the leeward side, the kiosk was totally enclosed. Built-in benches lined the walls and circled the room around a center table. The benches, padded with striped corduroy cushions, had a couple of blankets tossed across the backs. Jon picked one up, wrapped it around Kate's shoulders and led her to the far side of the room away from the entrance.

Kate huddled beneath the fleecy cover as rain pounded the roof and thunder rumbled across the darkened heavens. Lightning danced on churning waves and sent vibrations along the ground. Jon lifted the blanket slightly and slipped in beside her. Neither spoke as he pressed her back on the seat and their bodies molded together. His mouth came down and closed over hers with a need that seemed to match the raging elements around them. Kate pulled his head closer and gave herself to the kiss. She could feel the steam rising from the wet clothes that covered their fevered bodies. In the distance, the roaring of the wild surf mingled with the roaring in Kate's ears. The male hardness of Jon's body pressed against her leg as his hand moved under her skirt and touched the edge of her underwear. He hooked a thumb into the elastic band of her panties and she felt a gentle tug. Ever so slightly, she raised her hips. Over the roaring in her ears, she thought she heard another sound. Suddenly, Jon pulled away.

"Yoo-hoo," a voice called. "Are y'all there?"

Jon sat up, pulling Kate with him. They hurried to straighten their clothes and he brushed her tumbled hair back from her brow. A face appeared in the doorway.

"There you are. Figured y'all had got stranded out here in this sudden downpour so I brought an umbrella."

She stepped inside and smiled a big grin that said she knew she was appreciated. "No need to thank me, it's all part of the job. I'm Lydia," she said, extending a hand. "Been Judge's housekeeper for more years than I care to remember. He called and said y'all was comin' down and told me not to bother about gettin' out here for a few days. But heck, I'd have none of that. Any guests in this house has a right to be taken care of proper-like, and that's my job."

"You were much too kind to come after us." Jon looked at Kate and smiled. "We would have managed fine by ourselves."

"I won't hear of it," she insisted. "I'd've been here sooner but I didn't know y'all needed me. But I'm here now and I'm goin' to look after your ever need. You want somethin' you just tell old Lydia, and it's yours." Her mouth was set in a determined line that said she would brook no resistance from them.

An hour later Jon and Kate were on their way north. The brief interlude in the gazebo was very much on Kate's mind, but neither of them brought it up. It was as if there was an understanding that anything of an intimate nature was not to be discussed in open conversation. Yet Kate could not help but wonder if they would pick up where they left off once they got back to *Brandywine*.

It was after midnight when the gates swung open to allow them entrance. The moon was hidden by an overcast sky and the knoll lay in such darkness that one would never guess there was a house at the top. As the car curved up the driveway, the headlights swept across the hill and filtered through the trees. Jon parked the car and helped Kate gather their things. Somewhere from the woods, an owl hooted and there were rustlings of nocturnal creatures as they crept about in their furtive activities. Through the inky blackness, Jon guided Kate across the terrace and pulled back the sliding door. As they stepped into the darkened room, a musky odor, heavy and oppressive, permeated the room and assaulted the senses. Jon came to an abrupt halt, and Kate could hear him pull in a ragged breath.

"Oh, God," he whispered.

TWENTY

*K*ate groped for Jon's hand in the dark. "Jon, what *is* that smell?"

He pulled her head against his chest and buried her face in the front of his coat before flipping on the light. Kate could sense the tenseness of his whole being as he stood for a moment and held her tight. At last, he turned her loose, and they looked around the room. Everything was in place and looked normal except for the over-powering odor of the musky perfume.

"I'm going to put these things away and then get out the air freshener," Kate said and headed toward her bedroom.

The room was dark and she felt her way around the bed and over toward the nightstand to switch on the lamp. The first thing that caught her eye was the rumpled bedclothes. The pillows were bunched on top of each other, and the spread wadded and twisted, hanging half off the bed onto the floor. Kate ran a hand across her furrowed brow. She thought she made up the bed before they left. She turned toward the dresser. There, emblazoned across the mirror, was one scarlet word: *Whoremonger!* She took a step forward and touched the glass. The letters, written in lipstick, smeared beneath her touch. She jumped as Jon turned on the overhead light from the doorway.

"Jon, who would do such a thing?"

"I know who's responsible. Silas."

"Silas would never do a thing like this. What reason would he have?"

"Not *do it!*" Jon spat the words. "*Allowed* it to happen. The grounds are secure. There's only one way in and that's through the security gate. Silas has the only other remote control." He slapped the doorframe. "He had to have let someone in—which was directly against my orders."

"How's the rest of the house? Has anything else been disturbed?"

"I don't know. I've only checked the living room. Everything there's fine. We might as well go ahead and go through the rest of the rooms." His shoulders drooped slightly. "Maybe this is the extent of the vandalism."

"Is that what it is, vandalism?"

He cut his eyes at her. "What else would you think it might be, Kathleen?" For some reason he seemed angry with her.

"I don't know, Jon. I'm asking."

"And I'm telling you, it's the work of a crazy person."

The remainder of the house looked untouched. The only room still to be checked was the pool room. When Jon opened the door, a vile stench rushed outward and caused them to retch. Jon held a handkerchief over his nose as he pushed through and turned on the light. The pool was a floating sewer. Meat from the freezer lay thawed and rotting in the warm water. Empty paper sacks, once containing meal and flour and sugar, floated on top of the soupy mess. Little containers of herbs and spices bobbed like fishing floaters. The water took on the coloring and consistency of a swamp.

Kate stared at the devastation, anger heating her blood and charging her internal survivor battery. Her eyes were drawn to the far wall. As she gasped, Jon's eyes followed hers to the message painted in foot-high letters: *BE SURE YOUR SINS WILL FIND YOU OUT!* Beside the message, a giant penis outlined in scarlet, dominated the room. Blood-engorged veins ran the length of the eight-foot high drawing and seemed to pump life into the obscene erection. A wispy garland of daisies surrounded the base and lay upon knotty, over-sized testicles. Like a prestigious work of art, a border of bright yellow sunflowers framed the whole thing, and Kate remembered the artwork from the farmhouse.

"We've got to call the police," she said and turned to leave the room.

"No!"

"But, Jon—"

"You heard me, Kathleen. No police."

"Then you'd better get a cleaning crew in here to take care of this mess. And while you're at it, you might as well call the pool man because the filter's not running."

"I'll take care of the filter. And the two of us can clean the place up."

"Are you crazy? We'll never be able to get this stuff out of here."

"What's the matter?" His voice was heavy with sarcasm. "Not afraid of a little hard work, are you?"

"What's come over you? I'm not responsible for this mess, but you seem to be blaming me for it. Jon, do you know who did this—what the message means?"

"Don't ask me questions, Kathleen. I hate questions." He turned around in the room and looked toward the ceiling, studying. "If I retract the skylights and keep the door closed, the odor will stay out of the rest of the house. I'll deal with it and I don't want to hear any more about it. Go to bed."

Kate carried a bottle of glass cleaner and paper towels to the bedroom. The red letters streaked and ran like blood when she sprayed the mirror. She swiped the soft paper towel across the glass until all traces of the message was gone. The bedclothes were heavy with the odor of musk. She stripped them away, dumped them in the washer with detergent and bleach. Pulling an extra blanket from the top shelf in the closet, she curled up on the chaise lounge to wait for morning.

When daylight finally crept in around the drawn drapes, Kate rose from her cramped position and hurried for a shower. When she entered the kitchen, Jon was nowhere to be seen. She left there, walked down the hall and pushed open the door to the pool room. He was busy at work. To the right of the room, black plastic garbage bags, filled to the top, sagged against the wall. Jon was skimming the top of the water and dragging out hunks of garbage. She walked over and stood beside him.

"You've worked all night?"

He nodded without speaking.

"I want to help, Jon. What do you want me to do first?"

"I don't need you here right now. I want to get as much debris as possible out before I open the drain. You'll need to run into town and do some shopping." He looked at her face but Kate could tell he was avoiding her eyes. "I'm afraid you'll have to start from scratch. There's nothing left in the refrigerator or freezer and all the shelves are empty." He lifted a soggy box of cornflakes from the net and dropped it into the bag.

"I'll be back in a couple of hours," she said.

When Kate returned from her shopping, she spent the rest of the morning restocking the pantry and cabinets. Pounds of poultry and seafood and meat had to be divided and rewrapped for the freezer. At one o'clock she stopped to make sandwiches for lunch. Jon was still skimming when she called him to eat.

They sat at the table without speaking. Any intimacy they had ever shared seemed to be lost in a nebulous world that defied explanation. Kate feared with all her heart that the delicate bond that had taken months to build could never be put together again. Her despair was at its lowest ebb.

A tap sounded on the terrace door. Silas stood on the other side, grinning. Kate heard Jon draw in a violent breath. She was afraid for all of them. She rose and followed Jon to the door.

"Mr. Ames. Ma'am. Glad to see you back. How was your trip to North Caro—"

"Silas." Jon's voice stopped him cold. "Did you let anyone inside the gates while we were gone?"

"Only the pretty lady." His smile faded. "She said she had something she'd promised you, and wanted to drop it off. She said you were expecting it. Did I do wrong?"

"Wrong?" The raging fury in his voice was unmistakable. "You have the nerve to ask me that? My God, do you think I went to the trouble of installing a security system just so some buffoon could throw open the gates and let in the whole wide world?"

"But the lady said—"

Jon raised his fist as if to strike Silas. "I don't give a damn what was said."

Kate touched his arm. "Jon, please—"

"Shut up, Kathleen. This is between Silas and me." His eyes glared at Kate before he turned back to the little man in front of him. Silas seemed to shrink before Kate's eyes. "You had no right to allow anyone in while we were gone. You betrayed the trust I put in you."

"I'm sorry."

"That's not good enough. Get your things together and get out, Silas. You and your wife are fired. If I catch either of you within these gates again, I'll have you arrested."

"Jon," Kate said. "Emily's going to have a baby."

"Well, I didn't get her pregnant." He slammed the glass door and stalked away.

Kate was rooted to the spot where she stood. She would never have believed Jon capable of such cruelty. She watched Silas as he walked toward the old pickup. His limp seemed more bothersome than usual, and she ached for him. She knew he could no more understand Jon's anger than she herself could. By the time she joined him back in the poolroom, he seemed to have calmed somewhat. Kate decided to give him time to cool down further before she talked to him about Silas.

The odor had improved considerably. The retractable ceiling allowed fresh air swept down and helped cleanse the room. On the far wall, the obscene drawing lay buried beneath a cream-colored coat of wet, glossy paint. In the pool, the last few inches of brackish water was draining away, and the filthy sides showed the amount of work still ahead of them. Jon was busy with screwdrivers and wrenches, dismantling the filter. He looked at Kate as she approached.

"Don't say anything, Kathleen. I don't want to hear it. I know you like Silas; I like him, too. But what he did was inexcusable. And I don't want to hear any more about it." He glanced at the sinking water in the pool. "It'll drain out pretty fast. If you want to help there's scouring powders and sponges over there." He motioned his head toward a box of cleaning supplies. "It's going to take a lot of scrubbing to get it clean. You don't have to help. It's up to you."

"Of course, I'll help. It's just that I don't understand. Jon, who was the lady that Silas was talking about?"

"Silas made a mistake. There was no lady. Now, if you want to help, I suggest you get busy. You'll have to hook up the water hose. It's over there in the corner."

Kate started to turn away, then stopped and took a step back in Jon's direction.

He stopped turning the wrench.

"I'm only going to say this to you one time, Kathleen. What happened in this house is never to be mentioned again—*not even hinted at*. Not with me. Not with anybody." His eyes blazed against hers, hot and unblinking. "Do you understand that? Because if you can't erase it from your mind, then you'd better find somewhere else to live. There's no room for you here. As far as I'm concerned *it never happened.* Therefore, there's nothing to remember."

"But—"

"Leave it alone, Kathleen."

Kate nodded without speaking and turned from him again and set about to do her work. She pulled on rubber gloves and boots and dragged the hose down into the shallow end of the pool where the water had already drained away. Globs of chocolate had gathered into one spot and clung to the tile; flour made a pasty mess and bonded tight; blood stained the grout between the tiles and had to be scoured with a stiff brush. Kate scrubbed the rest of the day and hardly got further than one corner.

The rest of the week passed with her down in the cavernous shell of the empty pool. Nights found Kate with aching shoulders and stiff hands from the hard scrubbing. She and Jon rarely spoke. Kate felt a certain sense of victory the day they finished the cleaning and filled the pool with sparkling clean water. It seemed at last the nightmare was finally behind them. Jon turned on the electrical system and the familiar hum of the filter sounded soothing and musical.

Supper that night was taken in the now-familiar stony silence.

Jon glanced up from his plate. "How about a game of Scrabble after supper?"

"I don't think so," Kate murmured. "I think I'd just like to go to bed."

"Are you okay?"

"I'm tired."

"You go on to bed and let me clean up here."

Kate needed no urging and left for the solitude and comfort of her room. After a shower, she sat on the edge of her bed and thought about her life. In spite of her resolve, she began to weep. Once the tears started to come, she found it impossible to stop them. She wept for her exhaustion, for her pain and confusion. She wept for Emily and Silas, and the baby. Mostly she wept for the closeness she and Jon had shared, and lost.

"Kathleen?"

Kate raised her head from her hands and forced her sobs into silence. She wiped her stiff fingers across her cheeks.

Jon stepped into the room. "Why are you crying?"

Kate shook her head and stared at her red, roughened hands. "I'm just tired, I guess."

He walked around in front of her and took her hands in his. "You'd never cry from being tired. No, it's more than that. Forgive me for making you so unhappy." He slipped to the thick carpet at her feet and laid his head in her lap. "I never meant to hurt you—not in a million years would I hurt you."

Kate let the tips of her fingers touch his hair. She dare not say the wrong thing. "It's not just me. It's Emily. I worry about her and the baby."

Jon raised his head and looked at her. "Do you want me to see Silas and try to get them back? I will, you know. I'll apologize to him. I overreacted—I know that now. I wouldn't blame him if he never spoke to me again." He rose. "But first I must apologize to you and ask your forgiveness. I had no right to treat you as I did. I promise you now: I'll never raise my voice to you again in anger."

She rubbed her crinkled brow, not really understanding. "You had your reasons," she said. "But having Emily and Silas back would be the nicest thing."

"If it's within my power they'll be back tomorrow." He leaned toward her and kissed her cheek. "Good night, my dear. Sleep well."

For the first night since their return from North Carolina, Kate slept the night through. The sleep was deep and dreamless.

The next morning she looked up from wiping off the breakfast table and listened. There it was, the familiar clatter of the old pick-up Silas drove back and forth to work. The truck pulled into view and Kate hurried to the door and waited. She saw Emily wrench open the truck door and rush across the yard. Kate met her on the terrace and opened her arms.

TWENTY-ONE

There was an extended break in the weather and Jon spent time outdoors with Silas discussing the placement of new shrubbery. On the morning of Kate's party for her friends from the office, the two men were busy planning a rock garden and waterfall.

"Kathleen," Jon called, stopping on the rug placed just inside the door. "We're running into Wilson's Nursery to order some things for the garden. Do you need anything?"

Kate glanced at Emily. "You finish polishing the silver, I'll be right back." Going through the breakfast room, she met Jon at the doors leading to the terrace.

"You can pick up a couple bottles of wine. I think we have enough, but you can never be sure. Now don't forget, our guests will be here at eight."

He smiled at her with good-natured patience. "I'll be back in plenty of time."

Kate watched as Jon joined Silas in the old truck and they rattled away. She rejoined Emily, who continued polishing the diminishing mound of silverware. "I don't know who loves gardening more, Jon or Silas." Kate said. "Just give Jon some dirt to stick his hands into and he's happy."

"Silas would never be happy doing anything else," Emily said. "It just about broke his heart when Mr. Ames fired him." She laid down the polishing cloth and looked at Kate. "You know, he would never talk about it. The only thing he ever said was that it was his fault."

"It wasn't his fault, Emily. I'm not sure it was anybody's fault."

"Well, I only know we're happy to be back." She laughed. "Plus he doubled our salaries."

"I didn't know, but I'm not surprised," Kate said. "He's really a good man."

"Yes, he is. And guess what, we bought a car—a real car, which we'll need when the baby comes. It's not new, but a really good one." She smiled. "Lordy, I missed you."

"And I missed you, too," Kate said with a smile. "And the baby." Then the smile faded and she looked serious. "But as I cautioned you the day you and Silas came back to work: we must never talk about that particular time. Jon will not allow it to even be mentioned and we have to accept his wishes." Kate patted her on the arm and smiled before gathering up the gleaming silver and lining it on the buffet. "Now, let's see about starting on the food."

"Who did you say is coming?"

"Old friends. Friends from where I used to work." She looked at Emily and smiled. "Wonderful, dear friends."

"Do you miss working?"

"No. But I do miss the people. They're the closest thing I had to a family, until I met Jon. And, of course, now I have you." She stopped and patted Emily on the stomach. "And before long, the baby."

Emily laughed. "I bet you're looking forward to seeing them—" Her words were cut off by the ringing of the telephone.

"Will you get that?" Kate asked as she buried her hands into a bowl of unpeeled shrimp.

Emily picked up the phone. "Ames' residence," she said. "Hello." She waited. "Is anyone there?" She hung up and turned.

Kate's head jerked up. "Who was it?"

"I don't know. But they were there. I could hear breathing. Then they just hung up."

"If it was important, they'll call back," Kate said. But the call made her uneasy. *Seems like a lot of things make me uneasy these days*, she thought. Throughout the remainder of the day she caught herself glancing at the phone on the wall. It did not ring again.

Marty and Dixie were the first to arrive for the dinner.

"Kevin's going by to pick up Sally," Dixie said and nudged Kate in the ribs.

"Lord, help us," Marty said. "There she goes, presuming again."

Dixie handed her coat to Kate and turned to look at Jon. "So, we meet at last," she said.

"You must be Dixie."

"Guilty."

"I'm pleased to meet you." Jon said, and looked at Marty. "I feel as if I already know the whole bunch."

Kate turned from hanging up the coats. "So I guess introductions aren't necessary." She motioned to the sofas and chairs. "Can I get anybody a drink?"

Jon led Kate to a chair. "Why don't you sit down with your friends and let me tend bar," he said. "Besides, I'm very good at mixing drinks."

Dixie laughed. "I bet you're good at a lot—"

Kate jumped to her feet and grabbed Dixie by the arm. "Why don't you help me bring in the hors d'oeuvres?"

"*What'd I do*?" Dixie sputtered as Kate dragged her through the doorway into the kitchen.

"What were you going to say?"

"That he was probably good at a *lot* of things." She grinned. "And I bet I'm right."

Kate handed her a tray of food. "Dixie, please behave."

She patted Kate's arm. "Of course, my dear. But if it wasn't for Marty, and I was a few years younger, friend or no, I'll be damned if I wouldn't try to drag him off to my lair. Lord, Kate, he's mighty fine."

Any reply Kate might have made was interrupted as Sally and Kevin arrived and she and Dixie rejoined the others in the living room. As the evening progressed, Kate was aware of Dixie's intense scrutiny of Jon. She seemed totally fascinated.

The evening wound down all too soon for Kate. Around eleven the guests started gathering their coats to leave, but it was closer to eleven-thirty when all the good nights were finally said and the last one out the door.

"It was a good party, wasn't it?" Kate asked after they had gone.

"A very good party. I'd like to get to know your friends better," Jon said. "I was impressed with Marty. He really knows the financial markets."

"I'm glad you like them. They mean a lot to me," she said. "And thank you for giving the party just the right touch. You put everyone at ease. That, sir, is the requirement of a good host, and you filled the role perfectly."

He seemed pleased by her praise and dropped a light kiss on her up-turned lips.

"Why don't you go ahead and lie down. I'll tidy up here," he offered. "Besides, you must be awfully tired."

"You're sure you don't mind?"

"No, of course not."

Kate lay down on the bed and pulled the corner of the bedspread over her legs, not meaning to sleep. But she did. Sometime later, the ringing of the telephone awakened her. In the distance, she could hear Jon talking, occasionally raising his voice. She reached for the phone on the bedside table and eased the receiver off the hook.

"...or I'll come up there, Jonnie. I swear to you, I will." The voice was throaty and sensual; a Marilyn Monroe voice.

The slam of a receiver sounded loud in Kate's ear.

"Jonathan, you bastard," the voice said. "Don't you dare hang up on me." The line seemed to crackle with anger.

Kate held her phone a moment longer, but the line had already gone dead. The house was cast into blackness when Jon turned off the lights in the other rooms. She heard the studio door open, then close again.

Kate tossed and turned the rest of the night. She kept hearing the voice on the phone. When daylight finally arrived, she was already up and showered. She would give Dixie a couple more hours before she showed up on her doorstep.

Jon was still behind the closed door of his studio.

A little after nine Kate left the house. She intended to stop by and invite Dixie to go shopping and treat them both to a fancy lunch. There was so much she couldn't tell Dixie, but the nearness of her old friend would offer a measure of comfort. Later, when she rang the Martin's doorbell there was no answer. So that the trip to town would not be a total waste, Kate swung by the market and shopped for groceries. She was gone less than two hours when she drove back up the driveway and parked the car.

She opened the door and dragged the sack across the seat. Just as she picked it up and turned around, Jon pushed back the sliding door and stepped onto the terrace. He was wearing his topcoat and carrying a small travel bag. The color drained from his face.

"Where are you going?"

"Kathleen, I'm sorry but something's come up." He shifted his gaze from her and hefted the bag in his hand.

Kate felt foolish as she stood there holding the sack of groceries, a stalk of celery sticking out the top.

"Will you be back? You're not coming back, are you, Jon?"

He took a step toward her. "Of course, I'll be back. Probably tomorrow. I left you a note on the table." He looked tired as he seemed to search for something else to say. "I have to go now. The plane's waiting."

"You're flying?"

He nodded. "A small charter. It's all in the note." He tossed the bag up on the front seat of the Navigator. "If something happens that I can't make it back tomorrow, I'll call."

"It's another woman, isn't it, Jon?"

"Kathleen, please. There's no other woman in my life." He climbed into the car and slammed the door. He didn't look at her again as he started the engine and turned around.

"I don't believe you, Jon," Kate said as he drove away.

She carried the groceries inside and set them on the table. Jon's note lay propped against the napkin holder. Basically it said what she already knew, adding only that he would be staying at the Hearthside Hotel in Washington if she needed him. Kate folded the note in half and ran a thumbnail down the crease. Anger swept over her in a tidal wave, anger toward herself, but mostly anger toward Jon. She deserved better than this. The trip had to be in response to last night's call. Kate knew she *had* to find out what was going on. She reached for the phone directory, found the number and dialed.

"Eastern Direct Shuttle Service."

"What time is your next flight to Washington D.C.?"

"We have a noon flight."

"That's less than an hour from now."

"Yes, ma'am. Would you like a reservation?"

Kate knew if she stopped to think about it, she'd lose her nerve. She would have to hurry. "Yes, please. I'll be right there. The name's Kathleen Ames."

Still wearing her coat, Kate grabbed her purse and keys, closed the door behind her and hurried to her car. As she drove away, she remembered the ice cream in the bottom of the grocery bag. It was chocolate and would make a mess when it melted. *Damn him*, Kate thought. *Damn him for making me do this.*

A short time later the plane landed in Washington. Kate entered the terminal and wondered which way to turn. She followed the exit signs to the street and was relieved to see a taxi. The driver motioned her in.

"Can you take me to the Hearthside Hotel?"

"You got it."

Speeding through the traffic, Kate wondered if she had lost her mind. *What am I going to do when I get there? What if I see Jon? Worse yet, what if he sees me?* Just a few short hours ago, she was safe in her own home surrounded by all the things that mattered to her. Now here she was in a city she knew nothing about, and facing God knows what. *So you'll wing it,* she told herself. *You're a smart broad, Kate. Improvise.*

"Here you are, lady," the driver said as he stopped the cab in front of a three-storied Georgian structure. "That'll be thirty dollars even."

Kate handed him a fifty. "Keep the change."

"Hey, thanks lady."

She looked at her watch as she entered the hotel lobby. It was almost two-thirty.

"May I help you?" asked the desk clerk.

"I'd like a room please."

"Certainly." He handed her a pen to sign the registry, stretched over the counter and looked around. "Luggage?"

She signed her name and handed the pen back.

"The airline lost it." The lie came easy.

The clerk turned the register around and read the name.

"Here you are, Miss Spencer," he said, sliding the key card across the counter. "Room 202, directly in front of the elevator. That'll be one seventy-five."

Kate counted out the money and handed it to him. Then she picked up the card and headed toward the elevator. The second-floor light went out on the number pad over the doors just as she pushed the button. On the way up, Kate's legs threatened to collapse beneath her weight. The elevator stopped on the second floor and the door whooshed open. She stepped out. A man with silver-streaked hair brushing the collar of his chesterfield topcoat, was making his way toward the end of the hallway. Kate gasped. *Jon!* She stepped back and felt for the doors behind her, but they had already closed. *Lord,* she silently prayed, *don't let him turn around.* To Kate's relief he continued on to the end of the hall, opened a door and disappeared inside.

Kate stepped across the hall and forced her shaking fingers to fit the card into the slot and slide it down. Once inside, she sat on the edge of the bed and hugged her arms around her chilled body. In spite of the gnawing hunger in her stomach, she knew if she tried to eat she'd throw up. Slipping off her shoes, she lay back against the pillows and humped up inside her coat. Slowly she began to unwind and straighten her body on the bed. She had to find out what was going on. She owed it to herself and to Jon, to their marriage. A calming began to settle over her and the rapid beating of her heart slowed.

She rested for a time, then carried her purse to the bathroom and spilled its contents on the counter. By the time she washed her face and ran a comb through her hair, her hand was steady enough to put on fresh makeup. After piling the things back into the purse, she ran her hands over her dress and tried to smooth out the wrinkles in her coat. She slipped on her shoes, went to the door, and opened it just a crack. No one was around. At the end of the corridor, a door led to the stairs. Kate slipped out of the room, held the knob so the catch wouldn't make a loud click, and closed the door behind her. She darted down the hallway and vanished into the stairwell.

Seconds later, she opened the door and stepped out into the lobby. Everything seemed normal. A couple was checking in at the desk. Outside, a light snow was falling. Kate picked up an abandoned newspaper from a sofa, walked across the room to a dimly lit corner and planted herself in a winged-back chair partially concealed by a fig tree. The chair faced the elevator. Holding the paper in front of her, she waited.

The minutes ticked off. Kate crossed her legs and pulled the paper closer. Each time the elevator door opened, she peeked around the edge of the paper. Few people were coming and going. The hotel was not doing a brisk business. Suddenly a sultry laugh floated across the room. Kate lowered the paper just enough to see over the top. And then she saw them. Julie and Jon. Their arms were linked and Jon had an intense look on his face as he gazed down at the lovely creature beside him. The four-inch heels on white kid boots brought the little head almost to Jon's shoulder. Julie was wearing a longhaired white fur coat and white gloves. The coat was opened up the front showing the pink turtleneck sweater-dress underneath. Platinum hair, fluffed around an oval face, framed dark eyes and a beautiful mouth. Kate was reminded of a pink and white powder puff.

They walked across the floor and entered the dining room. Kate took several deep breaths before she dared to rise from her chair and, using the newspaper as a shield, wander casually about the lobby. Her hands were clammy as she headed for the entrance to the dining room. She glanced in. Jon and Julie were sitting in a booth against the far wall. Jon had his back to the entrance. Julie sat across the table, facing the room. The booths were high-backed and separated by planters that trailed vines and ivy across the top. The booth adjoining theirs was empty.

There was no hostess on duty. *I can do this, I can do this*. Kate kept the mantra going across her brain as she waited until the server was at Jon's booth before she strolled into the room and in their general direction. She kept her head low and seemed to be lost in the article she was reading, when she found herself at the booth connected to the back of theirs. Julie's eyes never wavered from Jon's face. Kate felt her empowerment expand and she was more than a little impressed by her audacity: the old Kate would be home in Woodway curled into a fetal position and whimpering. She sat down with her back to Jon and fought back a sudden desire to giggle. When the server arrived to take her order, she kept her voice low and ordered coffee. After the coffee came, Kate settled back in the booth and turned her ear slightly to one side. The room was quiet and nearby conversations easily overheard. Even whispered conversations, if one took the pains to listen.

"...then why did you come, if you don't intend to stay?" The voice sounded childish with a touch of pettiness.

"To tell you one more time that it's over." Jon's voice sounded masculine and firm. "My God, how many times do I have to tell you?"

"Until you make me believe it. You still love me, Jonnie; we both know that. You won't leave me again."

"I'm going back to Woodway tomorrow."

"Back to *her*," the voice hissed.

"That's where I belong. There's nothing for me here. I shouldn't have come this time. I'm sorry I did."

"I'm here. Am I not enough?"

"At one time maybe, but not anymore."

"I can't live without you. You do know that, don't you?"

"You'll find somebody else. You always did before."

"But they didn't mean anything to me. It was always you."

"Then why didn't you leave the others alone? God Jules, you even slept with Georgy. Do you have no self-respect? You know the dangers of free sex, all the bad stuff that's floating around out there on the streets—stuff that can put your lights out."

"I'll stop. I promise, I will."

"No, you won't. It's just like your coke habit, you can't give it up. You're hooked and you know it."

The laugh was deep and throaty. "Well, have you not turned into a self-righteous do-gooder. Just what has made you so pure, Jonnie? Has your new wife turned you into a prude?"

"Leave my wife out of this."

"Come on, Jonnie, tell Julie all about her. Is she good in bed? Is she as good as I am? Does she do the things that I used to—those special things you like?"

"Shut up, Jules."

"What do you see in her, Jon?" The voice seemed to mellow. "What did she have that you found so irresistible. You owe it to me, to at least tell me that."

"It's hard to explain. And I'm not sure I even want to."

"Well, *try,* lover boy. Tell me about this precious princess who's turned you into a blithering idiot."

"She's not a princess," Jon said. "And I'm sure as hell not a blithering idiot."

"Point taken," Julie said. "But please, Jonnie. Tell me about her."

"She's a good person, Jules. She reminded me of a simpler, more honest world; a world where people really care about each. It would never cross her mind to cheat or lie. I don't think she knows how. I'm not sure, but maybe she reminds me of my mother in a lot of ways."

"Your mother? Jonathan!"

"Don't go there, Jules. Don't even think it. It's something you wouldn't understand in a million years."

"But did you have to *marry* her?"

"I had to get out of the fast lane, it was killing me—the booze and drugs. The sex. I was becoming desensitized, and I couldn't take it. As a matter of fact, the first time I saw her was after one of our many fights, and I think I wasn't caring if I lived or died. It scared the hell out of me." He paused for a moment. "What I wanted, and what I thought was so important, suddenly meant very little. I want a quiet life. And I want a family."

"And I can't give you that."

"No."

They were silent for a moment. Then Jon spoke again.

"I'm just a farmer, Jules. A farmer who's getting on in years. I'm not cool and I'm not a playboy and it was time I quit trying to act like one."

"Do you love her, Jonnie?"

Kate turned the coffee cup on the saucer and held her breath. She was afraid if she breathed she wouldn't hear his answer.

"Yes."

"The hell, you do."

"Listen to me, Jules—it's over for us. I'm going home to my wife and I won't be back. You can choose to believe it, or choose to ignore it, the decision is purely yours."

"Don't be mad at me, please." The voice sounded like a small child begging for approval. "I'm sorry I'm being bitchy. When you left me this time last year and said you wouldn't be back, I didn't believe you. But this time I do."

"Then you'll leave me alone? No more phone calls. And no more trips to the house—that little bit of drama was vulgarity in its highest form."

"I'll promise, if you'll let me stay with you tonight."

"I can't do that. I won't put everything I have on the line. It's not worth it."

"You're saying *I'm* not worth it. Well, I remember the times you were glad to spend the night with me. You certainly paid enough for the privilege." The voice increased in pitch. "Now you don't want to dirty your hands on me."

Kate could detect movement behind her.

"Sit down and lower your voice. You're making a scene."

"I'm leaving, Jonathan. You left me the last time, now it's my turn. Go back to Hicksville and your slutty little wife. You both deserve each other. You're common, Jon. Common and crude. You've turned into a conservative monster. My God, I wouldn't be surprised if you've not turned into a Republican. Like I said: *a blithering idiot*. Right now I find you the least attractive man on the face of the earth and I hope I never see you again."

Almost before Kate realized what was happening, a blur of white brushed past her booth. Like a prancing pony, its nose in the air, the proud head thrown back, a defiant chin jutted forward. There was a lingering odor of musk.

Behind her, Kate heard the sound of ice cubes rattle against glass. "Oh, Miss," Jon called out. "Would you bring me another brandy— make it a double."

Kate waited until the server was at Jon's booth with his drink before she slid out of her seat and slipped away. She went straight to her room and called the airport. There was a flight leaving at seven. She made the reservation and called downstairs for a taxi. She left the hotel, had dinner at the airport, and at seven-fifteen the plane lifted off the ground and she was on her way home.

TWENTY-TWO

Exhausted almost to the point of immobility, Kate found it nearly impossible to move the next morning, and stayed in bed a long time. Jon returned home around noon but made no mention of his trip. Kate asked no questions. He spent the remainder of the day in his studio, not emerging until late afternoon. When he did, it was as if nothing out of the ordinary had happened.

"How about a swim before supper?' he suggested.

"Sure. I hadn't planned on cooking anyway since we have all those delicious leftovers from the party the other night. I hope you don't mind."

"I don't mind anything you do," he said.

Kate didn't realize how strained she was until the warm water closed in over her body. Slowly the tension drained away as she stretched out and let the water support her weight. Jon swam up beside her and dribbled water over her head.

"By the way, I stopped by the telephone office today," he said. "I thought maybe we needed an unlisted number. You know, to keep away the crank calls." He dove under the water before she could reply. They swam and splashed for the next hour. The telephone wasn't mentioned again.

A week later snow flowers pushed their heads through the thawing earth. Bright spots of lavender and gold dotted the area outside the terrace doors. The shrubbery Silas had planted with such loving care, had taken root and the delicate green lace of new growth was beginning to show around the edges. Kate felt revitalized as she stood in the doorway and looked at nature working her finest miracles. Silas came around the house and up the steps.

"Good morning, Silas."

"Morning, ma'am." He pulled the old hat from his head. "Is Mr. Ames here?"

Kate nodded. "He's in his studio."

He seemed worried. "Could I see him a minute?"

"I'll get him for you." Kate turned away and walked to the closed studio door and tapped lightly. "Jon, Silas is here to see you."

Shortly, Jon joined the gardener on the terrace and the two men talked for several minutes. Kate saw Jon slip something into the smaller man's hand and Silas tried to push his hand away, but Jon was insistent.

"If there's anything we can do just let us know," Kate heard Jon say as he closed the door. She looked through the glass and saw Silas heading for his truck.

"Is anything wrong?"

"Emily's sister has had a heart attack and they need time off to go up there," he said. "I don't know which scared him more, the sister's illness or having to ask me for permission." He frowned. "I wish he wouldn't be afraid of me. But then, I guess that's my fault." Jon looked sad as he spoke. "Anyway, there's nothing around here that won't keep, and I'll help you with the house. I told him to take all the time they need and their jobs will be here when they get back."

"When are they leaving?"

"First thing in the morning. He said there were several things he needed to do today, just in case they have to be gone more than a few days."

"I saw you give something to him. What was it?'

"Just a little extra money for the trip. It's about a three hundred mile drive upstate and you know how much gasoline's gone up. I almost couldn't get him to take it."

Kate touched his arm. "That was kind of you. You're a good person."

"No. No, I'm not. It was nothing."

"Nothing to you, maybe. But to Silas, I bet it meant a great deal."

The compliment seemed to strike a responsive cord. He put an arm around her waist and pulled her against him.

"Lady, I don't want to even think about what I would do without you." He held her close for a moment before turning her loose and changing the subject. "How about going out tonight? It's time you got out of the house and away from the kitchen."

"To the Inn?"

"Why don't we try the Country Club for a change. We haven't been there in ages and I hear they have a great new band."

"Maybe I can get you to dance?"

"Maybe."

That evening Kate heard Jon stirring around while he waited for her to dress. He put a

Mancini disc in the player and *Moon River* drifted through the wall speakers into the bedroom. *He's changed,* she thought. *He seems almost happy. Maybe tonight...*

"Don't ruin it by trying to push him too fast," she whispered to her reflection in the mirror. "Let him make the first move, in his own time, his own way."

Later, they drove down the lighted driveway. The heavy gates swung open and closed again behind them. Silently Jon reached for Kate's hand in the darkened car. There seemed no need for words.

The atmosphere at the old-fashioned County Club was relaxed and mellow. The new band was good, playing tunes from their generation; easy listening, easy dancing tunes. Jon held Kate close as they danced on the dimly lit floor. He was drinking more than usual. As the evening wound down, the band played *Good Night, Irene.* Kate could hear him humming under his breath, next to her ear. He kissed her as the music finished and the lights returned to normal.

"This is nice," he said as he continued to hold her. "Have you had a good time?"

"Lovely."

"I think maybe I'm a little drunk," Jon said. "Would you mind driving?"

"Be happy to."

On the way home, Jon hummed a list of tunes that the band had played earlier in the evening. Kate smiled to herself as she drove through the night. The lighted driveway beyond the gates welcomed them. Once inside the house Kate was still feeling hopeful. Choosing the gown she had been saving for some special reason, she's just never been sure why; until now. Drawing the black satin over her head, the gown cascaded around her. The side-split exposed her shapely leg to the thigh, making her look more daring than she felt. A slinky fringe at the neckline rained down over the bodice. *Sexy.* Kate cringed. *Bodies without all their girl parts can't be sexy,* hissed across her mind. She heard the tinkle of crystal and knew Jon was having another drink. She turned off the lamp and slipped beneath the sheet. And she waited. The room was lit only by lamplight from the living room. Shortly, a form was outlined in the doorway.

"Kathleen?"

"Come in, Jon."

He crossed the room, turned the edge of the covers back and slid in between the sheets. The odor of brandy was heavy in the room.

He reached for her. "I just want to hold you," he said.

Kate closed the space between them and felt his arms go around her.

"I adore you, Jon," she said. The great burden that had been weighing her down, lifted from her heart. At last she was free. "I think I've always loved you."

His arms tightened. "I know you do. I love you, too," he said. "Much more than I ever thought possible at one time."

Kate pressed the length of her body to his. She felt him stir beneath her touch. Jon buried his hands in her hair as his mouth came down over hers, and she melted into the kiss. He tasted of brandy and tobacco. Running his hand down the curve of her hip, he touched the smooth flesh of her leg. The heat from his hand seared like liquid fire. Kate touched the lapels of his silk dressing gown and realized that he was naked. She trailed kisses across his chest. He gasped and pulled her beneath him. Her world was spinning out of control and she clung to him for her life—for her survival.

"Kathleen." He breathed against her hair. "My darling, Kathleen."

Kate fought back the urge to hurry him, as she felt the hardness of his body against hers. He moved his hand across her taut stomach and dipped between her legs where dew-drenched petals lay waiting to blossom. She felt pressure from his throbbing erection and instinctively tightened against the final invasion of the core of her being. He pulled back slightly as if questioning her acceptance of him. Then her body molded to his, and she gave herself over completely, and was filled with a sense of well-being and completeness. A oneness.

The melody made by the surrender of two hearts directed the rhythm of their universe. Their breath and blood mingled, giving life to each other—and a reason for being. The dim room seemed infused with an aurora of transfiguration and their passion reached the ultimate peak.

"Don't turn me loose," Jon pleaded. "I'm drowning."

Kate locked her arms and legs around his body and together they gave in to a nova of brilliant and utter devotion. Then the natural order of the galaxy began to right itself. Jon kissed her closed eyes and whispered his love, before moving away to lie beside her.

"Only now do I understand what it means to be born again," he said. "Here with you, within these walls of peace and trust and tranquility, I've found an easing of my mind, a calming of the spirit far greater than anything I ever expected. And I feel like the unraveling has finally stopped. I'm a whole person now and you made it happen." He pulled her close to him. "You've been so patient. There's much to overcome, so much to put behind me."

He touched her chest, his fingertips caressing the scarred tissue.

Kate knotted her fists and stifled back a curse.

"Please don't be embarrassed, not with me—not ever with me. You should never feel unworthy, my darling. God gave you more beauty and perfection than anyone I know."

He touched her chin with his forefinger and turned her face toward him. His eyes held hers.

"Don't take unto yourself the sins of the world, Kathleen. You're not strong enough. Nobody is." He leaned over and kissed her rib hardened chest.

Tears brimmed in Kate's eyes and spilled down her face. "Jon." Her lips were stiff and tight as she forced herself to speak. "Can we talk about Julie?"

He pulled away ever so slightly. "Not yet. But soon. I promise you, soon." He drew her against him and covered her shoulders with the sheet. "Now we sleep."

"Yes, my darling. Now we can sleep." Kate smiled to herself and remembered her wish from the *Trevi* fountain in Rome. It had finally come true.

Throughout the night, Jon cradled Kate in his arms. The warmth of his body kept her safe and she slept in an innocent presumption that the evil of the world was far away.

Sunlight streaked through the windows when Kate woke to an empty bed. She moved with an unfamiliar stiffness as her body reminded her of the wondrous lovemaking. Memories of the night before flooded her mind and she blushed. Slipping into a negligee, she padded to the kitchen.

"Good morning," Jon said, smiling.

"Good morning to you. How long have you been up?"

"Hours, sleepyhead. Coffee?"

"Love it."

"You sit down right here," he said, pulling out a chair. "I'm going to make our breakfast."

"You don't have to do that."

"Sssh. I know I don't *have* to, but I want to. So humor me." He pushed a loaf of bread in her direction. "Here, I'll let you slice while I do the rest."

Kate pulled out one of the cabinet drawers and looked inside. "Wonder what Emily did with the bread knife?"

"It's hard to tell." He picked up a carving knife from the counter and handed it to her. "Use this one, but be careful. Silas had a sharpening fit the other day and sharpened every knife on the place. Don't cut yourself."

Kate sliced the bread and Jon hummed as he cracked eggs into a bowl and whipped them for

French toast. They took a long time eating. For once Jon ignored the morning paper and centered his attention on Kate. They talked of unimportant things, occasionally touching, a cheek, a hand.

"Let's leave the dishes for later and go for an early swim. How about it?" he asked.

Had he suggested boarding the space shuttle for Mars or trekking to the Swiss Alps to yodel, Kate would have considered it a perfectly reasonable request.

At the edge of the pool, Jon took her hand and together they jumped into the deep water. Surfacing at the same time, he swam to her side. Touching her face, he brushed the wet hair back from her eyes.

"Race you to the other end?" he challenged.

Kate laughed "Okay. But don't let me win like you always do."

"You got it." He flipped over and disappeared beneath the water.

Reaching the far end ahead of her, he hung onto the edge of the pool and waited.

"Slowpoke," he said, disappearing beneath the water and grabbing for her legs.

Sputtering Kate bobbed like a cork before finally being yanked under. She kicked at him, but missed. They frolicked and flirted and teased until sexual arousal pulled them together.

"I'm afraid I'm going to find it difficult to get my fill of you," he said.

Before she could respond, the doorbell from the terrace sounded.

"Damn," Kate muttered.

"It's just Silas. Nobody else could get in. Stay here. I'll see what he wants."

Climbing out of the pool, Jon took his blue and white striped terrycloth robe from the rack. Slipping his arms into the sleeves, he turned and smiled.

"Stay away from the deep end until I get back," he warned.

Kate smiled and silently crossed her heart.

Jon had absolutely forbidden her to swim alone. The few times he had to leave the pool, he always cautioned her to stay in the shallow end.

"But I can drown just as easily in the shallow end as the deep," she always protested.

"No, you can't," he continued to insist.

Kate had never failed to obey his wishes and today was no exception.

She turned on her back and drifted aimlessly on the water, waiting for him to return. The hum of the filter was the only sound in the room. Visions of the previous night filled her mind and set her heart to racing. Kate was as close to complete happiness as she could ever remember. She floated. She waited.

"What's taking him so long?" she wondered aloud.

Fearing something bad had happened regarding Emily's sister, Kate climbed out of the water and reached for her robe. As she opened the door and stepped into the hallway, puddles of water ran from her feet and spread like dark stains on the parquet flooring. She made her way to the breakfast room where unwashed dishes still cluttered the table.

"Jon?" she called.

The house was still. Peering through the glass doors, she saw the terrace was empty. Both cars were in their usual places. The decrepit old pickup truck was nowhere to be seen. Unreasonable fear prickled her spine. She had a nauseous chill.

"Jon," she called again, louder this time. There was no answer.

She turned back toward the main part of the house. Each room she checked was empty. Standing in the living room she glanced toward the studio. Almost cautiously, she approached the door. "Jon?" she whispered

The door swung open in response to her light tap. Then she saw him, seated at his desk with his back to the door.

"Jon, thank goodness I found you." She stepped into the room and walked around in front of him. "Is anything—"

He sat slumped in his chair, his head tilted forward. There was a trace of crimson on the blue material just where his robe came together. And protruding from his chest was the wooden handle of the knife Kate had used just a short time earlier.

TWENTY-THREE

Reality, time and space ceased to exist. Kate raised her head to scream, but an all-consuming fear reduced the scream to a pitiful whimper. She clinched her fingers and bit into the knuckles to fight back the bitter bile that frothed up in her throat and threatened to cut off her breath.

"Don't you dare faint," she ordered herself in a voice that was hard and demanding. "Think about Jon first. He needs help and like it or not you're the only one to do it."

Her sharp words kept her mind from shutting down, and forced her into motion. Legs, heavy with near-paralysis, carried her to the telephone in the living room. Almost calmly she punched in nine-one-one.

"9-1-1. What is your emergency?"

"I need an ambulance and a doctor. My husband's been hurt."

"What's the name?'

"Kathleen Ames. Mrs. Jonathan Ames."

"And where do you live, Mrs. Ames?"

Kate gave the operator precise directions to the house. "Hurry. Oh, please do hurry," she begged.

The next few minutes seemed an eternity.

Kate could feel her eyes, like burning coals, searing wounds into her brain and leaving it damaged beyond repair. She covered the distance from the front door to the door of the studio, and back again, and petitioned God for mercy.

"Let him be all right," she prayed as she twisted the damp belt of her robe. "Don't let him be dead. He's a good person, really he is, and I love him so much." She paced. She fought to breathe, to keep moving.

"Don't take him from me," her litany continued. "Not now. Not when he was starting to love me. Please let me keep him. I'm sorry for all the times I blasphemed Your holy name, and wasn't allowed to have a baby. But if you'll let me keep Jon," she offered a desperate covenant, "I'll be good and never ask for anything else as long as I live. I promise. You don't need him as much as I do. Please God, I'm begging, don't let him die."

The siren sounded faint at first, seemingly far away. The clanging increased until Kate felt her body vibrate with the powerful high-pitched wailing. The intercom buzzed as the yellow button lit up on the control board. She ran to open the gates. Rushing out the front door, she was momentarily stunned as a cold blast of air hit her damp body. Lights flashed from the green and white vehicle as it careened around the circular drive and the screams of the siren faded away.

"Hurry," she said as the attendants retrieved a stretcher from behind the wide door in the back. "He's in there." Kate clutched the arm of the man nearest to her and showed them the way. "Is there a doctor?"

"Yes, ma'am." The attendant motioned to the car just pulling in.

A slightly slumped figure toting a tattered black bag, climbed out of the car and hurried toward her.

"Mrs. Ames." Kate's appearance told him who she was. "I'm Doctor Alden."

"Hurry, please doctor." Kate pushed him across the marble portico and inside the house, immediately behind the rescue squad attendants.

Time crept as she stood still, hands folded in front of her, and waited for word. She heard the phone in the studio being used.

"Inspector Bowman, please." Kate recognized the doctor's voice. "Charlie? Better get over here. Looks like we have a homicide. And bring Al with you. Yeah, DOA. No, Mrs. Ames is here." He paused, listening. "I don't know, Charlie, you'll have to ask her." Kate heard the receiver being replaced.

Dropping into the nearest chair, she rocked back and forth. *Homicide? DOA? What is it all about?* The doctor found her there, slouched in the chair, her head buried in her hands.

"Mrs. Ames," he said, touching her shoulder, "I'm sorry. There was nothing I could do."

Kate looked up through glazed eyes, not understanding. "Is it bad?' she whispered.

"Mrs. Ames, your husband is dead. I'm very sorry." He looked at the two attendants standing in the doorway of the studio. "Davy, you and Terry go on back to town, there's nothing you can do here. I'll stay with Mrs. Ames until Inspector Bowman and the coroner arrive."

The two young men nodded silently and returned the empty stretcher to the vehicle parked outside.

The latch on the studio door clicked as the doctor pulled it shut. He went to the door and looked out over the grounds. They waited.

Promptly, and with much authority, Inspector Bowman came striding through the doorway. Close on his heels was the squatty county coroner.

"Charlie, glad you got here so fast." Doctor Alden extended his hand. "Al," he said with a nod to the coroner, "afraid we've got one for you."

"Mrs. Ames?" the inspector asked, motioning in Kate's direction.

The doctor nodded. "She's in a pretty bad way. She doesn't seem to understand exactly what's happened."

"For real, Doc?"

The doctor shrugged his shoulders. "Seems so, Charlie. But who knows," he said. "Who ever really knows?"

"Mrs. Ames, I'm Inspector Bowman," he said to the vacant staring eyes. He led her to a chair and looked back at the doctor. "I see what you mean." He straightened up and breathed heavily. "Well, show me the body."

The doctor took the two men into the studio as an additional team of serious-looking officials entered the house.

"In here, men," the Inspector said. "And somebody bring in the coroner's stretcher. Oh, and you, Ken, See about closing those gates. We don't want a bunch of reporters and curious spectators tromping all over the place. Everybody and their brother'll be out to see what's going on." He snorted. "People do love a good tragedy, as long as it's not their own."

From what seemed like a million miles away, Kate could hear the efficient-sounding voices of the experts as they set about to do their work. From somewhere beyond the door, flashes of light crept into her peripheral vision. She was vaguely aware of the doctor's nearby presence.

"We're ready to move the body now," she heard a voice say.

The doctor came to stand beside her. He touched her shoulder. "Mrs. Ames would you like to go into another room?"

Kate shook her head. Activity in the doorway of the studio caught her attention and she stood. The wide stretcher was being carefully eased through the narrow opening. A stark white sheet was heaped atop a vague outline that looked like a snow bank. Kate's brain refused to accept what her eyes told her as truth. Blackness engulfed her and she sank to the floor.

From what seemed like a great distance, Kate heard her name being called and fought against the intrusion. Soft cushions cradled her head and she wanted to sleep. She felt a light tap on her cheek.

"Mrs. Ames, it's Doctor Alden. Can you hear me?"

Kate forced her eyes open and looked at the doctor. "Jon's gone? They took him away?"

"Mrs. Ames, your husband's dead."

"No," she hissed. "Why are you lying to me?"

Doctor Alden shook her shoulders. "You must listen to me and hear what I'm saying. They've taken his body. Whoever's assigned to the investigation will be here soon to question you. Do you understand?" He handed her a glass of water and helped her to sit erect on the sofa.

Tears spilled over as she accepted the glass. A look of encouragement showed on the doctor's tired face.

Kate put her bare feet on the carpeted floor and took a couple sips of water. She set the glass on the coffee table and looked at the doctor, her pleading eyes floating on a bed of liquid.

"Is he truly dead? Might you be wrong?"

"I'm sorry. Mrs. Ames, but you must be strong for the ordeal ahead. The others will be back soon and there'll be many questions asked. Would you like to change your clothes?"

Only then did Kate realize how cold the wet bathing suit felt against her body. She hurried from the room and slipped into the warm fleecy sweats that gave a measure of needed comfort to her over-exposed body. The buzzer sounded from the front gate just as she came back into the living room.

"That'll be the investigative team now," the doctor said.

Shortly, a stranger came through the doorway with an assistant trailing along behind.

"Mrs. Ames, I'm Lieutenant Simon and this is Sergeant Cowan," he said. "We've been assigned to the case and will be asking you some questions. I hope you feel up to answering."

"Gentlemen," Kate nodded to acknowledge the introductions. "I'll do anything I can to help."

The questions continued until early evening. Kate repeated everything she could remember leading up to the time she found Jon in the studio.

"Did your husband have any enemies, Mrs. Ames?" Lieutenant Simon asked while his partner and Doctor Alden looked on. "Someone with whom he'd recently quarreled?"

The obscene message, the wrecking of the pool room, flashed across Kate's mind. After the passage of weeks and no police record of the incident to back her up, would they be likely to believe her *now*? How would she be able to convince these professionals, seasoned doubters all, that she was not conveniently making up the whole thing?

"No, Lieutenant. Not that I know of."

"Were the security gates closed all morning?"

"I'm sure they were."

"Who had access to the house and grounds?"

"My husband, myself, and Silas Hawkins. We each had our own remote."

"Who's Silas Hawkins?' the lieutenant continued to question. "And why would he be allowed to have a control device?"

"He's our gardener. Because he was always coming and going at all hours, Mr. Ames, thought it advisable for him to have free access to the grounds. Jon trusted him completely—and so do I."

"How do I contact this Mr. Hawkins? Do you have his address?"

"I'll get it for you, but he's not home right now. His wife's sister was suddenly taken ill and they left this morning to see about her," Kate explained. "I don't know where the sister lives. Somewhere upstate, I believe."

"Now think hard, Mrs. Ames. Is there nothing else you can tell us, leading up to the time you heard the doorbell ring, while you and your husband were in the pool?"

Kate shook her head. "Nothing."

"And you heard no sign of an altercation while you waited for him to return? No raised voices? No sounds of a struggle?"

Again, Kate shook her head.

"Did your husband seem particularly agitated or worried this morning?"

"Quite the opposite. He was extremely relaxed and perfectly at ease."

The lieutenant stood up and flipped closed the note pad on which he had been writing.

"Well, thanks for your time. I'm afraid for the next few days we're going to have to intrude upon your privacy. The whole area inside the fence will have to be searched for signs of entry and escape. We'll try not to bother you with opening and closing the gates any more than absolutely necessary."

"Lieutenant Simon," Kate said. "Is there any reason why your men can't have one of the remote controls? It certainly would be more convenient for them."

"You wouldn't mind?"

"No, of course not. I'll get it for you."

Kate returned with the control and handed it to the lieutenant.

"Thank you, Mrs. Ames. You've been most helpful. In the meantime, if you think of anything, no matter how slight, that you consider relevant, call me immediately." He handed her a business card.

"The same goes for me, Mrs. Ames," the doctor said. "If you need me, don't hesitate to call. I'm in the book."

"Thank you Doctor Alden," Kate said and showed the men to the door.

TWENTY-FOUR

Kate turned back to the room, letting her eyes drift to the police tape running across the studio door. She had been instructed not to enter the room pending further investigation. The silence of the house was deafening. A deep chill permeated the rooms and caused Kate to shiver. Her head ached and exhaustion crept over her body. Taking two pills the doctor had given her, she shrugged out of her clothes and stretched out on the bed. Late afternoon eased into pale evening, evening into bottomless blackness. The heavily sedated sleep kept her through the night.

Kate awakened with a start, events of the previous day flooding her mind. She lay still, refusing to move and set in motion the reality of her life. The ringing of the telephone forced her to rouse. It was Sally.

"The morning paper just arrived and Mr. Martin insisted that I call. Oh, Kate, how awful. Is there anything we can do? Can I come over and stay with you today?"

"Thank for offering, Sally," Kate said through lips that felt numb and did not move easily. "But I don't think so."

"You shouldn't be alone right now. We're so worried about you."

"Please don't be. If I need anything I'll let somebody know, I promise."

"Okay then, if you're sure. I'll call you later."

"Thanks, Sally." Kate hung up the phone, lay back against the pillows, and listened to the silence of the house. She could hear the ticking of the grandfather clock in the other room. The ticks stopped and the clock struck nine. When she pushed back the covers and stood, a terrible weakness washed over her. She dropped to the edge of the bed and waited for her strength to return. Moments later as she started to the kitchen for a cup of tea, the buzzer sounded from the gate. Kate was in no mood for company.

"Who is it?" she asked into the intercom.

"Kate. It's me. Now open this blasted contraption and let me in."

Kate was standing in the doorway when Dixie barged up the sweeping front steps. By the time she cleared the front door she was huffing for breath.

"I'm getting too old for so much commotion," she wheezed, tossing her over-sized handbag onto a nearby chair.

The sight of the old friend touched an emotional cord in Kate, and she could hold the tears back no longer. Dixie gathered Kate into her arms and led her to the sofa.

"What a despicable thing. What an utterly despicable thing," she said. "How dare someone do this to you." Cradling Kate's head against her remarkable bosom, she smoothed down the uncombed, matted hair. "There, there, my darling, you go on and cry all you want to."

"I don't think I can bear the pain, Dixie. So help me God, I don't believe I can live through this. It's too much."

"You can, Kate. I know you, especially your strengths."

"I'm not strong, not anymore. Loves makes you weak, and the harder you love the weaker you get."

Dixie agreed and handed Kate a handkerchief from her coat pocket.

Kate dabbed at her eyes. "You knew, didn't you?"

"Knew what?"

"That he didn't love me."

"He loved you."

Kate frowned. "Do you really believe that, Dixie?"

Dixie shook her head. "Not believe—*know*. But he *did* have a past."

Kate nodded. "There was someone else."

"I'm not surprised. It was in his eyes."

"But it was over, Dixie. I'd swear it was finished."

Dixie appointed herself in charge of Kate for the rest of the day. At noon she prepared a lunch and wouldn't listen when Kate insisted she wasn't hungry.

"Nonsense. Of course, you're hungry. There's never been a problem yet that an empty stomach helped one whit."

They ate and they talked. The day passed.

"How are things at the office?" Kate asked.

"Kevin gave Sally an engagement ring—a real eye-popper. I was impressed. The boy's got style."

"I'm happy for them. They'll be good for each other. But what about the business, Dixie? How's it going?"

"Not well, I'm afraid. Marty tries not to act concerned, but I haven't lived with him for forty years for nothing. He's worried. He just lost one of his largest accounts to a firm in New York."

"The Deaver account?"

"Yeah. How did you know?"

"Well, I haven't been gone that long. I had a feeling it was going to happen. It's a shame, too. Marty made that man a lot of money."

"I don't think that's what it was, the performance of CI, I mean. The prestige of having representation from a firm in New York was just too much of an enticement. The bad thing is, it may set a dangerous precedent. I believe that's Marty's main concern—that others will follow."

Kate nodded. "Men of Marty's caliber don't come along often enough that we can risk losing them, not in this day and time with all the insider trading going on, and unscrupulous men running Wall Street. It's much too important."

Kate got up from the sofa and went to the window. "I'd no idea it had gotten so late," she said, peering into the twilight. "Dixie, you must go. You make me feel terribly guilty for having kept you so long. Besides Marty will be wondering where you are when he gets home and you're not there."

"I suppose I should. Kate, are you sure you're going to be all right? Why not come out to the house and let Marty and me take care of you through all this?"

"Thank you Dixie, and I love you for offering." Kate shook her head. "But this is where I belong. This is my home."

It was almost nine o'clock when Kate stepped from the shower and reached for her robe. As she wrapped a towel around her wet hair, the phone rang.

"Kate. Walt Hampton. I just this minute heard the news and I'm on my way over." He hung up before Kate could reply. She made coffee while she waited for him to arrive.

Thirty minutes later, they sat in the den in front of a cold fireplace, their cups on the table in front of them. The judge turned to face Kate.

"Do they have any leads? Anything substantial to go on?"

"I don't know. They were here almost all of yesterday, and I see them occasionally walking around the grounds, but I've spoken to no one today."

"Well, I'll nose around down at headquarters and see if I can find out anything. My doctor's going to have a fit." He tapped his chest. "I've been in Vanderbilt all week, prodded and pumped and primed." He frowned. "Such nuisances, tests. I only got home tonight." He shook his head in disbelief. "Shocking. Such a waste. Jonathan was a rare talent. It's my firm conviction that the digital age would've never dawned as quickly as it did had it not been for some of his designs. He was brilliant."

"I didn't know the extent of his work."

"You wouldn't. He wasn't one to brag about his achievements. Don't get me wrong, he was proud of his accomplishments, as well he should've been. But he was raised from humble beginnings and I don't think it ever completely left him." He set his empty cup on the table and stood. "I must go. I've been ordered, *ordered,* mind you, to be in bed by nine o'clock and it's after that now. Promise you'll call me if you need anything."

Kate nodded.

The next morning she opened the door for Lieutenant Simon and Sergeant Cowan, followed by a couple of unfamiliar faces. She wondered if the parade of strangers through her house would ever cease. The strangers entered Jon's studio and Lieutenant Simon motioned her to the sofa. The sergeant continued to stand.

"Verification has been received on the whereabouts of the gardener," the lieutenant said. He consulted his note pad. "Silas Hawkins. He and his wife are upstate in Laurel Glen. A neighbor, a Mrs. Parker, talked to Mr. Hawkins on the day of the murder."

Kate winced at the word.

"It seems that Mr. Hawkins remembered a shipment of shrubbery that was scheduled to be delivered to his house within the next couple of days. And since his sister-in-law doesn't have a telephone, he stopped at a gas station and called Mrs. Parker to ask if she would accept delivery of the merchandise. From there he and his wife were to continue on to the sister's house, which I understand is pretty far out into the country."

"There's no doubt that the call came from Laurel Glen?" Kate asked.

"None. The origin of the call was confirmed through records of the phone company. Silas Hawkins has been removed as a possible suspect."

"I'm glad," Kate said.

"The autopsy's been completed, Mrs. Ames," the lieutenant continued. "The body will be released tomorrow. You may proceed with any funeral arrangements you care to make. As you know a search of the grounds is continuing, but so far nothing's been uncovered. Sorry it's taken so long but you have a large estate and a lot of space to cover." He paused and looked at her. "Has anything come to mind? Anything at all that might help speed up the investigation?"

Kate, knowing it was well past the time to reasonably recall anything of any significance, didn't hesitate in her reply. "No. Nothing."

The other team of men emerged from the study with a couple of boxes and headed for the door.

"You still have my card?" Lieutenant Simon asked.

Kate nodded.

After they'd gone, she sat on the sofa and waited for time to pass. She knew she was going to have to start rebuilding a new fortress for her life—a new battlement—one stone at a time and with great effort and diligence. But not just yet. She'd have to rest a while first, get her strength back. At long last she rose as if in a trance and moved through the house. She crept silently, as moving through a thick fog.

Kate was still learning of the impact of Jon's death upon the scientific community. There had been calls from the media, seeking information on the funeral and any memorial services planned. Determined to preserve the dignity of Jon's memory, Kate chose to keep the service away from the spotlight. She explained, as best she could, while not wishing to deprive friends and associates of the opportunity for paying their final respects, that the funeral would be closed and private. In a press release, she respectfully requested no flowers be sent, and for those wishing to acknowledge his death, that donations be made in Jon's name to the American Cancer Society. Telegrams and cards had been received from the White House, senators and governors, as well as NASA representatives. With the help of her dearest friends, Kate dealt with the monumental task as best she could.

A mist hung heavy in the air the day of the funeral. The small procession, bearing its burden, wound its way up the slope of the hill to a gaping hole in the ground. Jon's grave, beside his mother, was crowned with a marble tombstone. The stone was simple: name, date of birth, date of death. Kate knew of no epitaph, no sentiments, worthy of his life.

Words filled with love and remembrance were spoken by Judge Hampton. The few personal friends in attendance comforted Kate as best they could. Sentiments came hard and were awkwardly expressed, but she understood. She refused all offers to drive her back to the house, said her good-byes at the main road, and walked up the long, winding driveway. Once inside the house the sob that had been clawing at her chest all day finally broke free.

TWENTY-FIVE

It was the next afternoon when Kate first spoke to anyone from New York.

"Mrs. Ames," an efficient-sounding voice came over the line. "Hold for Mr. Bradden."

"Phillip Bradden here, Mrs. Ames." His works were clipped and hard. Concrete words. "May I extend my condolences, and indeed that of the entire firm of Abnerathy, Morefield and Clarke, on the loss of your husband. Terrible tragedy," he went on. "Mr. Ames was a very special person to us, a remarkable man. Truly a visionary without equal."

Kate doubted the sincerity of the hollow-sounding words, and wondered why Jon's firm in New York was calling.

"Thank you, Mr. Bradden."

"Since we have always handled your husband affairs, and naturally will continue to do so, we are currently in the process of the dispensation of Mr. Ames' will. The reading is scheduled for ten o'clock on the third." He paused. "I trust this is convenient for you and that you'll make arrangements to be here?" he asked, seemingly as an afterthought.

"I will."

"You'll not need counsel, but of course that's your decision. In the meantime if we can be of any assistance to you, please let us know."

"Thank you for calling," Kate managed to get out before the line went dead.

The following morning Lieutenant Simon arrived with the ever-silent Sergeant Cowan.

"Good morning, Mrs. Ames," the lieutenant said from the doorway. "Sorry to bother you again, but I have a couple of questions that need answering."

"Please come in and have a seat. Can I get you something? Coffee?" Both men shook their heads as they settled on the sofa.

"Mrs. Ames," the lieutenant began. "How did you and your husband get along?"

Kate was startled. "Fine, Lieutenant Simon. We got along just fine. As you know we were only married a few months."

"I know. Were there arguments—any jealousies? Someone else. Another woman, perhaps?"

Kate thought about Julie. *Yes, there was another woman!* she wanted to shout in answer to the prying questions. *Another woman who intruded into my life and my happiness: another woman who soiled and sullied this beautiful home with acts of unspeakable evil: another woman whom I spied upon and then hated myself for doing it. Yes, dear God, there was someone else.*

"No."

"This has been a most difficult case, I must admit to you." He rubbed his forehead. "We have uncovered nothing that would indicate that anyone, other than the two of you, were on the premises that morning. There was no sign of a struggle, which suggests that your husband knew the assailant."

He glanced at his notes. "Robbery has been ruled out as a possible motive since there was a considerable amount of cash on his desk in plain view. The murder weapon was a knife from your kitchen, containing your own fingerprints. There were no foreign prints found in the room and no sign of forced entry into the house."

"Of course the knife had my fingerprints on it. I used it that morning to slice bread." For the first time, Kate felt alarm. "Furthermore, Lieutenant Simon, forced entry wasn't necessary. I told you, the doorbell rang and my husband went to answer it. Beyond that, I can't explain."

"Mrs. Ames," the lieutenant's voice dropped slightly, "do you know the terms of your husband's will?"

Kate shook her head. "I don't."

"A copy was found in the top drawer of his desk," he said, motioning his head toward the studio. "The entire fortune, valued at well over a hundred million dollars, is left wholly and exclusively to you. You were not aware of this?"

"No." Kate was shocked by the enormity of it all.

"The will was there for anyone to see, yet you maintain that you didn't know of its existence?" He seemed to find the idea a little hard to believe.

"Lieutenant," Kate's voice started to rise. "Mr. Ames' studio was his own private room. I was in there very little, and only then when he was present. My husband spent a great deal of time in there studying books and drawings, things that meant nothing to me. I had no reason to search through his things, as you seem to be suggesting."

"Mrs. Ames," the lieutenant said, his words pointedly measured and guarded, "while I'm not accusing you of anything at this time, it might be advantageous for you to retain an attorney. It's not my job to frighten you, but to be honest things do not look good. We've interviewed dozens of people, here in Woodway and in Washington where Mr. Ames spent so much of his time, but we've come up empty. Frankly Mrs. Ames, if the man had an enemy in the world we've been unable to find out about it.

"We'll go forward with our investigation, of course. We don't intend to give up just yet. In the meantime," he concluded and stood up, "take my advice and seek counsel."

Kate's legs trembled under her weight as she showed the two men out.

When the door shut behind them, icy fingers of fear clutched at her heart. Her first impulse was to contact Judge Hampton, but immediately ruled out the idea. Kate was not willing to risk jeopardizing his health further. *"Promise me if you ever need help, you will contact my firm in New York,"* Kate remembered Jon insisting. Hurriedly she searched through her purse until she found the card that he had given her months earlier. She dialed the number and waited for an answer.

"Abnerathy, Morefield and Clarke," the voice said.

"Mr. Phillip Bradden, please," Kate said.

"May I tell him who's calling?"

"Kathleen Ames. Mrs. Jonathan Ames."

"One moment."

"Mrs. Ames." The voice of Phillip Bradden came across the line. Still crisp. Brittle. His professional voice, Kate figured. He wasted no time in ascertaining the reason for the call. "What can I do for you?"

"Mr. Bradden, I'm afraid I need the advice of your legal department. It seems that I may have become a suspect in the death of my husband."

"Oh my, that is serious. I wish I could help you, Mrs. Ames, I really do. But unfortunately our attorneys lean more toward the corporate side; mergers, that sort of thing."

"You have no one familiar with criminal law, Mr. Bradden?"

"Well yes, I suppose we do have a couple that deal with that sort of thing." Kate could visualize distaste showing on his face. "But I'm sure they're terribly busy."

"Could you recommend someone? Perhaps someone here in this area?"

"I'm afraid not." He sounded as if he thought the idea was ludicrous, and his voice contained a hint of impatience. "Woodway is quite a distance from New York and we really have very little contact with it. Oh, by the way Mrs. Ames, under the present circumstances, I think it advisable to delay the reading of the will until this matter is cleared up. You understand, I'm sure."

"Of course."

"I'll contact you later regarding any newly-scheduled proceedings. In the meantime, we'll continue to monitor the situation from here. Good-bye, Mrs. Ames."

Kate hung up the phone. It was plain she would receive no assistance from those quarters. The authorities would find the one responsible for Jon's death, of course they would. She was so confident in her belief that she dismissed from her mind any idea of retaining an attorney.

The remainder of the week dragged. Sally made her daily calls and Dixie came by often to fume and fuss at the incompetence of the local officials. Judge Hampton, despite the order to curtail his activities, called regularly. None of her friends were aware that she may have become a prime suspect in the case, and Kate saw no reason to burden them.

On Sunday morning, the sun tried to break through a heavy layer of clouds and there was an unsettled restlessness that pressed down on Kate's shoulders. After pulling on heavy boots and tying a scarf around her head, she put on a coat and went out the door. Wind whipped around the side of the house and up the steps as she crossed the terrace to the parking area.

Stubby branches protruded from bushes beside the road and scrubbed against the side of her car as she drove the narrow lane. She must remember to have Silas get someone to trim the limbs back. She parked at the bottom of the hill and walked up the incline to the cemetery. Nearly a month of inactivity had taken a toll on her disciplined body and she began to tire before reaching the top. The gate creaked as she pulled it back and she felt like an intruder.

The few flowers and greenery she had placed on the grave the day of the funeral lay withered and dying atop the mound of fresh earth. Bending, she righted a toppled vase and wiped the headstone with a tissue from her pocket. The day was suddenly darkened when the sun disappeared behind a black cloud. The wind rose with a murmuring and caused her to catch her breath. A chill shook her body as she remembered the dream that had frightened her after her first trip to the cemetery. Kate turned her back on the small plot of land and hurried away.

She could hear the phone ringing as she crossed the terrace. She opened the door and rushed to answer. It was Lieutenant Simon calling to inform her that he would call on her at ten o'clock the following morning. His voice was authoritative in his instructions for her to make herself available. It was then that Kate knew she would be charged with murder.

TWENTY-SIX

"Mrs. Ames." A voice brought Kate back to the present. She realized the car had stopped and she opened her eyes.

"Mrs. Ames," Lieutenant Simon repeated. He stood beside the car, his hand on the opened door. "Here, let me help you out," he said and reached for her arm.

Kate extended her hand and let him help her from the back seat. He guided her across the parking lot at the rear of the building. Sergeant Cowan pulled back one of the metal doors and stepped aside to allow Kate and Lieutenant Simon to enter.

The wheels of due process were set in motion as Kate went through the standard booking process: fingerprints, photographs, I.D. bracelet. Since the Woodway jail was such a small facility with no provisions set aside for the overnight retention of women, it was decided that for the time being Kate would be able to wear her own clothes and forego the mandatory full body search, shower and delousing. Afterwards, when she was given permission to make a call, she dialed Judge Hampton. He was not at home, so she left a message on his machine. Then she was led down a series of hallways, deeper into the belly of the building. Kate knew, on her own, she would never find her way out again.

Stopping in front of the first of two cells, the matron pulled back the door on a small room that looked relatively clean, and motioned her inside. Kate sat down on a mattress covered in navy-striped ticking and stuffed her cold hands beneath her thighs. Although the building was overly warm, the shivering that shook her body wouldn't stop. She sat there in her coat, her feet flat on the floor, until a guard brought food to her.

She ate. The tray was retrieved. She sat again.

"What the hell's going on here?" a voice bellowed from the hallway.

Judge Hampton's face was a bright crimson by the time he reached her cell. In a state that bordered dangerously close to cardiac arrest, he huffed while he waited impatiently for the matron to open the door.

"My dear," he said rushing to Kate and holding out his arms. "Are you okay?"

Kate nodded, feeling reassurance from the bulk of the embrace of this man she had come to love so much.

"Asinine," he ranted. "That's what it is, pure and simple." Clearly, his breathing was troublesome.

"Please," Kate said. "Don't get yourself upset. Remember your heart."

"Well, yes, I suppose I must." He led her to the cot and pulled a straight-backed chair to her side. He held her hands in his. "Have you engaged counsel?"

"I contacted Jon's firm in New York, but it seems they were too busy."

He snorted. "That bunch of over-paid imbeciles probably wouldn't have done you much good anyway."

"Do you have any suggestions?" She stopped short. "Wait, you're not going to be involved in this, are you?"

"Not this time. My doctor has just ordered me back into the hospital for more tests." He rubbed his chin. "But I do have a recommendation. My niece, Melanie, and her husband are just opening a new office here. Matter of fact, they're just out of law school and setting up practice; cracker-jack kids, specializing in criminal law. With your permission, I'll send them over."

"You have my grateful permission," she said.

"Fine. Fine. I'll contact them immediately." He rose from the chair. "Don't you worry, dear lady, everything will work out. You'll see."

Kate gave the big man a hug. "Now you take care of yourself and do what the doctor tells you. I don't want to lose you, too."

"Doctors. Bah!" He kissed her cheek and left.

The setting sun sent feeble rays through the barred window, creating shadows on the tiled floor. Kate lost track of the number of times she had counted the thin dark stripes. There were seven. From another part of the building, she could hear voices. Sounded like an argument going on. Nearby, a door opened and voices sounded in the hallway. The matron appeared with two blue-jeaned youngsters in tow.

Looks like it's going to be a busy night, Kate thought, and was glad that the other cell was empty to receive them. Bleak as it was, she hated the thought of having to share her cell with strangers. The matron stopped before the door to Kate's cell and slipped the key into the lock.

When she pulled back the door, the couple stepped inside.

"Mrs. Ames." The voice was soft. "I'm Melanie Anderson. And this is my husband, Michael."

Kate looked at the couple wearing paint-spattered jeans and jackets. The girl looked like a child: sparkling blonde ponytail, emerald eyes that gave new meaning to the word optimism, a lopsided smile coaxing dimples from cheeks that were flushed rosy from the cold. The lanky, bearded boy was not good-looking but he had an interesting face. His nose, slightly hooked, humped out between high cheekbones protruding below clear blue eyes that mirrored a serious countenance.

"Please forgive our appearance," she said. "But when Uncle Walton called we dropped the paint brushes and hurried over."

Kate found her voice. "You're babies. Just babies."

"Mrs. Ames," the husband man spoke. "Granted, we are young and, as yet, inexperienced. But you've got to believe me; we'll give you everything we've got, and then some." He pulled his hands from the frayed Air Force jacket that bore his name and dug his fingertips into the bearded chin. "The bottom line is this: what we lack in experience we'll make up in dedication and hard work."

"I'm sure you will," Kate said. "And I trust the Judge implicitly. If you'll have me as a client, I'm all yours."

The young couple looked at each other. While it was plain that they were trying to maintain a professional decorum, it was plainer still that their enthusiasm and energy was straining to break through. Their young faces beamed with fire and determination.

"The first thing we have to do is try to get you out of here," Michael said, his serious look returning. "I'll petition the court in the morning to set bail." He looked around the cell. "We don't want you in here any longer than necessary."

"In the meantime, Mrs. Ames, is there anything we can get for you?" Melanie asked. "Anything at all?"

"No, but thanks for asking, and please call me Kate. Mrs. Ames is so formal for such an informal setting."

"And, again, I'm Melanie." She pointed to her husband. "And this great guy is Michael."

Kate grinned. "So, I've got M&M's looking out for me."

Melanie grimaced. "Please, you don't know how many times we've heard that one."

"Sorry," Kate said. "My brain's gone a little mushy."

"You *do* know that this will be the first time we've defended a client accused of murder?" Michael said. "Heck, this is the first time we've defended a client, period."

"The judge said you'd just hung out your shingle. And since this is the first time I've been accused of murder, I guess that makes us even."

Melanie smiled. "We appreciate the fact that you're placing your trust in us on something of such an immense magnitude." Her ponytail bounced as she turned her head and looked at her husband.

"Kate," Michael said, "I know it sounds trite, but try not to worry. Let us do that for you. We'll see you first thing in the morning after our petition's been heard." He looked at his wife. "Well Melanie, I guess the rest of the painting will just have to wait."

"Thank goodness," Melanie said. "I was beginning to get awfully tired of the color." She pointed to a bile-green spatter on the leg of her faded jeans.

Kate smiled. "It is pretty bad, isn't it."

Melanie gave a dimpled grin. "Michael's convinced the landlord bought it at a buy-one-get-one sale at an army surplus store."

The couple stayed only a few minutes more. After they'd gone, all the lights were turned off with the exception of a single bulb left burning in the hallway. Kate squirmed and twisted on the hard cot, but found it impossible to settle down enough to allow sleep to overtake her brain.

Rejection was evident on their faces, when Melanie and Michael appeared the next morning. They did not have to tell Kate that bail had been denied.

"The district attorney is going for second degree murder," Michael said. "Which is good for us, because if he'd charged first degree, they're no chance that the judge would let Mel and me have the case. As it is, we have to still have a standby consultant."

"Mr. Stanley, and old friend of Uncle Walt's offered his services," Melanie said.

"If they're so sure that I did it, you'd think they'd go for the highest charge," Kate said. "Throw the book at me and put me under the jail."

Michael grinned. "They're not nearly as sure as they want the public to think. The only motive they can come up with is money, and after talking to people who've known you for years, they're not even sure about that."

Kate smiled. "How did the hearing go?"

Michael frowned. "Bail was denied for right now. Even for second degree, you've been deemed 'high risk' because of your financial means. They don't want you skipping the country."

"We objected, of course and insisted on another hearing in ten days." Melanie touched Kate's shoulder. "We're being pretty stubborn."

Kate looked up from the cot where she sat. "You know, neither of you have asked me if I did it—if I'm guilty."

"Uncle Walton said you didn't," Melanie said. "So you didn't. Case on that question is closed."

"How is the judge?"

Melanie looked worried. "Not well. He's having more test, but he's being a bear about this case. The doctor has ordered complete bed rest and that means no visitors." She carried a chair from the corner and placed it beside the cot.

Michael pulled a chair along side the two of them, sat down and snapped open a brand new briefcase. "Your arraignment's been set for ten o'clock in the morning."

"Arraignment?"

Michael nodded. "The formal charge and they'll ask how you plead."

"When will the trial be?"

"Who knows?" Melanie smiled. "As Robert Frost would say, '*we have miles to go.*' We still have to get through the preliminary hearing and discovery and probably a couple evidentiary hearings."

Kate shook her head. "Sounds like Greek to me."

"But in the meantime," Michael said, "tell us everything that might have any bearing on this case. Don't leave out anything just because you think it's insignificant."

Kate spent the rest of the morning telling her new confidants about her life with Jon. The couple listened.

"Did you have a good marriage?" Michael asked.

"You could say it was a good marriage."

Michael's eyes narrowed. "You don't sound a hundred percent sure."

"Well, I guess there are shortcomings in all marriages."

Melanie's female intuition seemed to pick up some unspoken signal. "What are you trying to tell us, Kate?"

Kate looked at the couple and shook her head, unable to continue.

"Kate," Michael said, "I know we're entering personal territory here, but there's no other way, believe me. It's hard to open up to strangers, because that's what we still are, strangers. But please trust our discretion and full sense of client confidentiality. We're here for you. Nothing else is of any concern to us—*just you*."

"In my heart I know I have to tell you things I've never told another living soul." She twisted a button on the front of her cardigan. "It's just so hard."

"Take your time," Michael encouraged. "We're in no hurry. Tell us about Mr. Ames. What kind of man was he?"

"He could be funny and serious, warm and gentle, yet I've seen him cold and distant. And cruel—very cruel. He was such a contradiction."

Melanie touched her hand. "You loved him a great deal, didn't you? Were you close?"

Kate shook her head as if to brush away the cobweb memories. "Not at first. It took a while." Her reserve finally broke down. "The marriage wasn't even consummated until the night before Jon was..., before he died."

Melanie looked up from her notes. "Whose decision was that, yours? His?"

"His. But I played a part in it, too."

"How, Kate?" Melanie asked. "How did you play a part?"

"I had a double mastectomy several years ago and was left pretty mangled." She shook her head. "You can't know..." Her voice choked. "You don't know how difficult it's been. Oh, Jon knew about it before we were married. I wouldn't have *not* told him. He said it didn't matter, but of course it did." She frowned. "Breasts are all the rage, you know. And how could they not be, with all the silicone bouncing around out there, and the new owners so proud that they go to great lengths to show them off."

"You think that was the only reason—the mastectomy, I mean?" Michael asked.

"I'm not sure. I always had a feeling, from the time we first started seeing each other, that Jon was fighting an inner battle, a battle of such intensity that it had the capability to steer the very course of his life."

"These mysterious phone calls you mentioned, that started in February. Do you think they might've been connected with someone from Jon's past?" Michael asked.

Kate stood up, jammed her hands into the pockets of her cardigan and walked to the cell door. She stood for a second looking through the bars. "I know they were," she said over her shoulder.

"How do you know?" Michael asked. "Do you know who it was?"

Dark eyes and white fur flashed across Kate's mind. "Julie," she said. "It was Julie."

"And just who is Julie?" Melanie asked.

"A woman from Jon's past. Too lovely to be so wicked—too wicked to be so lovely—but she was: wicked, vile and obscene. And *beautiful*. The word was made for women like her." She laughed. "As mysterious as this sounds, I don't think she has any bearing on this case. The last thing she said to him was that she never wanted to see him again."

"Tell us about her, then we'll all decide together whether or not she's important."

Kate told them about the vandalism of the house, and how Jon refused to report it to the police. "He became cruel and hateful, a different person, someone I didn't even know."

"And there's no record of the incident? No witnesses?" Michael asked.

"None."

"Why do I get the feeling you don't want to talk about her?" Melanie asked.

"Because I'm embarrassed by something I did."

Kate knew she had to reveal a side of herself that brought her shame. She told them about her trip to Washington to spy on Jon.

"I shouldn't have done it. I had no right. It was only that she was so important to his life, and I felt threatened. I somehow got the feeling that he never quite got over her." She shook her head. "Maybe that's why he kept the picture."

"What kind of picture?" Melanie asked. "A snapshot?"

"Not a snapshot. It was more like the black and white glossies taken in a fancy nightclub." She touched her lips. "And the ring. Oh, I nearly forgot about the ring."

Melanie and Michael scribbled on their pads as Kate told them about finding the picture in the cardboard box.

"Where's the picture now?" Michael asked.

Kate bit her lip. "The police may have it. They searched the studio pretty good."

"Perhaps they didn't find it," Melanie's eyes sparkled with intrigue. "Do you think it may still be in the box?"

"It was never unpacked. I remember seeing it pushed into the corner of the room. It looked just as it did the day Jon carried it from the farmhouse."

"We need that picture," Michael said. "As you say, Kate, it may not have any bearing on the case; then again, it may mean a great deal."

"Michael," Melanie said, clearly excited, "could we get inside the house and look for it?"

"We can try. Even though the authorities have finished their investigation they surely are keeping an eye on the place, so sneaking in is out of the question. No, we'll have to do it openly.

Kate," Michael said, "don't you need something extra from the house? You didn't get everything you needed when you left, now did you?"

Kate smiled. "I guess I didn't."

"Make it something good," Michael said.

"As a matter of fact, it is. Legitimate, too. There's some medication for anemia on my nightstand that I'm suppose to take every day. In all the confusion the day of the arrest I simply forgot it."

"Fantastic," Michael said. "We'll request permission to pick it up. Also, the remote control for the gate, do you still have it?"

Kate shook her head. "They took most of my things."

"We can get it from the officer in charge. That won't be a problem." Michael gathered his notes together, pushed back his chair and stood up. "Let's get to it, Melanie. Kate, we'll see you again before bedtime."

TWENTY-SEVEN

Michael and Melanie hadn't been gone but a short time when the matron appeared at Kate's cell door. She was carrying a large basket of fruit. Standing behind her, a deputy held an angel-wing begonia that Kate recognized as being from Dixie's beloved plant collection. He also carried a plastic shopping bag.

The matron unlocked the door. "Mrs. Ames," she said, "we have some things for you." They came into the room and deposited the items on the cot. "This also came." She handed Kate an envelope. It had been opened. As they turned to leave, the matron stopped just inside the door. "If you need anything, let me know and I'll see what I can do."

"Thank you," Kate said. "I do appreciate that."

Kate opened the shopping bag. Inside were books and magazines and a two-pound box of Godiva chocolates. She pulled the note from the envelope:

Kate,

Here are a few things to make your stay more bearable. They wouldn't let me in to see you, the dirty rats. I hope they all burn in hell.

Love, Dixie.

For the first time since Jon's death, Kate found a reason to laugh. She set the plant on the narrow ledge of the barred window. Tearing away the cellophane wrapper from the basket of fruit, she picked up a handful of grapes and reached for a magazine. For the next hour Kate forgot her surroundings.

Voices interrupted her reading and she jumped to her feet. Melanie had returned alone, gripping the ever-present briefcase.

"Well," she said, glancing around the room, "looks like you've been doing some redecorating since I've been gone."

"Here." Kate reached into the basket. "Have a snack."

"Thanks, I believe I will." Melanie polished the dark red apple on the sleeve of her navy blazer while she waited for the matron to lock the door behind her.

"We got the picture," she whispered. "It was in the box right where you said. Oh, and I dropped your medicine off at the infirmary. They'll be responsible for dispensing your dosages."

Kate nodded.

Melanie sank her teeth into the apple. "By the way, your house is spectacular. Was I envious!"

Kate's eyes clouded. "It is lovely, isn't it? Jon and I had such fun planning it together."

Melanie took another bite and laid the apple on the cot before opening the briefcase on her lap.

"This is the picture?"

"That's it. I only saw it briefly, but she's even more lovely in person."

Melanie nodded. "She *is* beautiful."

"Almost too beautiful to be real." Kate gave a slight laugh. "Now don't ask me what I meant by that, because I haven't the slightest idea. And there's the ring I told you about."

Melanie turned the picture over and studied the back. "What an intense inscription. But then from all you've told us, I get the idea she's a pretty intense person. I'm glad we have the picture instead of the district attorney. They could try to make a case based on unreasonable jealousy." She slid the picture back into her briefcase and picked up her apple. "Michael's waiting, so I've got to run. We'll see you in the morning—for the arraignment."

"Will it take long?"

"Ten minutes. In and out."

Melanie was right. The next morning the judge read the charges and asked how she pleaded. Kate's voice had been strong when she said, "Not guilty."

The consulting attorney, Eli Stanley, sat at the table with them but made no remarks other than to assure the court that he would be available for the duration of the trial.

Then Kate was back in her cell with Melanie. Michael was off, running down a rumor he'd heard.

"What happens next?" Kate asked.

"A lot of legal wrangling. You just settle in and try to make yourself comfortable—if you can." She smiled as she gathered her briefcase to leave. "I know that's asking a lot, but time will pass more quickly than you'd think. I'll see you tomorrow."

"I'll be here," Kate said.

Melanie stopped and turned. She walked over and put her arm around Kate's shoulder. "It's bad for you, I know. It may seem as if we're playing games, but believe me, we're deadly serious. The only concern we have right now, our only concern, is you."

"I know that, and I don't mean to whine. I'm grateful for the two of you."

Time ticked forward. Outside Kate's barred window, spring arrived. Summer would be along soon and she wondered if she'd be denied seeing autumn arrive on the knoll.

Then one morning a triumphant Michael entered the cell. His eyes fairly sparkled from the bearded face.

"There was someone else on the grounds of *Brandywine* that morning."

Kate sat on the edge of the cot, stunned by the revelation. "How'd you find out?"

He winked. "I have a friend or two in strategic locations. Silas Hawkins and his wife have just returned home. They didn't know about any of this until they got back. As soon as Silas heard, he went straight to the authorities.

"It seems he had stopped by your house that morning before he left. The weather reports predicted a freeze warning and he wanted to cover some seedlings so they wouldn't be damaged. He told the officials he entered the grounds and left the gates open while he was inside. He was crouched back in the shrubbery when he saw a black car come up the driveway. He didn't recognize the car, but he did notice the license plates. He said he saw a man go toward the terrace door and, assuming that he was an invited guest, didn't think anymore about it. He continued with his work, he thinks no more than five, maybe ten minutes, then went to put some things away in the caretaker's building. When he came out again, the car was gone. At that time he left, closing the gates behind him and put the entire incident out of his mind." Michael stopped to catch his breath.

"That must have been who rang the bell."

"No doubt," Michael agreed.

"Do they know who he is? Can they find him?"

"Oh, I'm sure they can," Michael assured her. "License plates are like fingerprints, there are no two the same."

"Then there really was a third person in the house that morning. I mean, I knew there *had to be*. I guess I thought there might be some other explanation. I don't know what, but something."

"It had to be someone your husband knew. If there had been a scuffle you would have heard, wouldn't you?"

"Not necessarily. Remember, I was in the pool with the doors closed. The pump was running and the water itself helps to soften sounds. There could have been a struggle and I wouldn't have heard."

"Well, Kate, looks like you were right about Julie. It appears that she has nothing to do with the case. Do you have any idea who the man might be?"

"None at all."

"He'll turn up, that much we can count on. By the way, Melanie wanted me to tell you that she had a call from her uncle this morning."

"He's improving then?"

"I'm afraid not. He insisted to his doctor that he be allowed one visit from us. Melanie said he demanded we come immediately. He said he had something to tell us about Mr. Ames—about this case."

"Wonder what it could be?" Kate pondered. "Remember I told you how angry they were with each other that night he came to supper. There was a gap between them. They cared deeply for each other, that much was apparent, but there was something separating them. It must have been awfully important for neither of them to give an inch. I often wondered what it was."

"Well, we'll find out soon enough. We're on our way to see him now. We'll check in just as soon as we get back." He started for the cell door, then turned back. "Oh, I nearly forgot," he said, pulling a piece of paper from his pocket. "This was left for you at the front desk." He put it in her hand and was gone.

Kate opened the envelope. It was a note from Emily: "*I wanted to come and see you but they wouldn't let me. Take care of yourself and I'll see you soon.*"

Kate dropped her head to her hands. "Oh, Emily," she sobbed. "Please take care of yourself the baby."

Kate tucked away her present circumstances into a corner at the back of her brain, and the rest of the day was taken up with her concern for the health of Judge Hampton and worrying about Emily. She had just finished supper and was dreading the long evening stretching before her, when Melanie returned.

Her eyes were unusually bright.

"He's gone," she said. Stark, bruise-like shadows stood out on the fair complexion.

"I'm so sorry."

"He died before we got there. Doctor Lawson said his heart just gave out."

"So you don't know what he wanted?"

"It was something to do with this case, I'm sure of that much." She clenched her hands. "Something he knew and felt he had to tell me. Uncle Walton was a closed-lipped kind of person. Years of being on the bench taught him that. Maybe it was a confidence he had been keeping all these years, and only now did he feel he could reveal it. Anyway, we'll probably never know."

"Where's Michael?"

"Sorry, I forgot to tell you. There's news on the grapevine that the mysterious man in the black car's been located. Michael's snooping around, undercover work he calls it." She smiled. "Sometimes I think my wonderful husband should have been a detective."

"Then we have reason to be hopeful, don't we?"

"Where there's innocence, there's hope." She smiled. "No little thing, *innocence*. And we have that on our side." Kate and Melanie turned their heads as they heard a door open.

Michael came bounding down the corridor, leaving the matron far behind. He caught his breath while he waited for the door to be unlocked.

"We've got trouble," he stated flatly. "The driver of the car's been found. His name's Julian Marshall and he's being held for the murder of Jonathan Ames."

"How can that be trouble, Michael?" Melanie asked. "Does that not clear Kate?"

"Afraid not, Mel. In his sworn statement he freely admits to having committed the act." He stuck his hands into his beard and ruffled the neatly trimmed hair. "But here's the kicker—he further states that our client here purchased his services."

"Purchased his what!" Kate exploded. "That's the dumbest thing I've ever heard."

"And the name—Julian Marshall," Michael asked. "Ring any bells?"

Kate shook her head. "None."

"Here's another piece of news," Michael went on. "Trial date has been set."

"Could we file for a continuance?" Melanie asked.

"We could, but why? We got as much now as we're going to get."

Flipping open her briefcase, Melanie sat down on the chair. "Okay you two, fun's over. Let's put our heads together and see what we've got to work with."

TWENTY-EIGHT

The courtroom was packed as reporters gathered for the bloodletting. Heads turned in her direction as Kate entered, flanked on either side by her young lions. She looked straight ahead, shoulders back, head erect, and steeled herself against the crowd. A line from *Macbeth* came to mind: *"...that struts and frets his hour upon the stage..."*

In front and to the left of the room, the defense table had been set with a pitcher of water and glasses arranged on a metal tray. Pushed against the table, three empty chairs waited. An elderly gentleman, looking slightly bored, sat at the end, facing the table's length. Eli Stanley, the standby attorney, Kate reckoned. Melanie took the third chair down and Michael pulled out the center chair for Kate. She sat down between them and watched as they opened briefcases and piled stacks of papers on the table. Melanie looked pretty in a red, button-front dress that barely reached her knees. Michael reached over and patted Kate's hand. She tried to smile, but the tight line of her mouth felt more like a sneer.

The room was stifling. Too many people crammed together, breathing each other's breath. Kate could feel dampness starting to gather on her upper lip and at her armpits.

A uniformed bailiff stood in front of the room: "Hear ye. Hear ye," he canted. "This court is now in session. All having business before this body draw nigh and you will be heard. Case Number Fifteen-Hundred-Thirty-Seven, the People against Kathleen Spencer Ames." He seemed concerned not in the least that he was setting in motion the considerable powers of the State, for the sole purpose of extracting from the defendant the justice to which the People were entitled.

"The Most Honorable Fleming L. Peterson, presiding. All rise."

A chamber door opened and an elderly man emerged and stepped up to the bench. He had a big head, wide across the brow, and the wire-framed glasses seemed much too small for his face. Slightly drooping jowls gave him the appearance of a friendly bulldog.

"Be seated," he instructed. "Mr. Holbrook, is the prosecution ready?"

"We are."

"Mr. Anderson?"

Michael stood. "Ready, Your Honor."

"Eli," the judge nodded to the third attorney, "much obliged to you for your able assistance."

Eli Stanley waved his hand to assure the court that it was nothing.

And so the proceedings began and pushed the morning along. Jury selection took less than thirty minutes. There were no preemptory challenges and only one dismissal for cause. It seemed that none of the people knew much about the case and there was an over-abundance of cooperation.

Technical and forensic witnesses came, gave testimony as to date, time, conditions, and circumstances. None of the material entered into as evidence by these witnesses was challenged by the defense. The jury showed little interest in the scientific terminology. Only when Doctor Alden testified, and the knife was introduced as People's Exhibit A, did they appear to become alert and conscious of their sworn duty. The doctor looked relieved when he finally stepped down.

The judge unhooked the glasses from his ears and looked at his watch. "It's nearing noon," he said. "Before we start with the next witness, we'll break for lunch. Court stands recessed until one o'clock." His gavel fell.

Melanie stayed with Kate while Michael hurried to get their food. They ate in a conference room behind the courtroom. Sitting across the table from the two women, Michael looked up from his burger and smiled.

"You're doing great," he said to Kate. "The best advice I can give you is to remain cool and confident. Try to show as little emotion as possible. Don't give the jury anything to chew on."

"Chew on?"

"A worried look, an angry outburst, tears—*especially* not tears, nothing that might stick in their brain and give them something to pick at."

Kate nodded.

"Silas Hawkins will be the next one up. The prosecution will move quickly until they get to the star attraction."

"Mr. Marshall," Kate said.

Michael wiped his hands and wadded the paper napkin into a tight ball. "And I can't wait to meet him," he said.

All the gallery seats were already filled when Kate and her attorneys re-entered the courtroom. Michael held the center chair for Kate. Melanie returned her briefcase to the table and took her seat on the left. Michael assumed the aisle chair and leaned toward Kate. "We have a few minutes before reconvening. You okay?"

Kate nodded. "Thanks to you two."

"By the way, I meant to tell you, you look nice in that navy suit and silk blouse—very legitimate and dependable."

Kate gave him a weak smile. "I've never been called legitimate before, but I guess it's okay. And you can thank Melanie for the outfit. She went out to the house and picked out some things."

Michael grinned. "In a court of law, anytime you can use the word *legitimate*, believe me it's very okay."

"Excuse me." Melanie interrupted them. "I see someone I need to speak to." Easing out of her chair, she left the table. She was gone only a moment. When she returned, she stopped beside Michael to speak to him. The chamber door opened.

"Here, Melanie," Kate whispered. "Take my seat, I'll move over." Melanie nodded and sat down in Kate's chair.

"Remain seated and come to order," the Bailiff said.

Michael's prediction proved to be accurate when Silas was the next witness called. Kate watched as he walked between the two tables. He tried to walk straight, but his hip refused to cooperate. His brown double-breasted suit was pressed to a shine and the creases down the trouser legs were as straight and crisp as Emily could make them. His voice was firm when he took the oath, but began to quiver as the questions were put to him.

"Now, Mr. Hawkins," District Attorney Holbrook continued, "had you ever seen this man before? The man driving the black car?"

"I don't think so."

"Would you recognize him if you saw him again?"

"I don't know." Silas shook his head. "I doubt it."

The prosecutor picked up a photo from the table. "I'm going to show you this picture. I want you to take a good look at it and tell me if it's the person you saw come up the Ames' driveway that morning."

Silas studied the picture. "I'm not sure. I was pretty far away."

"Did you recognize the car?"

"I'd never seen it before, I'm sure of that," Silas said with confidence.

"Was it a Maserati?"

"I don't know, sir."

"Was there anything distinctive about the car you can remember?"

"Yes, sir. The license plates."

"And what was on these plates, Mr. Hawkins?"

"Just two letters. There was a 'J' and then a little dash and then another 'J' and that was all."

"And you're sure about these identifying letters?"

"Oh, yes, sir. I'm sure about that."

"I have no further questions." The prosecutor turned and looked at Michael. "Your witness."

Michael rose from his chair. "Defense has no questions."

Silas stepped down from the stand and walked back across the room, his arms hanging limply at his sides. Just as he came even with Kate's table, he barely raised a tentative finger as if in a kind of greeting. Kate knew something of the pain he must have been feeling.

The district attorney picked up a sheaf of paper and shuffled them around. Seemingly satisfied with the order in which they were arranged, he cleared his throat and looked up.

"The State calls Mr. Julian Marshall."

The bailiff opened the door to the right of the courtroom and two uniformed guards ushered in the prisoner. Kate got her first look at the young man who had taken Jon away from her. Fascinated, she watched as he placed his hand on the Bible. He was of meager stature, the gray linen blazer compensating for his narrow shoulders, and navy-flannel slacks for his slight stance. Even so, he carried himself well, despite the appearance of being delicately constituted. His eyes were concealed behind smoke-tinted rimless glasses.

Watching him, Kate's basic maternal instinct replaced her ability to hate. He looked like a spoiled child: lovely, pouty, and vulnerable. It was hard to imagine one so innocent-looking as having committed such a heinous act. He looked incapable of mysterious secrets or harmful intent. He stared straight ahead while being sworn in, and seemed to hold the room mesmerized.

"For the record, would you please state your name and address," the prosecutor said.

"Julian Marshall." His voice was perfectly modulated. "I live in Washington D.C."

"And what is your occupation, Mr. Marshall?"

"I'm a diplomatic courier, currently assigned to a post in Washington."

"How long have you held your current position?"

"Since my return from South America. I was at the Embassy in Buenos Aires, Argentina for the past year. I only returned from there the first of February."

"And how long have you been in the employ of the U.S. Government?"

"All my adult life. I began as a congressional page just out of high school and continued all through college."

"I take it you didn't get where you are today without hard work and a lot of loyal dedication. Nobody pulled any strings for you, nothing like that."

"I don't understand your—"

"Credibility, Mr. Marshall. I'm trying to establish your credibility. Would you say you're pretty well thought of in government circles and among your peers?"

"Of course."

"Did you know the decedent, Jonathan Ames?"

The witness shifted in his seat. "No."

"You didn't know the deceased, yet you have stated in a sworn statement that you killed him. Will you tell this court why."

"For money." His voice was flat and without passion. "She offered me a deal I couldn't refuse."

Harrison Holbrook turned and looked toward the defense table. "When you say *she*, do you mean Mrs. Ames?"

"I do."

"Did you know this person—this Mrs. Ames at the time she called you? Had you ever heard of her?"

"Didn't have a clue," he said.

"How much did she offer to pay you?"

"One million dollars."

A murmur went through the courtroom. The jury sat spellbound, their eyes locked on the witness in the chair. Kate was immobile, her hands clenched in her lap.

"What did you think of that amount of money, Mr. Marshall?"

"I thought it was amusing?"

"Did you ever get the million dollars?"

"I did not."

"Now, Mr. Marshall, will you go forward and tell this court precisely how you were contacted by the defendant," the prosecutor instructed. "And how the offer was made."

Julian Marshall positioned himself in his chair and began.

"First, she called me on the phone. She said she would like to meet with me, that she had a business deal that would be very profitable for the both of us."

"Just a minute, Mr. Marshall," the prosecutor interrupted. "How did the defendant ever get the idea in the first place, that you might even remotely be interested in a business deal that could net you a lot of money?"

"Objection, Your Honor," Michael said, rising from his seat. "The witness is being asked to form a conclusion."

"Sustained."

"Very well," the prosecutor said patiently, "let's try it another way. Did she tell you, in so many words, why she thought you might be receptive to some get-rich scheme?"

The fragile-looking young man rubbed the back of his hand against his cheek.

"I wondered about that myself. She was vague on the specifics, only saying that she had seen my name on a business card and thought I was an enterprising chap who might be interested in a lucrative business deal."

"Business card?"

He laughed. "Yeah, *Paladin*."

"Paladin?"

"From an old television show back in the day—*Paladin: Have Gun Will Travel*."

"Please enlighten us, Mr. Marshall, about this card."

He looked sheepish. "It was a dumb idea that guys get when they've had too many rum and cokes and looking for time to kill." He waved a hand. "It was two—maybe three years ago. Frankly, I'd forgotten about it until she brought it up."

"Mrs. Ames?"

"Yeah."

"Tell us about it."

He shrugged. "Couple of buddies and I left a bar late—way late; it was after last call. And, like I said, feeling no pain. We wandered down a side street looking for something else to do."

"And did you—find something else to do?"

"We found this all-night print shop. Cubbyhole. I figured it was a front for shady documents—being open all night, and all. But what the heck we weren't looking for any forgeries, just some excitement."

"Please continue."

"We wandered around—it was an interesting place. Tacked on the wall was a fly-specked poster advertising calling cards from the old black and white television shows from the fifties, you know, *Maverick, Gunsmoke, Paladin*. There was even one from *Wanted Dead or Alive* that starred Steve McQueen. Really cool stuff."

"Then what happened?"

"My friends dared me to get a card printed with my name on it." He grinned. "I never could resist a challenge so I had a dozen of *Paladin* printed with my name and telephone number. Best I remember, I doled out one to each of them for souvenirs of the evening and kept the others."

"And these friends, do you remember their names?"

He shook his head. "Actually I never knew either of them. They were just a of couple guys I shared bar space with for some serious drinking and we hit it off." He grinned. "You know how fellows just sometimes click?"

"Thank you for the stroll down memory lane," Holbrook said. "Now could you continue, please, with how Mrs. Ames initially contacted you."

"Anyway, she called, introduced herself on the telephone and asked if she might visit me in Washington, to discuss the deal privately." He shrugged his shoulders. "I said, 'Sure, why not.'"

"And did she?"

"Yes, she visited on two separate occasions."

"Exactly what did she say to you? And now we're talking about the first occasion only."

"That's when she said she wanted her husband dead, and would make it well worth my time."

The prosecutor paused and looked at the jury, then turned back to the witness. "And you agreed, at that time, to enter into this alliance with her?"

"Not at that time. I told her flat out that I wasn't interested." He struck the arm of the witness chair. "But she kept after me—wearing me down. She wouldn't leave me alone."

"She finally succeeded?"

Julian Marshall nodded. "She did. The second time I talked to her on the phone, she practically begged me to do it. She assured me the plan was foolproof, that we'd both end up filthy rich. It was then I told her we had a deal. We arranged to meet later to work out the final details."

"And the second visit?"

"That's when she gave me fifty-thousand dollars. She said the rest would come when the estate was settled and she inherited her husband's entire fortune."

"Did she offer to aid or assist you in any way in this proposed removal of her husband?"

Julian Marshall smiled. "She drew me a sketch of the house, specifically the location of the studio where she said her husband spent most of his time. Then she gave me a remote control to open the security gates, but I didn't need to use it since the gates were already open.

She said the house was completely isolated and no one would see me enter or leave."

"When you got there did you have any trouble getting into the house?"

"None. The sliding glass doors were opened just as she said they'd be."

The prosecutor cut his eyes at the jury. "She left the doors open for you?"

Julian Marshall sneered. "Just like she said."

"Now tell us, Mr. Marshall, what happened once you were inside the house."

"I'd memorized the layout of the house, and as I passed through the breakfast room I picked a knife up from the table. I didn't have any trouble locating the studio. The door was open and he was sitting at his desk. He looked up when I entered the room and started to rise. Then I stabbed him."

"When you say *him*, you mean Mr. Jonathan Ames?"

"Jonathan Ames, yes."

"Did you say anything to him."

"I said, '*This is from the prissy slut you were dumb enough to marry.*' Then I went out the same way I came in, got in my car and drove away."

"You said *slut*. Why did you refer to her in that way?"

"Well, she had him killed, didn't she?" He smirked. "What would you call her?"

"Did you see Mrs. Ames during this time?"

"I did. Just as I was leaving, she stuck her head out from behind one of the other doors."

"Did she say anything to you?"

"She laughed."

"Laughed?"

"And gave me the thumbs up."

The prosecutor shook his head as if he found the conduct of the defendant to be beyond belief. "Now I ask you again, Mr. Marshall, this defendant," he said pointing at the defense table, "this woman paid you to murder her husband?"

"She did."

"No more questions, Your Honor. But for the record, prosecution wishes to reserve the right to recall this witness for redirect, should it be deemed necessary."

"So noted," the judge said.

Michael unfolded himself from his chair and stood. "Your Honor, if it please the court, defense would like to call a fifteen minute recess."

Judge Peterson unhooked the glasses from his ears and pinched the end of his nose. "Request granted. This court stands in recess for fifteen minutes." The gavel sounded.

"All rise," the bailiff intoned as the judge rose to leave the bench and the jury filed out. Courtroom security escorted Julian Marshall from the room.

TWENTY-NINE

Michael returned to the table and sat down. Kate reached across Melanie and clutched his arm.

"Michael, he's lying? I never called anybody a *chap* in my life. What reason could he possibly have for saying the things he did?"

"He killed Jon, Kate. He has to blame somebody, and who better than the person who stands to gain the most—the wife." He stuffed his fingers into his beard and scratched. "He seems awfully sure of himself, even though there are tremendous holes in his testimony. Kate, are you sure you've never seen him before? Maybe in a crowd, or at a party?"

A frown creased her forehead. "I would have remembered," she said.

"Of course, she would've remembered," Melanie said. "My God, Michael, you saw him, he's—" She looked at Kate for help. "He's what?"

"Unique?" Kate suggested.

Melanie nodded. "That's it, *unique*. She'd remember, Michael. Believe me, any woman would remember him."

Michael snorted. "If you say so," he said and looked at Kate again. "Something's bothering you. What is it?"

"I don't know," she said, nipping her lower lip. "There's something familiar about him; something beyond my grasp. It's like a piece of puzzle that's supposed to fit but doesn't, so you want to force it into place."

Attention was drawn back to the front of the room as the judge reentered and took his place at the bench. "Bring in the jury," he said.

The room watched as the jury filed in: faces grim, eyes straight ahead.

"Return the witness to the stand," the judge ordered.

Julian Marshall exuded confidence as he returned to the witness chair. The judge looked at him. "I remind you Mr. Marshall, you're still under oath."

Michael rose and advanced toward the witness.

"Mr. Marshall, when did the defendant make initial contact with you? I mean, when did you receive that first phone call?"

"Sometime around the first of February."

"Can you be more specific?"

"No. I don't remember exactly. It was just after my return from Argentina."

"Now," Michael continued, "from what you've told us, one would assume that you have quite an important job with the government. Do you by any chance have an unlisted telephone number?"

"I do."

"How do you suppose the defendant was able to secure that number?"

"From the Paladin card, she said."

"You put your private unlisted telephone number on a prank card? You, a member of the Diplomatic Corp, just put your number right out there?"

The witness shrugged. "Like I said, we'd had too much to drink. It was a stupid thing to do."

"Do you by any chance still have one of the cards? Maybe we could all take a look at it."

"I don't. No. It was a long time ago and I have no idea where the rest ended up. Probably in a wastepaper can."

"After she called, you testified that the defendant visited you on two separate occasions. When did the first meeting take place?"

"It was about a week after the first phone call."

"*About* a week, Mr. Marshall? Can you pin it down to a more definite date?"

"Like I said, I'm not very good with dates."

"In your job, one would think that you'd be a very precise person. You don't keep a day planner, any kind of schedule?"

The witness cracked a grin. "Not about this."

"Very well, tell us what was discussed at that first meeting."

"She told me what she wanted done and how much she was willing to pay."

Michael consulted the notes in his hand. "Ah, yes. The *amusing* one million dollars. That's an awful lot of money." He cocked an eyebrow. "You believed her?"

"I'd heard of Jonathan Ames. His picture often appeared in the newspapers, periodicals, magazines. Everyone in Washington knew he was worth a fortune."

The cross-examination continued with Michael seeming to gain little ground. The witness appeared to become bored with the questioning, leaned back in the chair and began to relax and glance around the room.

Kate and Melanie sat at the table listening. Kate made meaningless marks on one of

Melanie's legal pads, leaning over occasionally to whisper a remark. Melanie casually reached in front of Kate and leafed through the stack of papers. The corner of the picture caught her eye and she eased it out just as Michael brought the witness back to attention.

"I'm sorry," Julian Marshall said. "Would you repeat the question?"

"I asked you about the second meeting, Mr. Marshall. What transpired on that occasion?"

"That's when she brought the fifty-thousand."

"Was that when the final plans were made?"

"It was."

"How was it decided precisely when the deed was to be carried out?"

"She said she'd leave the details to me; said that was what she was paying me for. She drew a map of the house and gave me the remote control."

"So, you're saying that the defendant left the entire operation up to you. You were to pick the time and method?"

"That's right."

"If the exact time that you were to arrive was not known, Mr. Marshall, how do you suppose the defendant knew when to leave the terrace doors unlocked? Indeed, how could she be sure that her husband would even be home on the very day that you happened to choose?"

The witness shifted slightly in his chair. "She said the doors were always unlocked because of the security gates. She also said that her husband had become reclusive and never left the grounds."

Michael nodded. "Now, about the money, the fifty-thousand dollars you allege the defendant paid to you. In what denominations were the bills?"

"Hundreds mostly. A few fifties, but mostly hundreds. It was a lot of paper."

"What did you do with the money? Do you have records of a large cash deposits to your bank, did you purchase any expensive items, anything at all to substantiate your having received the money?"

"Your Honor," the prosecutor said, "I object. This line of questioning is totally irrelevant and immaterial."

"Overruled."

"Exception."

"Noted," the judge said. "Answer the question."

"I didn't do anything special with the money: paid some bills, bought a few clothes. I don't remember much more."

"You don't remember a lot, do you, Mr. Marshall?"

The district attorney jumped to his feet. "Your Honor—"

"Never mind," Michael said, waving his hand toward the bench, "I withdraw the question." He studied his notes. "Now, the remote control you say the defendant gave you. Do you, by any chance, still have it?"

"I threw it away."

"Where, Mr. Marshall? Where did you throw it?"

"I don't remember. Somewhere out in the country."

"I don't suppose you still have the map that you say she sketched for you either—" Michael looked at the jury "—do you?"

"No."

"Let's go now to the day of the murder," Michael said, changing his tone. "You say you used a knife from the kitchen table. How convenient. Why did you do that? If you went there with the premeditated purpose of killing Jonathan Ames, why did you not take a weapon? How did you propose to carry out the act?"

The witness tucked his brows and tugged on the point of his chin. He seemed to take his time studying the question. At the defense table, Kate and Melanie sat watching the proceedings. The stuffiness of the room made breathing difficult. Melanie gave a slight cough and reached for the water pitcher. She motioned the glass toward Kate, but she declined with a shake of her head. Melanie, taking a slow sip of water, turned her attention back to the proceedings.

"I had a gun in my pocket," Julian Marshall was saying. "But when I saw the knife on the table it just seemed to make more sense at the time. There would be no noise and nothing to trace."

The witness shifted his position in the chair, seeming to become more confident. Propping an elbow on the left arm of the chair and resting his chin against the back of his hand, he removed his glasses and let them dangle casually in his right hand.

"Now, Mr. Marshall, if you would tell—"

Suddenly the shared expectancy of the room was suspended when Melanie became strangled and was seized by a fit of coughing. The glass dropped from her hand and shattered on the top of the table. Water splashed over the papers, ran across the table and dripped onto the floor. Michael begged the court's indulgence and stepped to the table to see about her.

"Call a recess, Michael," Melanie whispered frantically as she continued to cough.

"Your Honor, may I request a recess for defense to compose itself?" he pleaded. "The testimony of this witness is far too important to be side-tracked by distractions."

Melanie continued to make choking sounds.

"Very well," the judge said, sounding slightly miffed. "Due to the lateness of the hour we might as well dismiss for the day. And because of a conflict on the calendar, there will be no court tomorrow." He glanced at Michael. "I know it's an inconvenience for you, Mr. Anderson, and I'm sorry to interrupt the testimony of this witness, but it can't be helped. We'll reconvene Monday at nine." He banged the gavel. "Court dismissed."

Melanie mopped at the spilled water on the table and continued to cough and gasp for air. Kate straightened the papers for Melanie and put them in her briefcase. The face of the witness mirrored intense hatred as he watched the activity at the defense table. He jerked his arms from the grasps of the guards when they reached to take him from the stand.

Michael's face was filled with disbelief. "For God's sake, Mel," he said. "What was that all about?"

Melanie smiled through watery eyes. "I'll tell you later. Right now let's get out of here, we have work to do." She patted Kate's arm before she and Michael turned and hurried away.

The matron came for Kate. An air of anticipation filled the courtroom as reporters and spectators filed from the room, talking among themselves.

Kate was near exhaustion when she reached her cell. Comprehension of it all lay just beyond the limits of her mind and she began to doubt her sanity. Supper was delivered and returned, untouched. After a tepid shower she collapsed on the small bunk. The sleepless nights culminated in an overwhelming need for release, and she slept a deep, dreamless sleep.

Without having court to take up her day, Kate woke early on Friday morning and lay still, wondering what turn her life was about to take. Breakfast was brought and appreciated, and she lingered over a second cup of coffee. She smiled when Melanie arrived around nine. Along with her ever-present briefcase she had a shoebox tucked under her arm and a coat hanger dangled from one finger.

"Little early for shopping, isn't it."

Melanie smiled. "Picked this up yesterday." She popped the hanger on a nail. "Something we'd like you to wear to court Monday morning."

"We?"

"Michael and me."

"Where is Michael?"

Melanie slipped her coat off and pulled one of the chairs over. She took Kate's hand.

"He went to D.C."

"Why?"

"Why not? Or better yet, what better time? Since there's no more court 'til Monday, my wonderful husband thought he'd spend a day or two snooping."

"Think he'll find anything?"

"Could be." She grinned. "Back when I first started law school, Uncle Walt took me to Washington to show me around and introduce me to some of his cronies. A couple of them I remembered as being uncommonly generous with their time. Last night I took the liberty of giving them a call and asked if they'd have time to meet with Michael, if he came to Washington right away. They both agreed."

"So, what's Michael going to ask them?"

"About Julian Marshall. Do they know the name or anything about him."

"Melanie, I'm sure the Woodway police have already done that."

"Can't hurt to double check. Who knows, sometimes one little trail will lead to something bigger." She squeezed Kate's hand. "So, who knows?"

On Monday morning, Kate took the wrapper off the dress and was surprised at what Melanie had picked out for her to wear. The navy blue jersey with white cuffs and Peter Pan collar put Kate in the mind of a school marm.

"Okay, Melanie," she said to herself, "you want prim and proper, how about a French twist to go along with it." By the time she finished and slipped her feet into the navy flats with the white buckle, she thought she looked pretty damn confident for somebody in her predicament.

THIRTY

The matron escorted Kate back to the courtroom. Melanie and Michael were already at the table.

"My Lord, what happened to the two of you?" Kate said. "You look awful."

Dark circles ringed Melanie's blue eyes and her appearance, usually immaculate, was quite disheveled. Her blonde hair looked in need of a good sudsing and she was still wearing the same red dress she'd worn on Thursday.

Michael looked in a little better shape. At least he had showered and changed clothes. "Don't ask," he said.

"Listen, kids," Kate warned. "I know what you're trying to do for me, but you have to take better care of yourselves."

"Hush, Michael." Melanie scolded. "Missing one night's sleep is not going to kill you."

Michael arched his back and stretched. "Well, maybe," he said and winked at Kate as if trying to lighten the tremendous load he knew she was carrying.

Melanie leaned forward in her chair. "Kate," she said, "do you mind if I sit next to Michael? I need to talk to him."

"Of course not." Kate moved over to the far seat, nearer Ira Stanley. He gave her a nod. Melanie sat down in the center chair and bent her head toward her husband. There seemed to be a conspiracy between them.

Melanie casually pushed her briefcase to the left of the table, putting it directly in front of Kate. She turned and took Kate's hand.

"I need for you to listen to me carefully," she said. "There will be some disturbing testimony today and you need to be prepared. A lot of things were uncovered over the weekend. Please," she said, her voice tinged with a note of desperation, "I need a solemn promise from you. No matter what happens, no matter what is said, I want you to promise you won't react. Can you do that? You don't know right now how much I'm asking of you, but Kate, believe me, your defense depends on it."

"If it's that important," Kate said.

"It is. Remember now, no reaction—*none*." She smiled. "Don't even breathe until you have to." Melanie patted her hand as the judge entered the room and everyone stood.

Michael began again with his cross-examination of the witness.

"Now, Mr. Marshall, with the court's permission, let's review your testimony from last Thursday." He looked at the notes in his hand. "You testified that the defendant told you that she found your telephone number on a Paladin business card. Is that what you said?"

"That's what *she* said."

"Your Honor, may I approach the witness?" Michael asked.

"You may."

Michael stepped to the witness box and held up a small white card.

"Is this the card to which you were referring?"

Julian Marshall's eyes widened behind the lens of his glasses. "Yeah," he grunted. "Where did you find it?"

"And the name and telephone number printed on this card is yours. Am I correct?"

The witness squinted. "Best as I remember."

"And this is where the defendant got your number—from this card?"

"That's what she said."

"What if I suggested to you, Mr. Marshall, that the phone number listed on this card is not your private, unlisted number? What if I tell you that the number printed on this card is for the National Weather Service?"

"I remember now." He nodded. "I did use that. I guessed they wouldn't mind getting a few wrong numbers now and then." He smiled. "Must be pretty boring just watching weather patterns."

"So then, do you have another explanation for how Mrs. Ames was able to contact you on your private number?"

"No. I only know what she said."

"But she did, for a fact, contact you."

"Absolutely."

"And offered to pay you a large sum of money—one million dollars to be exact—in return for your services. You further testified that you agreed to enter into this *alleged* conspiracy of death with her because she wore you down, and you wanted the money."

Julian Marshall nodded.

"Aloud, Mr. Marshall," the judge ordered. "The court reporter cannot record a nod."

He cleared his throat and leaned into the microphone. "That's correct."

"Yet, of the fifty thousand you say you'd already received, you can't remember what you spent it on. May I suggest to you, Mr. Marshall, that you can't remember because there was no deal made? That no money ever changed hands, and your testimony is a pure fabrication?"

"Of course, a deal was made. I didn't just pull the whole thing out of thin air. She wanted Jonathan Ames dead. All she ever wanted was the money."

Michael stepped to the defense table and picked up the photograph of Julie. Melanie cautioned Kate with a look.

"Remember your promise," she whispered. Kate gave an almost imperceptible nod.

Michael approached the witness. "Mr. Marshall, I ask you to look at this photograph—"

District Attorney Holbrook was on his feet. "Objection. Defense is presenting evidence to which prosecution has not been privy."

"Very well," Michael said, glancing at the judge. "With your permission, Your Honor."

"Permission granted," the judge said. "And might I inquire as to why this evidence has not previously been turned over to the prosecution, Mr. Anderson?"

"The importance of this photograph only came to light over the weekend, Your Honor. Defense did not deliberately withhold relative documents."

Judge Peterson waved away the plausible explanation.

Michael stepped to the prosecutor's table and handed over the photograph.

The prosecutor studied the picture and handed it to his assistant. "Great looking chick," the assistant said in a stage-whisper that carried across the courtroom, and returned the picture to Michael.

"May I, Mr. Anderson," the judge said, holding out his hand.

"Of course, Your Honor," Michael said and placed the picture in the outstretched hand.

With eyes that mirrored no hint of what lay beneath, Judge Peterson scanned the photograph. He made no comment as he handed it back to Michael.

"Now, Mr. Marshall," Michael said, handing the photograph to the witness, "I ask you to look at this carefully and tell this court if you recognize either of the two people."

Julian Marshall's hand shook with a slight tremor as he reached for the picture. He appeared to study it closely. "I recognize Mr. Ames."

"You're not familiar with the other person in the picture?"

"No." His voice had weakened almost to a whisper.

"Speak up, Mr. Marshall," the judge ordered.

"No." His voice cracked, but was stronger.

At the defense table, Melanie held her breath and reached for Kate's hand beneath the table.

"I submit to you, and to this court, that you do in fact know who it is, Mr. Marshall," Michael pressed. "Because the other person in the picture, the person identified by the inscription on the back as being Julie, is actually you. Am I not right, Mr. Marshall?"

The witness paled and licked his lips. "I don't know what you're talking about. Of course it's not me."

"Mr. Marshall, will you tell this jury, are you a cross-dresser? Are you an active member of the homosexual community?"

"Objection!" the district attorney thundered, his face flushed a bright crimson. "Defense is entering into dangerous territory which is clearly inadmissible."

"Don't try to do my job for me, Mr. Holbrook," the judge said. Taking off his glasses and folding his arms across his chest, he turned to look at Michael. "Mr. Anderson, you're on extremely shaky ground with this line of questioning. I'll allow the question to stand, but I must admonish you not to wander too far off the reservation. It would be prudent on your part, for the sake of your client, if you prove relevance as quickly as possible. In doing so, I advise you not to test the patience of this court. Objection overruled."

"Thank you, Your Honor," Michael said. Beads of sweat dotted his brow and across the bridge of his nose. He turned back to the witness. "I ask you again, Mr. Marshall, are you a practicing homosexual? "

"Yes. But what has that got to do with anything?"

"Just answer the question: *yes* or *no*," Michael said. "To continue, have you ever dressed and appeared in public as a woman?"

"Yes, but—"

"Have you ever been known as *Julie*? Used that name as a sobriquet?"

"Yes."

Kate felt her heart stop beating. Only the memory of Melanie's warning kept her from leaping to her feet and shouting a denial against all that was being said. Melanie withdrew her hand from Kate's lap and began to fidget in her chair. She clenched and unclenched her fists on top of the table, then she pulled a tissue from the pocket of her dress and blew her nose. Such an obvious display of anxiety on the part of her lawyer left Kate puzzled.

"Once more, Mr. Marshall, are you the second person in the picture? Were you and Jonathan Ames lovers?"

Julian Marshall strained forward in his seat. "Yes!" he exploded. "I'm the one in the picture. But she knew all about me. She found out about Jonathan and me and paid me to kill him. Since I knew I'd never get him back, and all she ever wanted was the money, I agreed to do it." He pointed an accusatory finger at the defense table. "I didn't know what I was doing, but she did. I tell you, it's all her fault."

Michael flicked a smile at the jury. "Buried in that statement is the first true testimony you've given during this trial: 'Since I knew I'd never get him back'; you killed Jonathan Ames in a jealous rage. You couldn't bear to see him married to a woman, and because of your intense hatred of the defendant, you came up with this ludicrous charge that she paid you to kill her husband."

"I didn't hate her. I didn't even know her."

"But you testified that she met with you on two occasions to procure your services," Michael reminded the witness.

"I mean, I didn't know her before she called me." He licked his lips. "Of course, I knew her after that."

"Mr. Marshall," Michael reasoned with the witness, "is it not true that when you learned the defendant had married her husband, your ex-lover, you swore revenge on both of them? Your plans were put on hold for a while because you were dispatched to a post in South America and could not make good the threat. But immediately upon your return, as soon as you could conceivably carry out your sworn vendetta, you entered the Ames' house, unbeknownst to the defendant, and stabbed Jonathan Ames to death. In your unreasonable hatred you thought the wife, whom you didn't even know, would be accused of the murder, leaving you to get away free as a bird. But, when your car was unexpectedly identified by the gardener, your only recourse was to alter your plan and concoct this preposterous story that Mrs. Ames happened to see your name on a *stupid*—your word, not mine—business card and contacted you at that number, which by the way was the weather service—about killing her husband. *Isn't that what really happened, Mr. Marshall?*"

"No!" he shouted. "I tell you, she paid me to get rid of him. She said she wanted him out of the way."

Michael stood with his back to the room, facing the witness. "You still maintain that the defendant initiated contact with you, even met with you on two separate occasions, for the sole purpose of securing your services to have her husband killed?"

"She did," Julian Marshall said. He glared at the defense table, repugnance marring the lines of his fragile face.

"Will you point to that person, Mr. Marshall?" Michael requested. "The person you met with, not once, but twice. The one who paid you fifty-thousand dollars."

Something akin to fear flickered across the face of the witness.

"Over there," he stabbed the air, "at that table."

"Which one, please, Mr. Marshall? Be more specific."

Julian Marshall hesitated, his eyes darting; frantic. At last he spoke.

"The one on the left." Michael did not turn, but continued to face the witness. He raised his hand to show that he was not yet satisfied. "On whose left, Mr. Marshall, yours or mine? And tell this jury what she's wearing."

Julian Marshall edged forward in his chair. Desperation mocked his fine features. A sheen of perspiration gave his face a dewy, ethereal glow. He drew a deep breath and played his final hand.

"On my left," he said. "The one in the slutty red dress."

"Your Honor," Michael said, still facing the witness, "may we ask the lady just identified to stand? The one in the *slutty* red dress."

"Please stand," the judge ordered.

Melanie rose from her chair.

Michael continued to face Julian Marshall, their eyes locked. "Will you tell this court your name and occupation?" he said to Melanie.

"Melanie Anderson. Counsel for defense."

Kate's body was beginning to suffer from lack of oxygen, when she finally remembered to breathe. She felt lightheaded.

Julian Marshall's composure crumbled, as his world seemed to break up around him. He fell back into his chair and fought unsuccessfully to hold back the tears that rolled down his pristine face.

"I couldn't let her have him. He wasn't supposed to belong to anybody but me." He sobbed. "He was the only person who ever really loved me."

A murmur went up from the room. The judge rapped for silence and ordered the witness taken away. Guards came forward, gathered the weakened Julian Marshall from the stand, and shuffled him away.

Order was restored and Michael approached the bench.

"Your Honor, in view of the revelations of the last few minutes, defense moves that all charges against the defendant be dropped forthwith."

"Mr. Holbrook, any objections?"

"None, Your Honor," the district attorney said with a wave of his hand.

"The case of the People versus Kathleen Spencer Ames is hereby vacated. The jury is dismissed. This court is now adjourned." The gavel fell for the final time.

Reporters broke for the door as a clamor rose from the crowd. Kate felt like a sleepwalker trying to bring herself from a nightmare.

"I'm so sorry you had to find out this way," Melanie said. "Are you okay?"

"No. But I will be. At least now I know."

Michael hugged the two crying women. "Is she all right?" Kate heard him whisper to Melanie.

"She just needs a little time to sort things out," Melanie said.

"Come on you two," Michael said as he bundled them together. "Let's get out of here. What we need is a cup of coffee, or maybe something a little stronger. I'm buying."

Microphones were shoved in their direction when they emerged from the courthouse.

"Mrs. Ames, may we have a statement?" one reporter asked. "Mrs. Ames," asked another, "did you know your husband was gay?"

"Gentlemen, please," Michael said, holding up his hand. "It's been a very long day and my client's tired. Later, huh?"

Propelled by her two protectors, Kate felt herself being pushed into the car. Cameras continued to click from outside the windows as they drove away.

THIRTY-ONE

At long last Kate was on her way home. She sat beside Michael in the front and Melanie leaned forward from the back seat and put her arms around their shoulders. She kissed Kate on the cheek and tousled Michael's hair.

"Did we do good, or what?" she said.

"For babies? You were more than just good," Kate said. "I'd say this case will send your careers into orbit."

"Yeah," Michael said. "Too bad it had to come at such a tremendous cost."

Kate fell silent, gripped with a sadness so overwhelming that she couldn't begin to know how to continue with her life.

"But you're going to be okay, Kate," Melanie said, patting her shoulder. "I don't think you have any notion of the inner strength you have."

"You sound like Dixie," Kate said. "You're right. I might turn out to be a tough old broad yet."

Michael laughed. "*Broad*, my dear lady, is a label I would never associate with you."

Kate turned on the seat. "Speaking of 'broads,' Michael, what tipped you off that Julian Marshall was actually Julie?"

"Melanie gets all the credit for that. I'm surprised that Judge Peterson didn't see through that little charade of hers when she went into that coughing fit. Judges know only too well that lawyers, especially defense lawyers, are notorious for their delaying tactics."

"Maybe if I hadn't had the picture right there in front of me, I wouldn't have recognized him," Melanie said, resting her folded arms on the back of their seats. "Or maybe it was the way the light struck at a precise moment and caught him in a specific pose."

"Oh."

"Suddenly it was crystal clear. You couldn't see it, Kate, because you were too close; too involved. It meant too much to you. Your mind rebelled and refused to make the connection." She laughed. "The funny thing is I really did get choked. But I knew I had to get Michael's attention, so I used it."

Kate turned to look at Melanie. "Thank goodness for your keen powers of observation."

"At last we had a starting point: an alternate lifestyle," Michael said. "It was at least different from anything we'd considered. I knew the answers had to be in Washington D.C. After Melanie set me up with a couple of appointments with K Street bigwigs I was off on the next shuttle."

"And they knew Julian Marshall?"

Michael laughed. "Nope. Wasn't that easy. But they did know the name. The first gentleman I talked to, Mr. Greenwall, knew that he worked for State, but nothing more. The second one, Mr. Tyler, on the other hand, not only knew Marshall but also knew Eric Dalton, his roommate.

Melanie patted Kate's shoulder. "And naturally roomies know everything about anything that has to do with their bunkmates."

"Trouble was," Michael said, "Dalton was out of town and I had to wait an extra day to get to talk to him.

"But you finally did?"

"Yeah. But it wasn't easy. The number of people who knew that Julie and Julian were the same person was exactly two, plus Julian himself. And Julian was afraid if it ever came out, he'd lose his job. So, for appearance sake and to protect both reputations Mr. Ames was never seen in public with Julian, only 'Julie'. Apparently they were a popular couple. But nobody, as far as Eric Dalton knew, was aware that Jonathan Ames knew Julian Marshall. And when Mr. Ames was killed, the two who did know about the relationship went into hiding. Nobody was talking to nobody, according to Dalton. Of course the whole thing drove the Woodway investigators crazy. They wasted weeks with nothing to show for their efforts."

"But why did Julian Marshall kill Jon, Michael?" Kate asked. "Why did it have to come to that?"

Michael glanced over at Kate. "According to Dalton, Julian was out of his mind when he found out that Jonathan had married. Not only had he married, but he'd married a woman."

Michael leaned forward and switched on the wipers to clear the windshield of a light mist starting to fall. Leaning back against the seat and readjusting himself behind the wheel, he picked up the story.

"Then a couple of weeks later, Eric said Julian swept into the apartment, still in drag, and said he'd just come from a meeting with that *whoremonger*—meaning of course Jonathan Ames, and Julian vowed that he'd make sure the son of a bitch got what was coming to him, if it was the last thing he ever did."

"That had to be when I followed Jon to Washington."

Michael nodded. "I agree, since that was the only meeting between the two of them after Jon had gotten married."

"So why did Mr. Dalton open up to you?" Kate wanted to know.

"By the time I got to talk to him and told him about the photograph of Mr. Ames and Julie, Eric knew that Julian's story would never going to hang together of trying to pin the murder on you. Heck, he knew more about the trial than I did. They might be a bunch of sophisticated mucky-mucks in that hellhole called The Seat of Democracy, but they love gossip and scandal. And the killing of Jonathan Ames was right up there at the top."

"So, tell her the rest," Melanie said.

"That's when Eric gave me the nail for the coffin—the Paladin card. You see, he was with Julian that night, him and some other dude he called Junior. All three were crazy drunk and thought Julian having a card printed would be the coolest thing in the universe. Of course Julian agreed, enny-mimy-miny-moed the three cards, and Paladin came up the winner. Julian gave both them a copy and stuffed the rest into his pocket."

"And Eric Dalton still had his copy, but he wasn't talking. What about this 'Junior' person?"

"Junior is the son, and heir apparent, to one of the most influential senators in Washington. Nothing, I mean *nothing* touches that man. So Junior was shipped off to while away the next year or so in Europe." Michael shook his head. "Junior was history."

"I still don't understand how you knew Julian wouldn't know who I was."

Michael grinned. "Part of that was dumb luck, part a roll of the dice. Remember, you said Jon returned from his last trip out of town in February, which was before you two really started going together. That had to be when Julian was sent to South America. You and Jon didn't really start seeing each other seriously until he was out of the country. By the time he got reassigned back to Washington, you were already married. That's when the calls started. According to Eric Dalton, Julian was convinced Jon had married some low life right off the streets who was only interested in his money. In Julian's words: *Jonnie had crawled into the gutter and mated with a sewer rat.* It was obvious from that description, Julian Marshall had never seen you, Kate. It wasn't until after I talked to Ray, that I had an inkling."

"Ray?"

"One of the guards who escorted Julian to and from the courtroom. Last Thursday when Melanie got choked and the judge called a recess, I ran into him in the parking lot and he wanted to know what Mr. Marshall had against my wife. He said Julian was ranting and raving about the bleached-blonde and how he hoped the water strangled her guts out: *'Then the bitch could have a reunion with Jon in hell and they could burn through eternity.'* He bragged to Ray that he'd see to it that you never got your filthy hands on a penny of the money. It was then that I knew: Julian Marshall had no idea who you were. He was thinking young, dumb-blonde trashy, and gold-digger."

Kate swung around in her seat and looked at Melanie. "So that's why you look like, well..."

Melanie laughed. "Like a sewer rat?"

"But a beautiful sewer rat," Michael said.

"Anyway," Melanie said. "That's the reason for the musical chairs. It's usually customary for the defendant to occupy the center chair at the defense table. Today we maneuvered to keep you away from that seat. We hoped that Julian would continue to believe that I was the one on trial." She gave a shaky laugh. "And it worked."

Outside the car, the mist turned to a light rain and Michael clicked on the wipers again. Kate looked at her reflection in the darkened windows. Her eyes were quieter now, more accepting of things she didn't understand: *the little fox no longer needed a place to hide.*

Michael touched her arm. "That you and Jon were more or less secluded out here in the country and didn't go out much, worked in our favor," he said. "We were counting on the fact that Julian was satisfied with his own perceptions of you, and had made no effort to find out what you really looked like. Besides, his main concern seemed to have been revenge. Since he'd met Jon, he'd been pampered like a princess—pardon the pun—and he wasn't about to give it up. Let's face it, he had to be a little crazy when he broke into the house and trashed it while you two were in North Carolina. And since he got away with that, why not go for what he really wanted—to get even with Jon for the ultimate betrayal."

"You think he was responsible for all the phone calls?" Kate asked.

"Oh, you know he was," Melanie said.

"I guess we'll never know exactly what happened that morning, will we?"

Michael swung the car off the main road. "No, Kate. I guess we won't."

Brandywine lay nestled in misty shadows as they drove through the gates. Kate felt the tall trees stretching forth their arms, beckoning her to come and rest. Never had solace been so imperative, freedom so special.

"I'd like to tell you two how much I appreciate all you've done," Kate said. "But I'm afraid I don't have the words."

"You don't have to," Michael said. "We needed you as much as you needed us."

"Well, you certainly got your careers off to a roaring start. I'm proud of you."

"It was quite a baptism of fire, wasn't it?" Melanie said.

Michael stopped the car and he and Melanie walked Kate to the door. "Are you sure you don't want us to come in with you?" Michael asked.

Kate shook her head. "I'd rather be alone just now."

"I'll call you tomorrow," Melanie said, handing Kate the angel-wing begonia.

"Keep it," Kate said. "Put it in your office as a kind of victory trophy. Dixie would be honored."

Melanie smiled. "In the meantime if you need anything or want to talk, call me."

"I'll be fine. You two run along."

Kate took the suitcase from Michael's hand. She stepped inside and closed the door.

She wandered the rooms, straightening a pillow, touching a lampshade. The door to the studio stood open, the cardboard box still sitting where it had been pushed into the corner. Its contents spilled over onto the floor, no doubt as a result of Melanie's hasty search. Kate snapped off the light and closed the door on the room.

Shimmering in its stillness, the water in the pool lay motionless. The room smelled of chlorine, the humidity a heavy shroud. Faint ripples ebbed like the touch of a dragonfly when Kate bent and dipped her fingers into the warm water. She walked to the deep end of the pool and stood looking down. With calm deliberation she slipped out of her coat and pulled her dress over her head. One by one the garments tumbled about her feet and Kate looked at her naked reflection. She sat down on the edge of the pool. Echoes of Jon's voice lingered in the dark hollows of her mind.

"Hurry up, slowpoke," she could hear him calling; hear his laughter.

Kate lifted herself from the smooth ceramic tile and eased down into the warm womb. The water closed in around her body and stroked her scarred chest like a lover's caress. She flipped over and pushed herself to the bottom of the ten-foot watery grave, and pressed the palms of her hands against the wall of the pool. *Stay here,* her heart whispered. *It's over. There's nothing up there for you, not anymore.*

Her brain, sluggish from lack of oxygen, was almost beyond the point of reasoning. Fire burned in her breast as her lungs struggled to breathe. A stirring of the water was like a feathery touch upon her face, and she could hear Jon's voice: *"Kathleen, don't take unto yourself the sins of the world."*

The realist side of Kate nudged its way through the layers of confusion, and her head cleared. Automatically she tapped her toes against the bottom of the pool and glided upward. Her face broke the surface of the water, and she gagged as she gasped for air.

Clinging to the side of the pool, she crossed her arms and made a pillow for her fevered brow. Uncontrollable retching tore at her body, and she fought against returning to the seductive lure of the water and blessed forgetfulness. She waited for the heaving to subside.

Boosting herself out, she dribbled water across the tiled floor to the rack beside the door. She unhooked one of Jon's robes and slipped it on. Kate could feel his arms closing in around her. She buried her face in the terry cloth. Even the chlorine odor couldn't remove completely the lingering fragrance of his body.

Kate drifted from the poolroom, passed through the kitchen where an ashtray on the table held one of Jon's pipes. Unconsciously, she picked it up, cradling it like a precious keepsake, and entered her bedroom. Here he had finally lain with her and his unraveling had stopped. *What demons tormented his soul while he waited for the jackals to circle?* she wondered. *For he surely knew they would.* The price was too high to pay because he wanted a quiet and simple life. Kate sat down on the lounge chair in the shadowed room and held the pipe, placing the stem against her lips, tasting where his mouth had been. The faint tobacco odor and stale taste brought tears to her eyes, but she refused to cry.

THIRTY-TWO

It was Monday the following week. Kate and Melanie stood on the sidewalk staring up at the imposing steel and concrete professional building before them. The business day was just coming to life.

"Shall we go in and let the air out of some tires?" Melanie suggested.

"Let's do it," Kate said.

A large floor-to-ceiling directory covered the wall between a bank of elevators. After studying the listings, Melanie slapped a button and immediately double doors opened. They stepped inside and were whisked upward. On the fifteenth floor, they emerged into the offices of Abernathy, Morefield and Clarke.

"Mrs. Kathleen Ames to see Phillip Bradden," Melanie said to the Max-Factored receptionist.

"Do you have an appointment?"

"Oh, I think he'll see us without one." Melanie pointed to the intercom system. "Just push one of those cute little buttons and tell him we're here."

"I'll have to see if he's in." She sounded annoyed as she rose from her desk, tugged the latex tube-dress down over her slim hips and slithered away.

"No doubt we've thrown her entire schedule into a tizzy." Melanie gave a wry smile. "Besides, she'd probably planned on doing her nails."

Kate's reply was interrupted by the opening of a door.

"Mr. Bradden will see you now," she said.

"I rather thought he might," Melanie said.

They followed the receptionist down a plush-carpeted hallway. Rich mahogany paneling covered the walls and gave off a warm glow that suggested many hours of hard polishing. A copper plaque on the door bore an engraved name: Phillip Bradden. The receptionist pushed through.

A young man approached them, buttoning the coat of his handsome three-piece Armani.

"Mrs. Ames," he said. "It's a pleasure to finally meet you."

Kate held out her hand. "Mr. Bradden, this is Melanie Anderson, my attorney."

"Pleased to meet you," be said, beaming appreciably. "Here, have a seat." He motioned them to chairs covered in butter-soft leather. "Now," he said as he settled himself behind the desk, "what can I do for you two lovely ladies?"

"Mr. Bradden," Melanie snapped. "We're not '*two lovely ladies*' as you put it. We're here on serious business. My client wishes to have the matter of her husband's will settled as expeditiously as possible."

"Well now," he said, leafing through the calendar on his desk. "Let's see when it can be scheduled. We have some time free on the twenty-seventh of next month. How does that sound?"

Melanie glanced at Kate. "It's your decision— you are the boss."

Kate nodded.

Phillip Bradden grinned, satisfied. It was evident that he was a man used to ordering people about in their lives. Telling them what they did, and did not, need, could, and could not, do. Kate felt a stirring of anger. How dare he dismiss her as if she were an insignificant insect to be shooed away. She was special. *Damn special.* Jon's love had made it so. Besides, had Melanie not just reminded her that she was the boss. She felt blood pounding in her ears.

"Just a minute." Kate rose and placed her hands on the top of his glass-covered desk. "No, that's not good enough, Mr. Bradden. I suggest you look at your calendar again and see if you can't possibly make time available just a wee bit sooner." Kate was vaguely aware of Melanie trying valiantly to conceal a giggle that was bound to interrupt the proceedings.

Phillip Bradden gave Melanie an appealing look, as if asking for help.

Melanie shrugged her shoulder and held up her hands.

"Don't look at me," she said. "I'm just here to hold her coat." She straightened herself in the chair, her serious look returning. "But you may as well know, Mr. Bradden, we have a copy of the will. The reading is a mere formality on your part."

"Well, yes, let me see." Color seeped from beneath the collar of his Turnbull & Asser shirt and crept across his face. "Oh, here's an opening for day after tomorrow. How could I have missed that? Will that be more convenient for you, Mrs. Ames?"

"Wednesday will be fine," Kate said and gathered her purse and gloves from the chair. "Mr. Bradden," she said, inclining her head in his direction. "Melanie, shall we go?"

Leaving Phillip Bradden in the middle of rising from his chair, they swept from the room, stood outside the closed office door and looked at each other. Melanie was the first to burst into a fit of laughter. Realizing what she had done, Kate joined in, and together they capped hands over their mouths to smother their enjoyment.

Kate pulled herself upright and wiped her eyes. "Was that me in there just now? I can't believe I was so rude."

"You, rude?" Melanie feigned surprise. "Never. I knew you had fire in your soul, I just didn't know how long it would take *you* to find out it was there. Well, now I can stop wondering. I'm proud of you. You were magnificent."

"I'm proud of me too, by God. So proud in fact, that I'm going to treat us both to the most expensive lunch in New York. How about it?"

"You're on. Stalking prey always makes me hungry."

Melanie took Kate's arm and steered her toward the elevator. On the ride down to the lobby, both women continued to glance at each other and snicker. It turned out to be grand day.

On Wednesday, the reading of the will took only a matter of minutes. The importance of Jon's fortune was not lost on Kate, but neither was she in awe of the enormity of it, as Phillip Bradden informed her that she was the sole beneficiary of Jon's estate. He retrieved a sealed envelope from the folder before he closed the file.

"At the request of your late husband," he said to Kate, "you are to receive this letter. The contents are unknown to anyone and it's to be delivered to you at the close of the reading of the

will. Now, I believe that concludes our business."
Phillip Bradden started to rise from his chair.

"Not quite, I'm afraid," Kate said, dropping
the letter into her purse and getting to her feet.
"I'm moving the account, Mr. Bradden."

"Moving the—Mrs. Ames you can't—"

"Of course I can."

"Listen—"

Like a mama tiger defending her young,
Melanie jumped to her feet.

"Don't badger my client, Mr. Bradden. She's
been through too much to have you rail at her.
You heard her intentions. I have been instructed
by Mrs. Ames to commence proceedings to have
the Ames' account moved to Consolidated
Investments in Woodway. The transfer is to
include, but not limited to, all securities,
properties, stocks and bonds. In short Mr.
Bradden, the entire portfolio. This transfer is to
begin as soon as humanly possible."

Stunned, Phillip Bradden dropped back into
his chair.

"What you're asking is inconceivable," he
said. "You don't realize the vastness of the Ames'
holdings."

Kate smiled. "Oh, but I do, Mr. Bradden.
Believe me, I really do."

"But we've always handled the Ames'
account. I don't think you've given this matter
enough thought, Mrs. Ames. Are you sure this is
what you want?"

Kate nodded. "I've given Mrs. Anderson full
control over the transfer. I don't want to be
bothered with it."

"Bothered! Mrs. Ames, we're the most—"

"Please direct any comments you have to my attorney," Kate said.

"But, Mrs. Ames—"

"Mr. Bradden," Melanie quipped, "I'll not tell you again: address your questions and comments to me, if you don't mind."

"Please," he said, holding up his hands. "Wait just a moment. I really must get Mr. Abernathy in on this." He pressed a button on the intercom.

"Bambi, would you get our guests some tea." He released the button and turned to Kate and Melanie. "Please, make yourselves comfortable. I'll be right back." His dignity seemed to evaporate from beneath the handsome Armani suit as he hustled from the room.

The receptionist brought the tea, set it on the corner of Phillip Bradden's desk, and left.

"*Bambi*," Melanie twisted her pretty mouth into a tight grimace and knuckled a dimple into her cheek. "Why am I not surprised."

Suddenly the door banged open and a blustering dynamo charged into the room. His florid face showed spidery blue veins beneath transparent skin stretched across angular cheekbones. He had the look of a man who had enjoyed too much rich food and far too many fine cigars. A heavy gold watch fob swung back and forth across his poorly concealed bulge. He reminded Kate of Humpty-Dumpty.

"Mr. Abernathy, I assume," Melanie said, rising and extending her hand. "I'm Melanie Anderson, legal counsel for Mrs. Ames."

"Little lady," be nodded in Melanie's general direction and bore down on Kate.

"Mrs. Ames—"

"What is it with you people." Melanie's voice sliced like a knife. "This fancy law firm has a lot to learn about common courtesy. You live in the most enlightened city in the world and you still address women as *'little ladies.'* Mr. Abernathy, if you please, direct your comments to me, not my client."

The man stopped short. "Nonsense," he sputtered. "What's this stupid idea about transferring the Ames' account to some two-bit firm in a hick town?"

Oh, my, Kate thought, *he shouldn't've used the word 'stupid.'* Now that would really get Melanie's back up.

"Mr. Abernathy," Melanie snapped, "since you don't know me, I'll overlook your gross and pitiful patronizing attitude and stick to the facts. Is it not correct that the estate of the late Jonathan Ames was left, in its entirety, to Mrs. Kathleen Ames? To do with," she said, raising a hand to stay his objections, "to do with as she sees fit?"

"Well, yes, but—"

"No conditions or stipulations were attached, I believe. Is that not correct?"

"Millions! You are talking about millions of dollars," he said as if trying to impress upon her the gravity of the situation.

"I know," Melanie said with a slow, solicitous smile. "We've engaged the services of a very reputable auditing firm who'll assist in the transfer. Please begin as quickly as possible to consolidate the Ames' portfolio. This afternoon is short notice I know, so in the morning will be soon enough."

She retrieved her briefcase from the floor where it lay propped against lovely mahogany Queen Anne legs.

"Now if you'll excuse us, neither Mrs. Ames nor I have had our lunch." She glanced at her watch. "And it's already past noon."

"Gentlemen," Kate acknowledged the two men who stood gaping. She took Melanie's arm and the two of them sailed from the room.

That night, surrounded by the gentleness of *Brandywine* and Mancini playing softly in the background, Kate sat at the red-cherry secretary in the corner of the bedroom. Muted shades of blue and green and red splashed from the Tiffany lamp on the nightstand and shadowed the room with flittering apparitions.

Holding Jon's letter, she traced the words on the envelope: Kathleen Spencer Ames. Kate smiled. He was always one to go for full measure. *No cutting corners for that man*, she thought, running her fingertips across the fine linen texture of the paper. She lifted the envelope to her nose, wanting to smell the lingering essence of him, the tiniest hint of his presence. But there was nothing. Through misty eyes, Kate tried to sort out her feelings as she looked at the large scrawl of Jon's handwriting. He had taught her how to love again; how to make he finally believe that there are no perfect people. And for that she was grateful. How would she ever get on with the rest of her life without him?

She pulled back the sealed flap and opened the folded page:

My Dearest Kathleen,

This letter is to come to you on the event of my death, and I find it difficult to write because by now you know the true me.

Just today you agreed to marry me, and from this day forward I am committed to you. I do not know what the future holds for us, I only know of my desire to make you happy. You love me, I can see it in your eyes. I love you too, my dear, but I'm afraid there will be times that you will doubt that love. At this moment you are the most important thing in my life and I look to you for a new beginning, a putting off of the old. I'll not apologize for what I am. I neither asked for nor granted it to be so. Some things we don't question. We just are. But now I make you this sacred promise: there will be no other love in my life. The past is buried—closed off by an impenetrable curtain. My devotion to you is complete. As you read this, I know you will be tolerant and understanding. I beg not for your hate, but if you are to remember me in years to come, I ask only that you remember me with love.

Jonathan

Kate refolded the letter and tucked it away in the bottom of her velvet-lined jewel case. She looked around the lovely bedroom and remembered their last night together. Such passion. Such splendor. She would not cry for her loss; rather, she would rejoice for the short time they had together. Kate reached a decision regarding her immediate future. Having reached that decision, she did not tarry. She dialed the phone and waited for an answer.

"Hello," Melanie's voice came over the line.

"Melanie, it's Kate."

"Is anything wrong?"

"No, dear. Everything's fine," Kate assured her. "I'm calling to tell you that I'm going away for a while."

"Alone, Kate? Are you sure?"

"I'm sure. Will you and Michael manage any legal affairs while I'm gone?"

"Of course, we will. You know you don't have to ask."

"Melanie, there's one other thing, but I hesitate to impose."

"What is it, Kate?"

"Will you and Michael keep an eye on *Brandywine* for me, perhaps spend some time here? This place means a great deal to me and I hate the idea of it being totally abandoned while I'm away. Silas will stay on. He feels responsible for Jon's death but he mustn't. Emily is to stop working but her salary is to continue. Marty will take care of her medical bills and the expenses for running the house. I don't know how long I'll be gone; it could be a long time. I'd like to visit Europe again." She laughed. "Give the *Trevi* another penny for granting my wish; go back to Capri. Also, I've been in contact with a doctor in Los Angeles. It's remarkable what they're doing with breast restoration these days. So I'll be coming back through California and give him a visit."

"Sounds like you've got it all mapped out."

"It'll keep me busy for a while. I guess that's what I need now—to keep busy."

"We'd be honored to keep *Brandywine* for you," Melanie said. "When will you go?"

"In a few days. I need to spend one day with Marty going over my finances, and I might as well have my doctor give me a checkup before I leave. I haven't been feeling on top of things lately. The anemia thing, I suspect."

"You have to take care of yourself," Melanie cautioned. "Why don't you stop by the office tomorrow and let's have lunch. Better yet, let's call Dixie to join us. After talking to her on the phone so many times during your trial, I look forward to meeting her. She's quite a character."

"It's a date, tomorrow around noon. Good night, Melanie." Reaching for the telephone directory, Kate looked up a number and made one more call.

The following week Kate's good-byes had been said to those people who were important to her, and she was ready to leave. Looking around the house for a final time, she collected her purse and coat. She knew now that her going would only be for a little while. Her life was at *Brandywine*, but not until some of the hurt went away. For now she had to go. Not to run from the past but to welcome the future. Closing the door softly behind her, she walked across the terrace and down the steps. She stood for a moment and looked at the glory that was the woodland. She cupped a hand protectively under her belly as a quickening stirred deep within her womb. Kate had shared her secret with no one, but held this moment for Jon and herself—the legacy he had left behind. She would be back when autumn came again to the knoll; be back to take up her life again and to have Jon's baby.

She walked toward the waiting car and settled behind the steering wheel. She looked at the house one final time. *Brandywine.* A home whose walls had witnessed love and death, and the creation of new life which would keep alive the one that was lost.

Slowly she drove down the long, winding driveway and the red glow from the taillights faded away.

Epilogue

The sun began its descent, casting long fingers through the limbs of the tall trees and sending shadows down the reaches of the knoll into the meadow. The final dying rays flickered across the lonely hill to the small cemetery where tombstones stood as constant reminders of those who had once lived, and loved, and left behind grief to witness their passing. As the last of the light died away, a single beam illuminated Jon's name on the brightness of the new marble. Beneath the name the newly-etched words: *Beloved Husband and Father. Remembered With Love.*

About the Author

Poet, short-story writer, novelist, Mary Ann Artrip published her first poem in 1989. Since then she has read from her work on PBS and has been featured in national and regional publications. Being a devotee of O. Henry and Hitchcock, her writing tends toward the unexpected. Blending surprise endings with love of the mystery genre, her first novel, *Remember Me With Love*, published in 1994, won the publisher's Golden Book Award for mystery/suspense After being out of print for a dozen years the novel was reissued in 2007. Her second book, *Moonshadows* came out in 2005 and was nominated for the Appalachian Writers Association Book of the Year.
Surrey Square, published in 2006 was a 2007 IPPY award winner.

"I didn't' start writing seriously until later in life," she says of her work. "I wasn't ready in my tender years. But I'm terribly envious of those who could, of those who had the talent and the enormous energy good writing requires. For me personally I had to remember the words of Solomon: *'To everything there is a season.'* So I had to be patient and allow myself time to mellow, to be warmed by the sun of passing summers, to ripen slowly. The trick was to strike a fine balance between ripe and rotten. No easy thing for a writer to do."

Author's website
www.maryannartrip.com

www.ingramcontent.com/pod-product-compliance
Lightning Source LLC
Chambersburg PA
CBHW020232180626
46810CB00006B/2149